Flexible Virtues

PATRICIA CRUMPLER

This is a work of fiction. Names, characters, places, and incidents are products of the author's imagination or are used fictitiously and are not to be construed as real. Any resemblance to actual events, locations, organizations, or persons, living or dead, is entirely coincidental.

World Castle Publishing, LLC
Pensacola, Florida
Copyright © 2025 Patricia Crumpler
Hardback ISBN: 9798288505522
Paperback ISBN: 9798891264236
eBook ISBN: 9798891264243
First Edition World Castle Publishing, LLC, July 22, 2025
http://www.worldcastlepublishing.com

Licensing Notes

Cover: Cover Designs by Karen
Editor: Karen Fuller

CHAPTER 1

Sandy had to look twice. If the back of the man's black cashmere coat didn't scream handsome, his face took care of that when he turned and smiled at her. *Men like that don't want women like me.* Standing in the vestibule of the library, he brushed a few of Manhattan's early-season snowflakes from his lapel. He wore the stamp of success, confidence, and good taste. By contrast, she was dull—right down to her name, Sandy Gray.

He caught her staring. She broke off the gaze and pushed the library cart into the reference section. Reference books often proved heavy, and Sandy needed both hands to lift and shove them into their proper spots. Engaged in shelving, she sensed someone behind her. After positioning the next volume, she turned.

"Excuse me." The captivating man in the cashmere coat addressed her. "Could you help me find some books on moldings? The kind used for woodworking."

"Of course," she said in her best professional tone. "That would be in the seven-hundreds under *architecture*. Is there something specific you're looking for?"

His lips turned up slightly, making her inner parts twitch. She imagined that the tiny gesture meant: *Yes, I would like you.*

"I'm doing some wood refinishing on my house. I need to research how one works with antique molding. My place was built in the 1870s."

Sandy progressed through the Dewey section, where the nonfiction and classic literature resided, to the books on architecture. Stopping where the information on woodworking sat on the shelf, she pulled a book halfway out and turned to him. Distracted by his gray-blue eyes for a moment, her internal voice gave her a shove. *Focus.* "You could find a lot more on the internet."

"I've already looked on the internet. It's awkward to take your screen and hold it up next to the crown molding. Besides, I like books. The internet feels cold. Libraries inspire me."

"Maybe you should take your coat off?" *Did I really say that?* She could have smacked herself.

"Good idea. I might be here a while. Thanks."

Sandy stiffened her arms, hindering the temptation to help him with his garment. He draped the coat over a nearby chair. No one could blame him for not wanting to hang it on the pegs in the vestibule, out of sight. Then she saw his suit. Although she didn't know much about designers, the charcoal jacket and pants must have had fancy labels on the inside. Her fingers touched the pearls she wore over her blue sweater. No label, just a sweater, but the pearls were real, left by her grandmother. Pearls, who wore *them* anymore? Her first thought regarding this man resurfaced. That kind of man would never notice her, a nondescript woman with a name sounding like it came from the label on a paint can. Like a slap in the face, she desperately wanted to change.

She pulled more books and put them on the table in front of the lovely, soft coat.

The man with the perfect face smiled and sat. Having completed her service, she returned to the reference section. Sandy concentrated on shelving and tried not to look his way. She clucked in annoyance each time she checked on him and could not restrain her pleasure as he nodded and turned the pages.

When her shift ended at six o'clock, she took her drab jacket from the backroom closet. The temperature outdoors had dropped since morning, and she pulled out the wool scarf wadded in the pocket. Outside at the bus stop, she thought about the man in the library and reflected on the details she committed to memory. If there were $500 haircuts for men, he had one. Neat and precise, the style kept his hair short enough to restrain the struggling curls but allowed a slight wave, ending with a sheared, curved line at the back of his neck. She touched her own hair, pulled it back, and secured it with a holder bought in the dollar store.

The bus exhaled noisily as it groaned to a halt. The other zombies at the stop made the same silent step into the metal monster. She looked up and down the aisle. This bus never had empty seats. There were usually spots available at her old bus, but then.... A little wave of sick passed through her as she thought about the other library. She had been transferred a few months ago to this branch after— She banished the memory of that early evening when she was pulled into an alley and— The wave of revulsion increased. Her stomach flipped. She winced at the thought of the day she would have to testify.

The bus halted abruptly, and the driver yelled, "Crazy cabbie!"

Horns blared, and her memories of the almost-assault vanished. She caught a whiff of cheap aftershave from the man holding the loop next to her, not the dreamy scent wafting from the hunk researching antique moldings. When did she become a man's cologne mavin? Maybe today. Two transfers later, she walked the quarter mile to the home she shared in Astoria with her friends Paula and Lorraine. A frozen Swanson meal heated in the microwave provided dinner. Bypassing the usual television shows, she went to bed early.

The next morning, she took a long look in the bathroom mirror when a knock sounded.

"Hey, hurry up, I'm going to need the toilet pretty soon," Lorraine said.

Sandy opened the door. "Okay, you can have it." As

Lorraine passed by, Sandy grabbed her arm. "Will you do something with my hair this morning?"

"Sure, if you'll let me pluck your eyebrows, too. And how about some makeup?"

"Okay," Sandy said.

Lorraine called Paula, who ambled down the hall. "Hey, Roomie, Sandy must have met someone. She's fixing herself up."

"Finally." Paula tossed her words toward Sandy. "Who'd ya meet?"

Sandy waved away the question. "I didn't meet anyone. It's time I started looking a little better."

"Nuh, uh," Paula scoffed. "There's a man behind it. Always is."

Lorraine threw a handcloth in the hamper. "That techie at the library?"

With a soft sigh, Sandy faced her two roommates. "No. He's too shy; just talks to me. Nothing happening there. But there was this Adonis type in the library yesterday. No one who would look at me twice."

Paula shook her head. "Hey, don't sell yourself short. You're pretty. It's a matter of advertising the merchandise correctly. Besides, beauty is skin-deep."

Lorraine went into her bedroom and came out with a black bag full of hair implements. "Let's do something with Sandy's skin-deep." She held out a pair of scissors and threatened the air with snipping motions.

"Do your best," Sandy challenged.

Sandy had the eleven-to-seven shift and arrived at the library fifteen minutes early. As she hung her jacket in the library's backroom closet, she caught a look at herself in the mirror. The pageboy cut suited the shape of her face, and the ten-minute conditioner made her brown hair shine. She turned right and left, examining as much as the reflection allowed. The small touch of makeup accentuated her coloring. "Not too bad," she muttered to herself, "for a plain girl."

She entered the computer area and approached the tech, who tapped the keys at a station. He looked up from the screen. "Hi, Sandy."

"Oh, hi, Oggie. More problems?"

"Always. But, that's job security." He stood as she passed. "Hey, you look nice. Uh, I mean, you always look nice, but, um, you look better than usual. Oh, I didn't mean that you don't sometimes look good, but—"

"Thanks, Oggie."

"Would you go to the movies with me?"

Sandy stopped and turned. "Really? When?"

Oggie raised his eyebrows, furrowed them, then cleared his throat. He sat hard behind the computer console. "This weekend?"

"I have to work Saturday, but we can go Sunday afternoon. What do you want to see?"

"Hold on." He pounded the keyboard. "You pick. Demons? Romance? Spy? Musical?"

"Surprise me."

Oggie's smile spread across his face. "Okay. I'll come by Sunday around one."

"You'll need my address."

"In Astoria?"

"Yes," Sandy angled her head. "How did you know?"

"I heard you say you lived there." He took his cell phone from his belt holder and pressed the keys. "I'll keep your address in here."

She recited her address.

CHAPTER 2

The emptiness of the library the next day made the staff edgy. Circulation statistics equaled funding. *Encourage check-outs,* directed the large handwritten admonition on the backroom door, and *Read* signs hung on every wall surrounding the stacks and reading room.

At three p.m., the Adonis returned and walked straight to Sandy. "Hi, remember me?"

"Of course, Dewey 723." A voice inside chided her. *So lame.*

A small grin appeared on his ideal lips. "Good memory." He folded the stunning coat over his arm. "I would like some information on shellac. I want to know about the original materials. Could you help me research?"

"Shellac? Hmm, I'd say 620s, maybe 698, but maybe—Hold on, let me see for sure."

She moved to the stacks in the six-hundreds, then waited while he draped the soft black overcoat on a chair back. He stood behind her as she read the spines, his scent enveloping her. She pictured a girlfriend or, *ugh,* a wife, choosing the expensive bottle at a high-end department store. He stepped next to her, scanning the books. She caught a quick look at his hands as they flew along the shelf. No band on his left hand, but he wore a class ring and a gold watch. This man wasn't afraid of jewelry and would be wearing a wedding band if he were married.

Sandy pulled a few books and piled them into his waiting hands.

"Thanks," he said.

"Anytime," she answered. She worked in the back for the

rest of the afternoon on acquisitions.

When she got ready to leave at seven, Oggie stopped her. "It's dark. Do you want me to wait with you at the bus stop?"

"No thanks, I'm okay." *Does he know why I was transferred here?* The library system had insisted on keeping her near-assault a secret. They didn't want it known that employees and patrons could be at risk outside of a branch.

She put her jacket on and slipped out the back door. The wind whipped the bus stop sign, making a metallic crackle. She pulled the scarf around her chin.

"Hi, there."

She turned to see the life-sized Ken doll from the library. "Oh, hi."

He pointed to a café across the street. "It's pretty nippy, and I'm going to get coffee. Would you like to join me?"

An instant flicker of fear gave Sandy a shiver. This was her late night. "No, I need to get home. My roommates would worry." What was she, fourteen? Not all men were potential attackers. But she had to be careful.

He gently took her arm. "Call them on your cell. I'd like the chance to talk with you, which we can't do in the library."

Her mental voice gave her a thump. *Come on, already.* "Okay."

She called the house phone. Paula answered. Sandy said, "I'll be later than usual. I'm having coffee with someone I met." She turned to the man who stood next to her.

"Cameron Morgan," he said.

She told Paula his name and rang off.

They sat at the one free booth in the café. He ordered soup, coffee, and hot dinner rolls for both of them.

"By the way, please call me Cam."

"I am Sandra Gray. Call me Sandy."

Cam said he was an attorney and told her about his house and the refinishing work he planned.

She had a flash of thought and swallowed hard. "Attorney? You don't happen to work for Curran, Farrand, Schwartz, and Gilden?"

"I know of them. They're criminal attorneys. I'm with Bache, Savage, Coward, and Franks."

"You're not a criminal attorney?"

"Only if one of our existing clients needs it."

"Oh. Do you have a specialty?"

"Not yet. I'm pretty new at the firm. I do what they tell me." A vertical dimple crinkled his cheek. "Do you like working in the library? Been there long?"

"Somewhat to the first question. No to the second." He was *listening*. "I used to work in another branch and got transferred here two months ago. This branch is all right, but I liked the other one better."

"Why not go back?"

She wasn't supposed to talk about the assault or the upcoming trial. Maybe it was okay to discuss it with someone not related to the proceedings, but she wouldn't take a chance and do something that would help the defendant. Even if the criminal had been interrupted before he could complete his evil purpose, he deserved to pay for his intentions. His rich father was doing everything possible to get the bastard off the hook.

"The library system transferred me. Bloom where you're planted, my grandmother used to say. So, I'm taking root in this flower bed and smiling."

"Good advice," he said.

Their order came. The soup and rolls were warm and filling, and they tasted divine.

A uniformed officer walked by the booth. "Hi, Officer Larry," Sandy said.

He stopped at their table. "Hi, Library Sandy. And Morgan. Surprised to see *you* here."

Cam shook his hand. "Nice to see you, Manelli. Last time we met was at Wallensky's wedding. Some party, eh?"

"Yeah. That's what us Italians have in common with the Irish. We like lavish, boozing weddings. The Callahans wanted a bash for their first daughter. Hmmm, good ole Dennis Wallensky, a promotion *and* a wife in the same year. The guy is gold."

Cam laughed. "Wally's the best."

"Gotta run," Manelli said. "Good to see both of you."

Cam buttered his roll and smiled. "Officer Larry? Library Sandy?"

Sandy shrugged. "He volunteers to bring in a group of at-risk kids once a week. He talks about crime; I read light morality stories and help them check out books. The kids love it."

"What is light morality?"

"When the good guys win. I read *Aesop's Fables* and old-fashioned fairy tales where someone must make the right decision or do the right thing against bad odds. Not this modern stuff where bad guys are the heroes." Sandy touched the napkin to her mouth. "How do you know Officer Larry?"

"Manelli was my best friend's partner until Wally got promoted. Then Wally got married, and I saw Manelli at the wedding."

When the bill came, he looked at his watch. "It's nine o'clock. I'm afraid I've made you late to catch a bus. I have a car. Could I take you home?"

The memory of the dark alley, the stranger's hot breath on her face, flashed like a strobe. She didn't like waiting for the bus at night, but was accepting a ride from Cam safe? He seemed nice. Officer Larry liked him.

Cam smiled, displaying two perfectly placed vertical dimples this time. "I'm totally safe. I'll show you my driver's license. You can give my tag number to your roommates."

"Does my nervousness show?"

"You would be foolish not to be careful. Things happen." He said it in an offhand manner.

"I'll let you take me home," she said and blushed at her own daring. "Maybe you'll regret your offer when you find out how far away I live."

"It's fine, don't worry. My firm provides an E-ZPass."

How did he know there would be tolls?

They walked to a nearby parking garage. A gold Lexus beeped when he pressed his fob. He held the door for her and then got into his side. At the exit, he used a card to make the metal arm lift. Turning the car onto the street, he said, "Where to?"

"Astoria." She feared the mention of the working-class address would prompt him to screech to a stop.

"Okay," he said cheerily.

She gave him her address, and he put it into his navigation system. Sandy listened to soft classical music on the quiet ride home. The ride beat the bus and subway time by forty-five minutes. Cam pulled up to the driveway of the house she shared with her roommates. The neighbor and landlady, old Mrs. Vreeland, peeked out the window as she always did when one of her *girls* came home.

"Nosy neighbor?" Cam asked.

"We don't mind. She's a darling. Makes brownies and gives advice. She never had kids, and she'd love it if we called her Mom."

"Sweet," he said.

His words sounded believable, the way he said them. *"I'll bet he's great in court.* If she sat on a jury, she would trust every word he said.

He came around to her door. "I'll probably be in the library Thursday. Maybe we can get something to eat afterward?"

She stepped from the car. "Good timing. Tomorrow is my

day off. I'll be back on Thursday. I get off at six."

"Perfect. It's a date, then."

He waited in the car until she went in. She moved to the window and watched the car back down the driveway.

Lorraine looked out the window with her. "Who was that? We were beginning to worry about you."

"Oh, sorry. I got involved. Remember me telling you about the gorgeous guy from yesterday? Him!"

Lorraine held her hands up. "My magic scissors. These fingers are blessed."

***

Cam drove the car at the speed limit until he reached the main road. He pulled into the parking lot of a drugstore and made a call from his cell phone. The call clicked on.

A man asked, "So, Morgan, any luck?"

"No," Cam said, "I didn't get much information. I need more time with her."

CHAPTER 3

On Thursday, Cam spent the last hour of Sandy's shift looking through architecture books. After work, she met him near the bus bench. He took her to a small steak place not far from the library. The waiter poured a Shiraz to go with the sirloins Cam ordered.

"Only a little for me, please," Sandy said.

Cam picked up his glass. "You sure?"

"I'm not much of a drinker. I'm afraid of saying stupid stuff when I get a buzz. Although I will admit I enjoy a buzz now and then."

"That's charming," Cam said, holding the glass up as a tribute to her. "Here's to a good buzz now and again."

Sandy clinked her glass to his and took a sip. "Mmm, nice."

As they chatted, Cam brought up her previous library several times. He mentioned the declining safety of neighborhoods and how criminal activity had increased since his youth. Sandy agreed with his views, but she didn't enlighten him with her personal proof.

At the end of the date, he drove her home, walked her to the door, and gave her a goodnight kiss on the cheek. Sandy's stomach did a flip-flop as his lips brushed her face. She could barely get the words "Good night" out.

"He's dreamy," Paula said as Sandy came in.

Lorrain remained at her post by the window, watching Cam walk to his car. "We'll hear Mrs. Vreeland's opinion tomorrow, no doubt."

Sandy closed her eyes, smiling. "He *is* dreamy, and I don't want to wake up." Her eyes opened wide. "I have a date with

Oggie on Sunday. Gee, I have a social life!"

"Auggie Doggie, the library tech?" Paula rolled her eyes back. "Lovely name."

"His name is Ogburn Goodhart Edwards. O.G.E. Calls himself Oggie. It fits. He's an Oggie and a nice guy."

Lorraine let the curtain fall back. "So, what does Oggie look like?"

"Hmm. Let me think. He's not someone you look at and really notice. You know, average height and weight, kind of boyish, medium dark hair, glasses. I wouldn't call him handsome, but not bad, just an *ish* kind of guy."

Lorraine plopped onto the couch. "Yeah. That's us, *ish* gals destined to end up with *ish* lovers."

Sandy sat next to her. "If they are good stand-up people, then we will be lucky to have them."

Paula took her place next to them. "That's our Sandy, shooting for the stars again."

CHAPTER 4

At one p.m. on Sunday, Oggie knocked at Sandy's door. They took a bus to the movies and afterward ate at a diner.

"I had fun, Oggie. Thanks," Sandy said as they walked up the front steps to her house.

"You'll go out with me again?"

"Why not?" Regretting her response, she rephrased. "Yes, of course." She waited a beat to see if Oggie would try to kiss her. When he didn't, she reached for the door handle. "Good night." Reading Oggie's discontent at being too shy to kiss her, she dismissed the urge to do the departing gesture for him. "See you tomorrow." She opened the front door. Oggie, easygoing and fun, albeit nerdy and shy, generated an odd attraction. She wanted to date him again.

Lorraine and Paula stood like Roman Centurions guarding the living room.

"What's up?" Sandy stopped in front of them.

Paula grinned. "You *do* have a social life. Mr. Universe called our house phone while you were gone."

"Cam? I didn't give him my phone number."

"Easy to get if he knew your address," Lorraine said. "How come you didn't give it to him anyway?"

"He didn't ask. What did he want?"

Paula handed her a paper with Cam's phone number. "He wants you to call him." Paula's grin turned into a sly look. "Don't do it. Make him call you back. They like it better that way. Being a little hard to get makes them want you more."

"Puh-lease," Sandy said. "Hard to get? Who wants to get

me?"

"Girl!" Paula said. "Cut it out. Two guys are asking for dates. Be aloof."

"Okay. Cam probably wants library advice, anyway."

Lorraine lightly slapped Sandy's head. Paula fake-punched her arm.

Later that evening, as Sandy put a load in the dryer, the telephone rang. Standing just a few feet from the phone, she picked it up. "Hello?"

"Hi, Sandy. It's Cam. I've been invited to a big gallery opening. Would you like to go? You'll need a formal dress."

Sandy thought for a few seconds. She would have to find a formal gown. She had not worn a fancy dress since her high school prom. *A gallery opening? When will I get another invitation like this?* She swallowed, cleared her throat, and then accepted.

At eight sharp on Saturday night, a limousine stopped in front of the house. Cam, resplendent in his tux, knocked at the door.

The residents and Mrs. Vreeland, too, were treated to the sight of Cameron's deep dimples when he took Sandy's hand and led her to the shiny black vehicle.

"You look lovely, Sandy. That dress is the perfect blue for you."

The car accelerated so smoothly that she didn't notice they were moving.

"Champagne?" Cam poured from the open bottle, beads of ice adhering to its Perrier label. Another bottle sat in the limo's built-in ice container.

"Just a little, please."

Cam added a bit more to the glass. "Is there something wrong? You don't look happy."

"Yes. Something happened today that distressed me. I don't think I'm allowed to talk about it."

"Maybe we could talk about it hypothetically. You might feel better."

She sipped, wrinkling her nose at the soft bubbles. "Well, what if there was a person whose testimony would put a rich but bad character in jail? And then, someone sat on the bus next to the witness and offered her $50,000 to withdraw the testimony. Do you think it would upset that witness?"

"Yes, it sounds upsetting. I would say if the witness considered taking the money, she should demand $250,000 because it's what the defendant would end up paying for a good law firm's legal fee. Then both parties benefit."

Sandy looked at him with her mouth open for a second. "I'm not taking any money! That is, the witness doesn't want the money. The criminal needs to pay for his crime."

"I agree." Cam patted her leg. "But, since the witness knows what she should do, she ought to forget the incident and go out for some fun."

"Okay," Sandy said, taking a long sip. "I'm not supposed to discuss it, so don't ask me any questions, please." The nagging voice inside said she had already talked too much.

"No questions." Cam took her hand.

They rode in silence, sipping the champagne and listening to the soft jazz the chauffeur had playing low in the limo.

Places Sandy usually saw from the bus whizzed past. The limo ride made the familiar route look better. *Is that how rich people see the world, through fancy car windows?*

The car slowed and stopped. Cam touched Sandy's hand. "Hey, we're here.

CHAPTER 5

The gallery overflowed with guests, each one more expensively dressed than the next. Sandy barely noticed the paintings and sculptures amid the sights and sounds of the party. A string quartet played, overshadowed by low chatter. A waiter came by with a tray of canapés and wine. Cam took two glasses and a plate of crackers dabbed with tiny dark spheres.

Sandy popped a cracker in her mouth. "Mmm, caviar, delicious. I've had it before, but it tastes better tonight."

"Beluga. My favorite," Cam said. "Aren't you going to taste the wine?"

"No, I had champagne in the car. I'll just pose with the glass."

Cam laughed. "Adorable."

A woman approached the couple and stopped too close to Cam. A marble statue of Venus behind her paled in comparison to this woman's beauty. The statuesque blonde threw her head back with a laugh. "On assignment, Cam?"

"Carter, may I present Sandra Gray? Sandy, this is Carter Logan."

Carter's smile curved up on the left side, making it both charming and sinister. The diamond danglers at her ears sparkled like prisms. Sandy extended her hand. The lady's bountiful cleavage blossomed in the swooping neckline of the silky red dress.

"A handshake?" Carter laughed and took Sandy's hand. She looked at Cam with undeniable sympathy. "You need a better job, Cammy." She walked on.

"Sorry about that," Cam said. "I'm bracing myself."

"What for?"

"For the fit you're about to throw."

"I'm not going to throw a fit. Why did she think you were on assignment?"

"It was an insult. Sometimes, the firm asks me to accompany clients to affairs. Carter is mean. She doesn't have to be like that."

"How do you know her?"

"We were together for a while. Actually," Cam sighed, "she broke my heart."

"She's stunning, Cam. I'll bet a lot of men fall in love with her. What happened?"

"I've known her since I was a kid. We dated on and off through high school and college. After law school, when I inherited the house, she moved in. I thought we'd get married. That was during her *decorator phase,* and she had outlandish ideas for the place. I kept saying no to her designs, and she dumped me. She didn't love me. She wanted a project."

"Poor Cam."

"You aren't angry over her comment?"

"No. Only the people I value can insult me."

"You're special, Sandy." He picked up her hand and pressed it to his lips.

A movement caught Sandy's attention. Carter leaned slightly away from a group of people and eyed Cam. He gave Sandy a delicate kiss on her forehead, then on her lips.

Sandy almost let go of the wine glass. Cam took the glass and hailed a waiter with a tray of empties.

"Excuse me," Sandy said. "I need to use the girl's room."

Cam escorted her across the floor to the bathrooms. When she came from the stall, Carter leaned against the sink. The woman stared at her own reflection in the mirror and asked Sandy, "So, how did you meet Cam?"

"I helped him research when he came into the library."

Carter refreshed her lipstick. "I used to date him."

Sandy washed her hands. "He told me."

Carter forced her eyes away from the mirror. "Cam is attractive and good where it counts. I guess you'll find that out. He moves pretty fast. He's a go-getter and gets what he wants."

Sandy dried her hands with a folded linen towel on the counter. "He didn't get you."

Carter's lop-sided smile broadened. "That's right, except for me. But I can get *him* any time I want. Nice dress."

"Thanks. Yours is exquisite." Sandy dropped the used towel into a basket. "Nice to meet you, Carter." Carter returned to her image in the mirror. Sandy left.

From his waiting place outside the restroom, Cam strode to Sandy and slid his arm around her waist. They left the gallery, and, in the lobby, he phoned for the limo. A few minutes later, the chauffeur opened the door for them. In the back of the limo, Cam popped the cork on a new champagne bottle. "Let's go to my place. I want to show you why I have been doing the research."

"Um. I don't know."

"I'm safe, Sandy. I want you to see it."

The limo let them off at the curb in front of an unattached three-story stone house. The vehicle then turned left down a sloped driveway. They climbed four stone steps, and then Cam pressed buttons on the lock and held the carved mahogany door for her.

She entered and scanned the rooms from her place in the foyer. "Gosh. It doesn't look this big from the outside. Where do you keep your car?"

"There's a garage in the rear. Originally a carriage house."

"You're doing the remodeling work yourself?"

"No. I thought about refinishing the paneling in the study, but I've decided to hire out."

"Oh, so no more research for you."

Cam didn't respond. He took her hand. "I'm not sure what I should do with the kitchen." He led her past the dining area and into a large room. "What do you think?"

White-framed glass doors lined three upper walls. The base cabinets with solid doors had a beige tiled counter. She walked into the butler's pantry, admiring the built-in cupboards and shelves. The kitchen looked like it had been remodeled during the Craftsman Era. "I like the kitchen as is. Only put in a dishwasher! Who did the dishes before you owned it?"

"Maids."

Sandy lightly smacked her forehead. "Duh!"

Cam touched her cheek with the back of his fingers. "You're funny. And nice and cute."

She wanted to believe the compliments.

Cam stepped close and nuzzled her neck. It felt good, but her nagging-ninny mind-voice cried foul. Sandy moved a few inches away. "The gallery opening, you go to places like that often?"

He made a face. "Unfortunately. The firm's clients send us invitations and one of us has to make an appearance. The partners go to really cool things like dinners with Hizzoner, but I attend the common things. Thanks for going with me. You made the evening bearable."

"Does Carter go to a lot of those things?"

"She lives for them. She's a dilettante, and dabbling in the arts doesn't occupy enough of her time. She's a malicious, spoiled brat. I didn't see that until we broke up."

"Whoa, she hurt you bad."

"It will never happen again."

"Gee, that's pretty cynical."

"Protective. Haven't you ever had *your* heart broken?"

"No."

Cam's mouth twitched. He looked away. "Maybe we should go."

In the limo, Cam poured more champagne. "Here, have some."

"Okay. Hey, be careful. I can't get this dress soiled in any way. It has to go back to the store tomorrow."

"You don't like it?"

She fingered the rich blue fabric. "I love it. I couldn't afford what really looked good, but Paula found it shopping yesterday and knew it was perfect. She wouldn't let me see the tag, but Lorraine said there was barely enough on her credit card to get it. Now, I don't go along with this sort of dishonesty, and I didn't know she planned to return it until she told me on my way out the door. Paula works at a dry cleaner and will run it through in the morning so she can get the charge removed when she takes it back."

"You're kidding?" Cam looked at Sandy and touched the material. He opened the cork and spilled a bit of champagne on the dress.

"Are you crazy?" Sandy grabbed the white towel from the chiller and dabbed at the dress. "Cam!"

He took out his cell phone. "Hi, may I talk to Paula? Good. This is Cam Morgan. Will you please tell me how much that lovely dress Sandy is wearing cost you? Come on. It's important. Please? Great. Thanks."

He removed his wallet from his jacket pocket, counted a number of hundred-dollar bills, then nodded. "You need to keep that nice dress. The dry cleaning can get that spot out. I've had champagne spots before. No problem. And don't worry, the law firm will pick up the cost of the dress. And the dry cleaning."

Sandy should have protested, but she wanted to own the dress. She fought the voice inside, and the voice lost.

When they arrived at Sandy's house, Cam walked her to

the door. He gave her a genuine kiss goodnight, touching his tongue to hers. He kissed her again. "You're a special person, Sandra Gray. I have been honorably lifted by your presence. Thanks for a wonderful evening."

Sandy opened the door. Cam called Paula's name, and when she came, he gave her a handful of hundreds. "Great dress, Paula." He put his hand to his forehead and saluted. "Good night, ladies." Then he walked to the waiting car.

CHAPTER 6

Cam called a few days after the gala and asked Sandy to attend a casual adult birthday party for Steve Little, one of the firm's partners.

He picked her up the afternoon of the event. "Lovely sweater," Sandy said. "You look like you could do an Irish Spring soap commercial. Don't they call those things fisherman's cable knit?"

Cam shrugged. "I don't know the sweater's pedigree."

"It shows off your shoulders. Good choice."

"I didn't select it. When Carter lived with me, she bought me gobs of clothes. I have enough to last me for years."

Sandy ran her finger over the curvy pattern on his arm. "She has wonderful taste."

Cam shook his head. "It took me a year to pay off my credit card. But I agree, she had good taste. In clothes. Not so much in some of the things she says or does."

The party, held on the terrace of a penthouse overlooking Central Park, brought complaints of boredom from Cam. Sandy loved the view and enjoyed the buffet of canapes and finger food. With a pleasant smile, Cam shook hands and chit-chatted for an hour. Then Cam lightly grasped Sandy's elbow, steering her in a retreat out the front door. "Let's go to my house. We'll cook something. Watch TV." They stopped at a grocery store and bought items to make roast chicken, braised Brussels sprouts, and baked potatoes.

At his house, the two of them worked in the kitchen together. The dinner was superb, and after cleaning up, they retired to the den to watch television. The TCM channel showed an old black-and-white classic, *Mr. Peabody and the Mermaid*. Sandy had seen it once a long time before and considered it lucky that she could see it now sitting next to Cam on the buttery white leather couch. A few minutes into the movie, Cam slid his arm around her. She tingled at his touch. Later, he put his nose on her neck and kissed upward until he reached her lips. Taking short breaths, her face heated from the excitement. Cam ran his hand under her sweater and massaged her breasts.

"Don't do that, please," Sandy said, forcing the words to come out.

"You don't like it?"

"I like it, but it's what comes after that I'm uncomfortable with."

"What's the problem?"

"I don't know you well enough. It's only been a few dates, Cam."

"Is there a magic number of dates?"

"I don't know you well enough. That's all."

"Sorry," he said.

Sandy didn't say anything. She was sorry, too, wanting to go further. But it didn't feel right. Not then. *When will it be right?* Her grandmother had advised her *to go with her heart.* Right at the moment, she wasn't sure if her heart had been overshadowed by the excitement igniting her insides that were triggered by Cam's attention. The outcome of the mental debate ended in *not now.*

They finished watching the movie holding hands. When the grandfather clock chimed its mellow strokes at nine, Sandy asked Cam to take her home, explaining that she had the early shift the next morning.

"Okay," he said. "Maybe next time you can stay longer."

Sandy, not being adept at innuendo, translated his statement to mean staying overnight. On the ride home with

Vivaldi playing on the car's radio, Cam's implied invitation provoked mixed emotions. Her body warmed with enthusiasm, but her mind flashed caution. She liked him a lot. Maybe more than a lot. Or deeper than liked. When Cam walked her to the door, he pulled her close.

"A goodnight kiss?" He asked.

She nodded. Their kiss turned into many. When Sandy came in, somewhat shaken, Paula and Lorraine attacked her with questions. Sandy stumbled with her answers.

Paula rubbed her hands together. "Sandy's in love with that handsome dude!"

"She sure looks like someone in love," Lorraine said.

Sandy sat down. "I'm not in love, or, oh, I don't know. Besides, his looks mean nothing. It's his personality. He's smart, witty, well-mannered, and a good kisser. He's confident but vulnerable."

Paula shook her head. "Nuh-uh. Guys who look like that aren't vulnerable. They're arrogant, and the smart ones can make you think whatever they want."

"Okay, he might be a little arrogant. I think it comes with the job, but he had a bad relationship, and he's careful now. That's vulnerability." She closed her eyes and breathed in. "And he smells so good."

CHAPTER 7

The following morning, Mr. Little, the firm's partner, told Cam a plea deal had been struck, and the friend at Curran, Farrand, Schwartz, and Gilden no longer needed Cam's services to work on the witness, Sandra Gray.

When two weeks went by without a word from Cam. Sandy wondered why he didn't call her. After reflecting on their last date and the crowd he moved with, maybe she wasn't his type. He was too good to be true. She still had Oggie. He took her to interesting places, like the Cloisters, and she had accepted a date for a Sunday afternoon picnic.

Oggie rented a car and drove to Valley Forge. In the freezing temperature, they discussed what it must have been like for General Washington and his poor soldiers. Oggie regaled her with trivia about the Revolution and spoke of his father's ancestor who lodged Washington during the campaign.

"I knew about the soldiers being in Valley Forge during the winter, but I hadn't thought about it. You made it real. Thank you."

"You're welcome," he sighed. "Hey, I'm getting cold. Want to go?"

As they sat in the warmth of the heated car, Oggie stared at Sandy.

"What is it, Og?"

"I wish I knew how to talk with women."

She brushed the back of her fingers down his cheek. "You do fine. Be yourself."

Without warning, Oggie leaned over the center console,

pulled her to him, and kissed her.

Reliving the attack, she screamed, "Stop!" pushed him away, and banged against the passenger side door. Her heart pounded.

He clutched her forearm to help her sit up. She jerked her arm away from his grasp.

Wincing, he collapsed against the driver's seat. "Oh, God. I'm sorry. I didn't mean to scare you. I just wanted to kiss you. See? I don't know what to do."

"I know you won't hurt me." She breathed in and calmed. When her heart returned to normal, she moved closer, brushed his lips with hers, and whispered, "Do it like this."

He kissed her a few times and held her in a tight embrace. "Sandy, I luh-uhv, uh, like you so much."

"I like you, too."

"I know you're dating another guy."

"He hasn't called me in almost three weeks."

"Be careful of him, the lawyer. He's not nice."

"Wait a minute." She glared at him. "How do you know about him?"

"I checked him out. You're better off staying clear of him."

"Oggie! You had no right to spy on me or anyone. Stop snooping."

"Sure, anything you say. I don't want to make you mad."

"Too late. Take me home."

On the way back, she thought about what happened. In the silence of the car, she played back the disastrous exchange with Oggie. *God, he is clumsy.* He meant well. If she hadn't been so frightened, it would have been humorous. He was correct about not being skilled regarding relationships. Was he the man she wanted? He was the one she currently dated. *A bird in the hand,* her grandmother had often said. In her heart, Sandy knew Oggie was a fine man. She enjoyed his kisses—almost as much as

Cam's. Maybe she should find out more about Ogburn Goodhart Edwards. "Tell me about your family."

"I don't have a family. No close relatives. I was a surprise gift to older parents who themselves had no siblings. My mother was in her late forties, and my dad was fifty-two when I arrived."

"Ah, maybe that's why you're uncomfortable with people. But you're so brainy!"

"You know us only-children. We tend to be bright."

Sandy moved back a few inches. "How did you know I was an only child?"

"Um, the *us* meant there are a lot of only children."

"Oh," she said and turned on the radio. They listened to NPR on the way back.

A few days after the picnic at Valley Forge, there was a commotion at the library. A half dozen black SUVs squealed to a stop in front of an apartment building across the street. Sidewalk bystanders gaped, and the library staff pushed against the window to get a look.

"Hey," Sandy said as a group of men was brought out in handcuffs. "That bearded guy is in here all the time. He spends so much time on the computer we have to shoo him off. I wonder what those men did to get arrested."

Oggie smiled as he turned from the window. Sandy made a mental note to ask what was so amusing. After the vehicles left, the spectators dispersed, and the library staff went back to their posts.

Shortly after the excitement, Oggie approached the checkout desk. Sandy, focused on the schedule left by the supervisor, held her finger up, meaning, *wait.*

"I have to leave right now," he said.

When she finished reading the last few words, she looked up. Oggie frequently put in long hours at the library, and he was entitled to comp time. With Delores, the supervisor, gone for the afternoon, Sandy was in charge. "Everything all right?"

"Sure," he said. "I have something important to do right now."

"Take off."

Sandy forgot to ask him about the smile. She didn't have time to think about Oggie's unexpected departure. With her early shift ended, Sandy needed to go. She didn't like to leave until everything was finished and moved at double speed to complete her work. As she waited at the bus stop, a gold Lexus pulled up to the curb.

Cam hopped out, rounding the front of the car. "Sandy, I owe you an apology. I should have called before, but things at work had me tied up day and night. I know that's no excuse for not at least calling. Let me take you to dinner. Somewhere nice."

A little shot of pleasure ran up her body, settling in her shoulders. Sandy's mind whirled. *He hasn't called in weeks, and now he just shows up?* Should she make it easy for him?

Cam opened the passenger door. "Please?"

She had dressed a little better and used makeup every day with the hope she would see him again. Here he was, apologizing and asking her to dinner. *What do I want?*

She stalled for time to think. "I'm not dressed up enough for any place fancy."

"Nonsense. You look terrific."

"My roommates are expecting me home for dinner."

"They'll understand. Please, I'm trying to say I'm sorry."

The argument in her brain came to an end. Sandy rose from the bench and moved toward the car. She got in.

Cam pulled away from the curb. "Is everything okay? My cop friend, Wally, told me they arrested suspected terrorists across the street from your library."

"Terrorists? Is that what was going on? Wow. One of the men came into the library almost every day to use the computers.

Do you think they're really terrorists?"

"Wally is the police liaison officer to the FBI. He said the feds had been watching them for months and found their plans to blow up New York City's electric grid. I worried about you."

"I hope the feds got them all. Thanks for worrying about me."

Although his concern made her feel good, her inner voice questioned how troubled had he been, not calling for weeks. "I've wondered why I haven't heard from you for a while."

"Work was causing me some hassle. Things are better now."

"Good," she said. *Good, you worried. Good, you came here. Really good to see you again.* She looked at his profile as he drove. *Really good.*

The restaurant Cam chose was casually elegant, glowed softly, with small candles flickering on the white tablecloths. The carpet and heavy drapes muted sounds, making the low conversation blend with the tinkling of glasses and cutlery. He ordered for both of them.

While they waited, Cam spoke of the recent case he settled where a seafood restaurant chef, suspecting fraud, had the fish DNA tested. Although the large corporate purveyors labeled the frozen pieces as snapper, mahi-mahi, and swordfish, the report exposed the identity of the real species as cod and catfish. The story fascinated Sandy and underlined Cam's charm.

When the meal came, the filet mignon tasted better than anything Sandy could remember. She savored the wine the sommelier recommended.

After the crème brûlée, she became quiet. No matter how hard she tried to suppress her internal alarm system, eventually, the thoughts surfaced, and she mulled over why Cam hadn't called. What about Oggie's warning? Not one to keep quiet when a thought banged around her head, she spoke. "Cam, I was the prime witness for a trial, but the bad guy took a plea bargain.

Right after that, I didn't hear from you. Will you answer me honestly? I want to know if you were involved in *any way*."

Cam bit his lip and took a moment. He nodded. "I'm sorry."

Blood drained from her face. "So, you didn't meet me by coincidence?"

Cam winced and shook his head.

"And Officer Larry? Did you set that up in the restaurant?"

A bump moved in his cheek before he unclenched his jaw. "I didn't arrange it, but I knew Manelli ate there often."

Sandy fished in her purse for a hankie. "I'm such an idiot." She wiped her eyes, and, realizing the job would be too much for the single sheet of tissue, she used the table napkin.

"Thank you for the honesty." Tears splashed. "Carter was right," her voice cracked, and she could hardly get the words out. "You need a better job, Cammy." She pushed back her chair.

Cam hastily took out three fifties from his wallet and placed them on the table. He moved fast to follow her on the trek to the front door. Both of them waited for their coats at the coat desk. Sandy donned hers on the way outside. Cam followed at her heel. At the curb, Cam grabbed her shoulder as he passed the car ticket to the valet. The touch brought back the image of being in the alley that awful evening. She wanted to escape. Flee her fears. Run from Cam.

"Sandy. Please."

The fears jumbling in her mind kept her from answering him.

"At least let me take you home."

Did she fear Cam? Or was she so terribly offended that she didn't want to speak? An internal debate warred over how she should react. If she refused his offer, she would be taking public transportation home. A cab was out of the question with what she had in her wallet. She concluded the inner argument.

She would be better off letting him drive her home. He owed her that, at least.

A blast of icy wind made her shiver. Cam stepped close and put his arms around her. She was too miserable to struggle, and as they waited for the car, she wept into that beautiful soft coat.

When they got into the car, she wouldn't look at him, turning her face to the window. Gaining control, she spoke. "Why did you ask me to dinner this evening? A pity date? Guilt?"

"I like you, Sandy. I took you out because I missed you." He slapped the top of the steering wheel. "Damn it. Damn me. Please, Sandy. I do like you. A lot. You are so far above the women I usually date. I feel terrible about this."

"Good. I hope you feel bad when you go out with those other women, then." *Oh, that was a clever comeback.* Sandy still had the restaurant's napkin and dabbed her eyes. She regretted the black smears on the white linen, noting the drawbacks to wearing makeup.

"Sandy."

She waved her palm at him. They were quiet for the rest of the drive. Not giving him time to open the car door in her driveway, she ran to the house and let herself in. She held her hand up to Paula and Lorraine, signaling that all questions should wait. She hurried to her bedroom.

The next day at the library, Sandy received an email from Oggie, which added more misery. *Dear Sandy, I have a new job and must be gone for a while. I'm not sure when I will return, maybe in a few weeks. I will call you as soon as I can. Take good care of yourself. I will think about you every minute. Still. OGE.*

CHAPTER 8

Sandy was bent over the computer in the back room of the library. When the door opened and closed, she smelled the distinctive aroma of Cam's cologne. She kept her back to the door, focusing on the keyboard.

"I've called for a whole week. You don't answer your cell?"

She didn't look up. "I do, but my cell has caller ID."

He put his hands on her shoulders. She flinched at his touch but didn't shrug him off.

"Sandy, my boss asked me to get to know you. I don't have to do that now. Can't I see you just because I want to?"

She let her breath out slowly, thinking, wrangling with her internal self, who was infinitely smarter. The battle did not last long. Here, he stood next to her, practically begging to see her. Didn't she want to see him too? She ignored the warning voice. "Yes," she said in a whisper and turned in her chair.

He touched her cheek. "Dinner tonight? Please?"

"I have three hours before I get off."

Cam held up his briefcase. "I brought work. I'll wait." He gave her a quick kiss and walked from the room to a table near the stacks.

Later, they ate in a tiny Italian restaurant where the quiet booths were barely lit, and the smell of garlic rolls and sausage had a warmth all its own.

"I missed you," Cam said, pouring Chianti into her glass.

Sandy was glad to see him but unsure about how she *should* feel. She almost said how much she missed him, but the words stuck in her throat.

"Will you go to a cocktail party with me next Saturday night?"

"Okay," she said before the voice inside her kicked in. "Cam, about the last time we were together—"

"Let's not talk about that. We are doing good right now. I'm afraid we'll get off course, and the last thing we need is an invitation for trouble. This ravioli is great. How's the eggplant?"

"It's delicious," she said and took a sip of the wine.

They lingered at dinner, engaging in small talk. When he brought her to her front door, he held her tightly. His embrace lasted a long time, imbuing a surge of pleasure from the prolonged contact. She ran her hands around his neck and relaxed in his arms, resulting in a tender kiss.

She sniffed his cologne that had transferred to her hand. "What is that delightful scent?"

"It's called Lucarelli, one of the few good things Carter did. I don't know where to buy it, and I can't find it in the department stores. When it's gone, that's it, I'm afraid."

She smelled her hand again. "I'll think of you until it's washed off."

Reaching for her wrist, he rubbed her hand across his cheek. "Now it will last longer. You can think of me all night." He raised his eyebrows. "I'll sure be thinking of you."

The contrast between his soft skin and the slight prickle of his whiskers made her smile. "Good night," she whispered and kissed him quickly before turning the door handle.

CHAPTER 9

Things were looking up. Sandy smiled all day because she had a date with Cam and received an email from Oggie saying he would be back in two weeks.

When Cam picked her up for the cocktail party, he gave her a smiling once-over. "You look great. Your dress doesn't have to go back tomorrow, does it?"

She laughed. "No, it stays. I'm sharing it with Paula and Lorraine. Luckily, we're the same size. At least we can all wear this one. And by putting our funds together, we can afford it."

"Good idea, recycling a cocktail dress. Is it your version of being green?"

She smiled because the dress was sage-colored silk. "Green. We help the planet and the three roommates. That is, as long as we don't go to the same parties."

On the long drive into the city, Sandy asked Cam to tell her about his work. He responded with details about his current case, a lawsuit started by a wealthy plastic surgeon against his son's private school. "The son, a swimming champion, and his friends disobeyed the basketball coach. The coach had been called out of the gym for a few minutes and told the students to wait for him on the bleachers. But instead, the students roughhoused on the court, and the boy suffered a leg injury. The damaged tissue would keep him from the Olympic swim team."

"Aw, that's a shame, poor kid."

"It is. I doubt the lawsuit will go anywhere because the students disobeyed the coach."

"Aren't you going to point out that the students were not

properly supervised?"

"Of course," Cam said. "But the situation boils down to behavior. Private schools like that one focus on teaching self-control. This boy didn't follow the rules and got hurt. That's why we have laws and guidelines, for the good of ourselves and others."

Sandy agreed. "My grandmother was strict, but, in the end, it did me good."

After parking in the underground garage of an apartment building on swanky Sutton Place in mid-town Manhattan, they took an elevator up one floor to the main lobby. Cam presented his invitation to the concierge, who nodded, pointing to a bank of different elevators that let them out on the twenty-sixth floor. Cam rang the doorbell.

While waiting outside, Cam said, "Our host is Aaron Feldman, a client of our firm. I don't know why I was the one invited to this party. I'm low on the totem pole."

A maid opened the door. The apartment took up the entire floor of the building. The elegant space easily accommodated the thirty guests and offered a breathtaking view of Manhattan's skyline. Muted chatter and tinkling glasses merged with piano entertainment. Cam and Sandy took drinks from the roving waiters and visited the buffet table. They had time to find seating and take a few bites before the host called the guests to attention.

Aaron waited for silence. "My friends, I have invited you here so I could make an announcement. I'm getting married, and I would like to introduce you to the incredible woman who has taken my heart."

Sandy said, "Aw," as the crowd made similar sounds.

Sandy and Cam stood to see the speaker. Aaron extended his hand to a woman who came to his side and kissed his cheek.

"May I present," Aaron said, and turned her to face his guests. "My fiancée, Carter Logan."

"Oh, God," Cam groaned. "I like Aaron Feldman. Poor bastard."

Sandy tapped his elbow. "That's not nice."

Cam's eyebrows came together in a deep furrow. "Truth isn't always nice."

After circulating the room for a few minutes, Carter left Aaron's side and made straightaway for Cam.

He flinched. "Congratulations, Carter."

She extended her hand to show the big diamond sparkling on her finger. "Hi, Cammy." She directed her attention to Sandy. "And, uh, Sarah, right?"

"Close. It's Sandra."

"Oh." She addressed Cam. "Hey, how's your buddy, that big ole hunk of cop meat?"

"He's fine. Just got married."

Carter made a face. "Oh, please don't tell me he's out of commission."

Cam tapped her ring. "Getting married usually means being taken out of circulation."

"It's like weeding out books when they aren't suitable for distribution," Sandy said.

Carter blinked, then regarded Sandy for a moment. "Weeding? How quaint. Oh, yes, you're a library clerk."

Cam's cheek muscle twitched. "Sandy is a librarian, Carter."

"Really?" Carter smirked. "So, what does one need to be a librarian? Did you take a certificate course at the junior college?"

Cam smiled. "Don't you have a Master's degree, Sandy?"

She nodded and recognized Cam's pleased expression.

"Oh, well," Carter put her hand to her mouth in a fake yawn. "Do give Officer Dennis my regards. Say, are you still making those nasty little wagers with him?"

Cam glared at Carter.

She deliberately looked at Sandy. "I see you are. Good luck to you." She winked at Cam. "You'll win."

Cam's gaze followed Carter's retreat. He spoke with clenched teeth. "Now I understand why I was invited. To make sure I knew. Let's congratulate Aaron and leave."

Cam shook hands with their host and introduced Sandy. Minutes later, they slipped from the apartment. Cam held her hand as they made their way to the parking garage.

After he helped Sandy into the passenger seat and settled behind the wheel, he started the engine. "Do you want to go to my place?"

"Not really." She chewed her lip. "Can I ask you something? When you first met me, were you supposed to talk me into not testifying against Chadwick Williams?"

"That would have delighted his lawyers. But no, they asked me to determine what kind of person you are. Williams had some heavy priors, and you would have made him look bad to a jury. After I met you, I knew you were a perfect prosecution witness. Williams didn't stand a chance."

"Is that why he took a lesser charge?"

Cam nodded. "Williams pleaded out because I told his law team that you couldn't be bought and your character was unassailable."

"Unassailable?" She thought about what that meant. Unconquerable, impregnable, unable to get past a barrier. A wave of anger made her neck stiff. "Were you supposed to get me in bed to suggest I was loose? So, his lawyer could say I teased that creep and asked for what he tried to do? Oh, God."

Cam jerked his upper body and turned to Sandy. "What the hell are you saying?" His volume increased. "Look, I admit my work isn't always principled, but how could you even think I'd do that to you? My job was to get to know you to see what you were like. That's it. Nothing more." Taking a calming breath, he said, "Making love with you was my own idea. No one else's." He lowered his voice. "Still is."

Sandy's inner voice tugged at the memory of Carter's words about Cam and his friend making nasty little wagers. She put her hands to her face, then dropped them and turned to him. "You just asked me to go home with you. Did you make a bet with your cop friend to get the uptight poor girl in bed by so many dates?"

"What?"

"You're not saying anything in defense. Did I guess right?"

"My lack of response is because I can't get my head around the things you're accusing me of or the kind of person you apparently think I am. Boy, you really know how to hurt a guy."

"Ask me about feeling hurt. I was a work project for you. You wined and dined me because you are the low man on the attorney totem pole. And Carter said you and your friend make nasty wagers. What am I supposed to think? Look, it doesn't figure, you and me. You're surrounded by beautiful, rich, chic women like Carter. Why would you be interested in me?"

"Why do I like you? For a lot of reasons, including the fact that you're the finest lady I've ever met. Women like Carter aren't fit to clean your feet."

"I wish I believed you," she whispered.

"Maybe you're right. Maybe this won't work," Cam said, anger clouding his face. He put the car in gear and shot out of the garage, narrowly missing a parked car. The ride and the walk to the house were wordless. Cam hesitated at the door. "I don't understand why you are so angry. I'm sorry. Good night, Sandy." He pivoted and walked back to his car, which idled in the driveway.

Sandy opened the door but turned, watching as he backed the car down the drive and peeled away.

Inside the house, Lorraine and Paula followed Sandy's trudge into her bedroom.

Paula grabbed Sandy's hand. "What happened?"

Sandy gently removed her hand from Paula's grasp, stretched to pull the back zipper, and stepped out of the dress. She grabbed her robe and wrapped it around her as if the terrycloth garment required punishment.

"Come on," Lorraine said. "Tell us."

Sandy returned to the living room, gave the shared dress to Lorraine, and then sat on the couch. The cushions made a huffing sound. "I can't stand him."

"Bull," Paula said. "What happened to vulnerable, good-smelling, and great kisser?"

"I don't belong in his world. We are too different. I don't know what to think. Am I too naïve? Or just stupid? The puzzle pieces don't fit. It's best I don't see him again. Oggie is more my speed. Please don't bug me about it, okay? It won't work between Cam and me. I want to trust him. But I don't."

Lorraine smoothed the silk dress over her arm. "Sandy, do you think you can just forget …." She snapped her thumb and finger. "Like that?"

Sandy snapped her fingers, repeating the sound. "Who?"

The next day, Sandy tried to put Cam out of her thoughts. She spent her time cleaning her room and reorganizing her closet. Since the work didn't occupy her thoughts fully, she offered to bake a coconut custard pie. Their refrigerator had the ingredients, and the milk would expire in two days. Win-Win-Win, she told herself.

On Monday, she stayed busy at the library working on new acquisitions. No one liked that job, but the complexity kept her thoughts from wandering. When her day at the library ended, she walked out into falling snow to wait for the evening bus. She sat on the bench as white blurs blew in waves one way and then the other. She took her cell from her purse and reviewed Oggie's latest email message. *Miss you. Wish we could be together right now. Can't wait to see you again. You're constantly on my mind. Still. OGE.* Was it snowing where Oggie was? He said he would be back in New York in a few weeks. The two people sitting on either side of her on the bench provided a bit of shielding from the wind, but a thought of Cam came to her, making the chill internal.

A gold Lexus pulled to the curb. When the passenger window rolled down, Cam stuck his head out and said, "Sandy." He hopped out. Steam pumped from the tailpipe as he came around to her. "Get in the car. Please." He bent close and touched her arm. "Come on. Get in the car."

The subtle force in his voice bothered her. Not that she thought he would hurt her, but since the attack, her unpredictable reactions to men surprised her.

"It's cold. I need to talk to you. Sandy." He gently tugged at her wrist.

The lady sitting on the bench turned to her. "You want me to call 911?"

Sandy shook her head. "It's okay." Biting her bottom lip, she got in the car.

Cam accelerated out of the bus lane and turned the corner, slowing into the parking lot of a store. He put the gear in park and kept the engine running. His seatbelt made a jangling whir as it retracted, and before the belt completely wound, Cam leaned over the console, pulled Sandy close, and kissed her.

While Sandy hit the button to release her seatbelt, a voice screamed in her head. *No! Don't kiss him. Stop!* She wouldn't listen to the voice and kissed Cam back with a fury she didn't know she possessed.

When the car windows were thoroughly steamed, Sandy pulled away and took a breath. "Cam—"

"No talking. Words cause trouble."

They kissed again and again until Sandy complained, "My lips are hurting."

Cam picked her hand up and pressed it to his cheek. "It hasn't even been forty-eight hours since I took you home. I couldn't stand it. I missed you."

In spite of her oath not to think about him, Sandy admitted, "Me, too." She opened the window to let fresh air in. "We shouldn't stay here."

Cam put the car in gear. "Let's go downtown. Rockefeller Center?"

"Okay." She couldn't allow the thoughts that screamed against being with him. He sat next to her, smelling good, offering warmth, the best kind of warmth.

Cam parked in a multi-layered garage several blocks from Times Square. They kept close together, strolling, looking in shop windows. Cam bought hot chestnuts from a vendor and later large pizza slices. The wind abated. Gentle snowflakes floated down like tiny feathers. They held hands as they watched the skaters at Rockefeller Center. The limited conversation suited Sandy, who feared even a hint of discord. After a few hours, she said, "It's ten. I have my early day tomorrow. I need to go home."

The fragile silence continued on the drive home. When the car stopped in the driveway, Cam walked her to the door. "When can I see you again?"

"I have Saturday and Sunday off."

"Okay, we'll go to a play. You'll answer my calls?"

She leaned against his chest. "I'll answer. Cam?"

He put his finger over her lips. "Enough discussion. It's dangerous." He kissed her, holding her tight between the goodnight kisses.

When Sandy came inside, Paula sat cross-legged on the couch with her hair rolled in flexible rod curlers. "Uh-huh," she said with eyebrows raised and a lot of white showing in her eyes.

"Uh huh," Sandy repeated.

"Oh, boy," Lorraine said and offered Sandy the cup of tea she just made. "Spill."

"We made up, that's all."

The roommates fixed their gazes on her, waiting for information.

"Okay, I am going out with him again." She let out a heavy sigh. "I don't understand it. I am not like the women he associates with. Most of them are rich and beautiful and don't even work. Compared to those women, I'm plain. Why is he seeing *me*?"

Paula rerolled the top curler. "Come on, Sandy. You said his looks meant nothing. You liked him because he was mannerly, witty, and intelligent. Maybe he's smart enough to like you for the same reasons."

Sandy put the cup to her lips. "Possibly. We'll see."

CHAPTER 10

Cam called Sandy every day until Friday night. He had tickets for them to see *Wicked* from orchestra seats.

She hadn't been to live theater since her high school graduation when a group of friends went to see *Rent*. But those seats had been at nosebleed altitude. Cam led her to seats she had only seen from afar. An extra delight was to be able to see the faces of the performers, their smiles, and the details of the costumes.

After the play, Cam said, "I want you to meet some friends. Okay?"

"Sure," she said, hoping they would be nicer than Carter.

He took her to a small bar called *Herman's*. When they entered, Herman sat on a stool near the door and gave Cam a salute. Cam nodded and said, "Two of the usual." He guided Sandy to the back room toward a couple who sat against a brick wall.

A tall, thick-set man stood and extended his hand, dwarfing Cam, who wasn't small in stature.

"Sandy, this is Dennis Wallensky and his wife, Marion. Meet Sandy Gray." Cam pulled a chair for Sandy. "Wally has been my best friend for, what? Fifteen years?"

"Yeah," the big man said, "ever since you beat my sorry ass in high school."

Sandy darted her gaze between the two men. "You? Beat *him* up?"

The man laughed. "He beat me in wrestling when his fancy prep school went up against my Catholic high. I was kind of slow with my teenage growth spurt."

"That explains it. I am glad to meet you," Sandy said.

Cam inclined his head toward the couple. "They just got married. Wally is one of New York's finest, and Marion is an editor for a publisher."

"Is he the one Carter asked you about?"

Marion made a face. "The man-eater? She's asking about Dennis?"

Wally put his hands up in defense. "Don't even think about it. I'm scared of that woman, and you know I'm not afraid of much."

Cam nodded. "I haven't seen you for a while. So, how is married life treating you?"

Wally put his arm around Marion. "Like a fat cat with a bowl of heavy cream."

"Can't you do better than that?" Marion asked.

"Okay, I'm the luckiest man alive."

Marion took a deep breath. "We are lucky. If we hadn't both come into the deli that day, we may not have ever gotten back together."

Wally chugged his beer and wiped his mouth with the back of his hand. "Honey, I knew you were there. I paid the cashier fifty bucks to call me the next time you came in."

"You did?"

"Yep," he said. "I had enough loneliness and wanted to see you."

"Why didn't you just call me?"

Wally finished Marion's beer. "You told me never to bother you again, remember?"

Marion looked at Sandy. "Don't they know we aren't serious in the heat of anger?"

Sandy didn't answer. *No means no.* Except, she did get in the car with Cam after she had said their relationship ended.

Thinking about the word *no* recalled the image of a dark alley and a man's hands dragging her down. He had ripped off her slacks and panties. Kneeling over her, he loosened his hand over her mouth while he pulled at his zipper. She bit his hand and screamed. A bum ran into the alley yelling, closely followed by two policemen who caught the near-rapist before he finished his intentions. Her breathing became shallow. A waitress with two glasses of white wine interrupted the horrible memory. Sandy picked the glass up and took a sip. Wally pointed to the empty beer glasses.

Marion wrapped her hands around Wally's ample biceps. "I was so happy to see him that day. I don't really care how it happened. Neither one of us could remember why we broke up. But," she sighed, "after I thought about it, I was reluctant to get back with him."

"Why?" Sandy asked.

Wally hung his head. "She said she wanted more."

Marion placed her cheek on Wally's shoulder. "I was disappointed he had never said he loved me and, well, I'm getting older. That day at the deli, when we talked, I told him I needed a commitment. As soon as I said that, he moved out of the booth and I thought he was leaving, but he went down on his knee, then said he loved me and proposed."

Wally nodded. "I would have asked her sooner, but she was so independent, I didn't think she was interested. I got so frustrated not seeing her, I asked my mother what I should do."

Cam's eyebrows made a vee. "You called your mother? I'm your best friend. Why didn't you ask my advice?"

"You? You wouldn't have told me to hunt Marion down, or when I realized I loved her, I should propose on my knee."

Cam looked into his glass of wine. "Probably not."

Two frosty beers made an appearance, and the subject of proposals dropped. The two couples talked until after midnight, when Marion said it was time to go home.

On the way back to Sandy's, Cam described his longtime friendship and how he was the only one who could call Dennis *Wally*. "We come from totally different backgrounds, but we understand each other. There is no one I trust more than Wally. I will admit it surprised me when he said he was getting married. Marion is good for him. What do you think about them?"

"I don't understand why they weren't honest with each other. They played games and almost lost their chance to be together."

"Mmm," Cam said. "Even though Wally is my best friend, I can't answer why he didn't tell her how he felt. I don't even know how I feel sometimes."

"I guess that's true for everyone. That's probably why we have the word *confusion*."

"Ah, that's my Sandy, a philosopher."

His Sandy. If only. "Enough with confusion. Tell me about another interesting case."

Cam's face lit up. "Okay, this isn't my case, but it will be a doozy. So, there's this fertility doctor who has a majority partnership in a sperm bank. One of the donors, Number Forty-two, has a Ph.D., speaks multiple languages, and is a musician, the perfect specimen. Forty-two is giving the doctor a hard time, no pun. The donor wants more money for his *material*. Our firm represents a wealthy family, and the males in that bloodline carry an unpleasant gene. Forty-two does not have that hereditary flaw and also has similar features like height, build, and coloring. The men in that family want ownership of the future supply of Forty-Two's material to father children free of the genetic problem. That way, all the siblings and cousins will be truly related. The donor signed a contract regarding payment but now refuses to produce material at the contracted price. The family made a deal with the doctor, but how can the doctor *make* Forty-Two provide the product?"

Sandy enjoyed hearing about Cam's work tales and the captivating way he explained the laws. Just before they reached her house, Cam asked her if she would go to a movie the next night. Thrilled at his request, she agreed.

After the movie and a late meal, Cam drove toward Astoria. Drifts of snow piled everywhere. The heavy Saturday night traffic slowed and then stopped.

In the quiet, Cam leaned over the console and rubbed his face lightly against Sandy's cheek. "I'm so glad we are together. I couldn't stop thinking about you. I got worried."

"What did you worry about?"

He reached for her hand. "That I wouldn't see you again. I care about you. And I know you care for me." He waited for her to speak, and when she remained silent, he said, "Say you care, Sandy."

Her voice became low. "I don't just *care*." She squeezed his hand. "I am in love —"

"Don't say *that*!"

"Why not, if it's true?" Sandy dropped his hand. "Are we playing games like Wally and Marion? It's all right to say we care for each other, but we can't say the word love?"

"Being in love has… commitment implications."

"Commitment implications. You are a damn, stupid, shit-headed fool, Cam. You don't know what you want."

"Don't be mad, Sandy. Hey, I didn't know you cursed."

Her irritation from his attempt to distract and diffuse her increased. "I don't curse. I guess my virtues are flexible. But I won't lie. You asked me if I cared. I do. I am in love, but since it's a new feeling, I'll get over it."

Sandy released her seatbelt, grabbed her coat from the back seat, and hit the door lock button. She jumped from the stopped car and then ducked into a store entrance to don her coat. The snow fell in horizontal gusts as she fled using long, quick strides. Two blocks away, the traffic flowed, and within a few minutes, she hailed a cab.

"Where to?" the cabbie asked.

She opened her wallet. "I'm headed to Astoria, so take me as far as you can for twenty dollars."

"Lady...."

Sandy began to cry.

His tone softened. "Boyfriend troubles?"

She swallowed hard. Pulling her tears away, she stiffened her shoulders. "Not anymore." As the cab moved through traffic, the driver eyed her in the rearview mirror.

"You look a lot like my daughter. She'd be your age about now. I ain't seen her since she was sixteen. We had a blowout, and she left. We never heard from her again."

"Oh," Sandy said. "I'm sorry. You could find her if you used a private detective. She is probably working, and if you have her Social Security number... There are ways."

"Yeah, I've thought about it. As soon as I saw you, I was hoping maybe, you know." He pulled into a bus stop. "Your money is up."

"Thanks," Sandy said. She slid across the back seat toward the door and handed him the twenty. "Find your daughter. I'm sure she wants to hear from you."

"Wait," the driver said. "I can't let you out in this kind of weather. This is the end of my shift. I'll take you to Astoria. I'll pay the rest. And tomorrow, I'm calling a detective. Thank you for reminding me of what I've lost."

The taxi drove into her driveway. She thanked him for his kindness. Luckily, the roomies were not in the living room to greet or ask questions. Sandy got ready for bed.

For the next few days, Sandy remained miserable, unable to keep Cam out of her thoughts. Weeks dragged. When Oggie texted and told her he would be back at work the next day, she perked up.

Oggie's goofy and witty personality entertained her. On his first day back to work at the library, the rain kept patrons away. During the lull, he offered to explain the Theory of Relativity and lost her after two minutes. They both laughed. Nerdy but affable, his intelligence might have put some women off, but his genuine innocence charmed Sandy. The Buddy Holly glasses complimented the unruly dark lock that fell over his forehead. A hint of mystery resonated.

Oggie took her to dinner a few times and once to the Museum of Natural History, where he delighted her with his vast knowledge. When she was with him, thoughts of Cameron Morgan rarely surfaced. Oggie's witty personality made her life bearable.

Then, with less than a day's notice, he left town again.

CHAPTER 11

For a month, Cam existed like a stunned ox. His world couldn't catch a breath, and a war waged in his mind. He imagined his near future and came up blank. He couldn't cope with the wrongness and took the day off.

Across town, Cam entered the small dry-cleaning shop near Sandy's house.

When the bell sounded, Sandy's roommate, Paula, came to the counter. "Hi. Great coat."

"Help me, and it's yours."

"Ha. I doubt it would fit, and you don't need to bribe me. What's up?"

His carefully scripted speech dissolved. "I want to talk to you about Sandy."

A noisy machine in the back room started up. "Not here." Paula leaned toward the open door to the next room. "Hey, Josh! I'm taking an early lunch."

A young man in a stained apron came from the back. He looked at Cam and scowled. "Who's that?"

Paula *tsked* at the man's question. "He's a friend. We're going out for a sandwich. I get an hour." She turned her back on Josh. "Let's go to the deli next door."

It was still early, and the midday crowd hadn't arrived. Cam headed to the back to pick the least worn-looking booth. The smell of corned beef wafted everywhere. His appetite kicked in. Paula slid in and unwrapped her rolled napkin. A waitress dropped off a three-bowl tray of pickles, coleslaw, and celery sticks.

Paula stabbed a squat pickle with her fork from one of the metal bowls. She bit off the end with a grand crunch. "These are great. Want one?"

Cam waved off, refusing the garlicky item.

"Yeah, yeah. I know. Bad breath and burps. But these are worth it." She chomped. "Besides, that's how come breath mints and antacids were invented." Her next crisp bite gave him a moment to speak, but he stared at the table while he selected his words.

"Okay, Cam, what can I do for you?"

"I want Sandy back."

She gnawed on the end of the pickle. "Do you always get what you want?"

"Usually, if I try hard enough."

"Why do you want her so bad?"

"I love her."

"Oh, yeah? See this?" She held the fork with the half-eaten stump close to his face. "I love this. And after I eat it, I can love another and another." She tapped a second metal bowl. "But then, after enough pickles, I start on the coleslaw, and I love that, too."

"Come on, Paula. It's not like that."

"Yeah? What's it like then?"

"I vowed not to get caught in a relationship so I'd never be devastated again. But I can't live without her. She is like no other woman I've met. I love her and want her to know it."

"Nah, she's not gonna believe you."

He took a breath. His shoulders fell as he exhaled. "I know. I really fucked— uh, messed it up."

"Your first word was right. Look, she's come home three times in tears after being with you. When she's with Oggie, she's happy and laughing. You know what that tells me?"

The arteries in his neck pulsed. "Who's Oggie?"

"The other guy she dates. He's great. Did you think you were the only one?"

A burn heated his face. He stared at Paula for a second. "Does she love him?"

"I think she likes him, but she hasn't gotten over you. That's what Oggie's doing, helping her forget you."

Cam sat silent for a short time. "I can't lose her to someone else. I have to think of something."

"Oh, yeah? Do you think there's anything you *can* do?"

He hesitated, half-staring at the metal bowls. "I think so. Do you know what size ring Sandy wears?"

"Ring? As in engagement ring?"

Cam nodded.

Paula pulled a silvery circle with a black pearl off her finger. "This is hers. We share stuff. Wanna borrow it?"

"Thank you. Can you keep her home this Wednesday?"

"It's her day off. And karma is on your side. Oggie is out of town for a few days. He works away sometimes. I'll make sure she's at home in the afternoon."

"Thanks, Paula." He stabbed a pickle and bit into it. "By the way, Josh likes you."

"You think?"

He took another bite. "I'm certain."

"Can't you guys just figure out how you feel and say it?"

"No. And it causes a lot of trouble."

CHAPTER 12

A knock on the front door sounded.

"Can you get that, Sandy?" Lorraine asked from the living room.

Sandy left her bedroom. "Why can't you get it? You're closer." She peeked out the sidelight window and backed away. "Oh, God, it's Cam. Tell him I'm out."

"No way. You answer it."

"Come on, Lorrie. I don't want to talk to him."

Lorraine put her book down, stood, and maneuvered Sandy gently into the corner next to the door. "What's wrong? Why don't you want to talk to him?"

Sandy shot Lorraine a pissy look, then dropped her head and whispered. "I don't know what's wrong with me. Since the attack, I react like a crazy woman. I can't trust men."

"You need to try harder," Lorraine said. At the second knock, she angled her head at the door. "Try."

"Let me in." Cam's voice filtered through the wood. "I need to see you."

Sandy cracked the door and stared through the gap, unable to summon the proper response. Paula rushed in and pulled Sandy away. Lorraine opened the door fully. Mrs. Vreeland came out of her house with lightning speed and followed Cam inside.

Sandy choked up. Words failed her. A sob that had waited a long time surfaced. Stifling another sob, she ran into her bedroom and flopped on the bed.

Cam stepped into her room, trailed by the audience. With trembling fingers, he raked his hair into place. "Sandy, please. I love you."

Sandy's stomach tightened. She sat up, wanting to say she loved him too, but the response stuck in her throat. She managed to say, "Cam...."

Cam approached the bed and then went down on one knee. "Sandra Gray, I love you." He opened a small black box. "Will you marry me?" He took the ring from its velvet slot and lifted her hand. "Sandy?"

Overwhelmed by his appearance, his declaration of love, plus the question, Sandy allowed the emotions of love and relief to mix for a few moments. She swallowed her throat lump away. "I...." Sandy rasped and regarded each of the three other ladies. She looked down at him. "I... Yes," and held her finger slightly apart as he slid on the sparkling ring. "It's beautiful."

Cam stood and brushed his pant knee. "It was my great aunt's. And now it's yours."

"Let us see," Lorraine demanded.

Mrs. Vreeland peered closely. "Rose cut diamond. Nice. My grandmother had something like it. It's Victorian." She looked at Cam. "Platinum?"

"It is." Cam took Sandy's hand and kissed her wrist. "I thought you would appreciate the style, Sandy. But if you don't like it, we can get something else, anything you like."

"I love it. Am I the first to...?"

Cam hugged her. "Since Great Aunt Mary-Lilly drew her last breath." Cam closed the black velvet box and put it in his pocket. "Ladies, would you be my guest for dinner as an engagement celebration?"

"We can be ready in ten minutes," Lorraine said.

While Cam waited patiently by the front door, Mrs. Vreeland hurried to her house. Sandy and her roommates ran to get ready.

In under the ten-minute timeline, all decked out for their

celebration, the ladies met on the front step. The group jammed into Cam's car.

After an hour's ride into the city, they dined in a rooftop restaurant where wall-sized windows and low lighting provided views of the East River. After a three-course dinner with no expense spared, including bottles of Dom Perignon, they made many toasts to the couple's happiness.

As Cam signed the credit slip, Sandy leaned to him and whispered, "Thank you for the wonderful meal."

He returned the whisper close to her ear, "Let's go to my place for an after-dinner treat. I've waited so long, I'm starved."

Sub rosa, she said, "I'm beginning to feel a bit peckish, myself."

He responded quietly so only she could hear. "Peckish?" Mimicking a movie gangster, he said, "I got your peckish right here!"

Sandy laughed. The other three ladies at the table could not have heard the entire conversation, but they laughed at her infectious snicker.

Cam called a car service to return the three ladies back to Queens. Driving up the West Side Highway to his Manhattan home, he turned to Sandy. "I know what joy is. I am happy. I thought I had been in love before, but it didn't compare to this. The first time I met you, something clicked. When we were apart, I felt empty. I know we were meant to be together."

She squinched as close to him as the console allowed. "I didn't expect something so poetic from you. But I know what joy is, too."

At a red light, he kissed her. "I think I might die if I don't make love to you tonight."

"Since we are engaged, am I responsible for your health and well-being?"

"Absolutely. My well-being is being threatened by lust."

He unbuttoned his collar and loosened his tie.

I thought you said you were experiencing joy?"

"Joyful lust. I can multitask."

"You are so talented, Cam, who knew?"

"Just wait. My many talents shall be revealed."

When he unlocked the house door, he brought her into the foyer and turned toward the elegant staircase, wide at the bottom, narrowing at the graceful bend with turned rails curving up to the landing. "I want to show you the house, this time in detail." He put his hands on her shoulder and kissed her neck. "But first, let me show you the bedrooms."

Portraits lined the wall adjacent to the stairs. Studying the faces, Sandy barely noticed her ascent with her hand in his. Cam stopped at an open door. "That's the master bedroom." He pointed to a door next to it. "And the master is connected to this small room by a wall door. Maybe it can be your closet."

She entered the small chamber. "I think this one will be the nursery."

"Hmm, see the effect that has on me?" Cam pulled her gently into an embrace, where she felt the effect against her hip. He guided her into the master bedroom. "Time for dessert." They stood next to his bed. He kissed her while working her buttons.

Sandy took off her skirt. "Here," she said, "Let me help you undress." Cam needed little help. He undressed in a flash.

She focused on his body. The only time she had seen a naked man before was in drawing class, an elective course in college. That model did not look like Cam. She eyed him from top to bottom, marveling at his curved shoulders and muscled torso. Golden silk curled on his chest as if a skilled artist had arranged the pattern. As her gaze traveled downward, she exhaled a half-gasp. She stood unmoving in her bra and panties. "Oh-oh."

He nuzzled her neck. "Hey, you're not afraid of me, right?"

She looked away.

He tucked her chin and turned her face to him. "Baby, you okay?"

She nodded, returned his stare, and gulped. "This is my first time. Please be...careful?"

He pulled her into his arms. "Oh, honey. I'm not sure what to say." He kissed her cheek. "But I'm not surprised." He sat and patted the mattress. "C'mere. No problem. Don't worry."

She sat. "I guess that sounds so...I don't know."

"Hey." He brushed a lock of hair from her face. "Everyone has a first time. We'll make it memorable."

"Do you remember your first?"

He nodded in an exaggerated movement. "Let's not get into that conversation."

"If you don't want to talk, it makes me curious. Tell me."

"Uh-uh. You really don't want to know."

"Oh yes, I do. I don't care about the girl's identity, wait — a *girl*, right?"

A vee formed between his eyebrows. "*Yes*. A *girl*. But—"

"Tell me."

"Oh, honey, this isn't a story that will do us any good. Please—"

"Cameron."

"It's going to get you out of the mood. Aw, shit."

"It won't affect my mood. Unless you *don't* tell me."

"Okay." He sighed. "One night, when I was fifteen, Carter, fourteen, called me and demanded I come to her house. An emergency. When I got there, she had on her mom's flimsy nightgown and said her folks were away. Since neither one of us had done it before, we were going to do it then."

"You said okay?"

Cam tilted his head. "I was a fifteen-year-old horndog. Of course, I said okay. Except she called all the shots. Told me what to do blow by blow, no pun. Even had condoms. Look, now you know. No more discussion. We walk a thin bridge sometimes when we talk."

Sandy put her head on Cam's shoulder. "Okay. No more talking."

Cam pressed a button on a panel in the headboard. The room lights dimmed into darkness. He gently pulled Sandy onto a pillow and scooted next to her, skin-on-skin.

Her heart hammered. The thumping increased as his hand brushed over her breast. The slight prickle of his chin against her cheek added to her excitement. One part of her couldn't wait for his next attention, but another part of her jumped at every touch, and she couldn't get a good breath. Each shallow inhale pulled her deeper into a self-imposed catatonia where nothing but the two of them existed. Cam's kisses, sometimes soft and gentle, transformed into hot pressure encounters at just the right time on just the right spot. With whispered directions, he guided her movements to provide his pleasure. The attention she lavished upon him gave her an additional jolt of arousal when he moaned or encouraged her touches.

Sandy had imagined making love with Cam. Actually, being with him, indulging in the enjoyments she dreamed about, far surpassed her fantasies. And Cam did some things she had never thought of. His tongue, applying the perfect touch, brought her a wave of indescribable delight. He lay next to her as the spasms imparted their sweet electricity. When she recovered, he reached over her and picked up something from the bedside table.

He ripped open a small metallic wrapper. "Here, put this on me."

Sandy had never held a condom before.

"Baby," he urged her. "On."

She held the wet plastic item against his shaft and brought it down. He groaned softly, got on top of her, and kissed her. A hollowness grew deep inside her, twisting open and demanding to be filled. "Do it."

"Honey,"

"Now, Cam, please, before I explode."

"Okay, but relax, Baby. And tell me if you want to stop." He moved to a kneeling position and nudged her legs apart with his knee.

She felt the condom's dampness against her. "Cam?"

"Honey, it's all right." Cam slid his hands under her hips. "Help me."

Sandy scooted up closer. "Now."

Cam held her firmly and pushed.

"Oh, God," she rasped. "No, don't stop." She hadn't expected the burning sting and bit her lip not to whimper.

Fully inside her, Cam put his lips to her ear. "All right?"

"Yes," she let out a faltering breath. "Yes."

Cam pulled out and pushed back inside. Stinging replaced the pleasantness of his previous passion. She was relieved when he stopped moving and groaned. He rolled to her side and embraced her. The demanding hollow inside her went silent. Maybe lovemaking had been overrated.

When he released his hold, he nuzzled her cheek. "Okay?"

She nodded. He turned the light on from the headboard button, keeping the illumination low, then left the bedside and went into the bathroom. In a few minutes, he came back with a warm washcloth for her.

Slipping past the awkward silence, Sandy sat against the pillows, elbows on her knees. "Cam—"

He moved close and put her head into the notch of his neck. "Not too good for you, right?"

"I'm fine."

He massaged her neck.

"Cam. Our relationship…everything has happened so

fast."

"Not really. As soon as I met you, I knew you were special. Even when they told me I didn't need to see you, I wanted to. And when you told me you wouldn't take money for not testifying, I couldn't stop thinking about you, so different from the women I know. It took a bit longer to admit you were the only one for me. And when Paula said you had another boyfriend, it kicked my ass. I couldn't let you slip away. But, damn, you can be so… mercurial."

"Oh, God, Cam, I'm sorry. I don't know why I—"

"It's probably backlash from your attack. Who wouldn't be afraid after that, not knowing what is around the corner? And I came on to you so strong. But know this for sure. I love you, and all of the worries about the past are over. We're together, we're getting married, and life will be wonderful for both of us. Oh, and the sex won't hurt ever again. You'll see."

"That's good news," she said. "You better be right."

Cam left the bed. "I'm right. Trust me. But now, let me show you your new home."

They both dressed.

Cam took her into each of the five bedrooms upstairs. Each room was elegant, not lavishly decorated, including the small one Sandy called the nursery. She had seen most of the downstairs, the entry, the parlor, the open dining room presided over by a chandelier, a room made into an office, the kitchen, and pantries. Then, he brought her into a library-like den and had her sit on an overstuffed sofa. He brought an old photo album from one of the shelves. For more than an hour, he flipped the pages, giving her the history of his family. The album had pictures of the house before the turn of the century. He closed the book and stood, extending his hand to her. "Let me show you what my aunt left."

Cam opened the doors of the built-in cabinets in the wood

paneling of the dining room. Sandy gasped at the beautiful pink and green Limoges china. She turned a piece of the sterling over in her hand as she admired the Gorham *Candlelight* pattern.

"There's more," Cam said. He opened glass pane doors showing thin crystal vessels etched with floral patterns. "We can change anything you want."

"I like it all, everything in the house, including the drapes."

Overwhelmed by the events of the evening and the tour of what would be her new home, Sandy said she had to leave. Her shift the next day started at ten. The two got into Cam's car for the ride back to Sandy's place.

It was two a.m. when Sandy returned. After the prolonged kiss at the front door, Sandy came inside to find Lorraine and Paula on the couch with the television on.

Paula snapped off the television and stood in front of her. "Okay, are you gonna give us the gory details?"

"No, never."

Paula grabbed Sandy's hand and made her sit between them. "Nothing? We waited up for a report, and you're giving us nothing?"

"Not a single detail," Sandy teased.

Lorraine jumped up and ran into the kitchen, returning with a white-topped cupcake hosting a small black candle.

"What's that for?" Sandy asked as Lorraine lit the wick.

"This is a requiem for your cherry," Paula said and snickered.

Sandy put her head up and sniffed. "You don't know…"

"Yes, we do!" Lorraine said.

Sandy rolled her lip. "I neither confirm nor deny. But he better *damn well* marry me."

The three young women fell on each other, laughing.

CHAPTER 13

Two days later, Sandy slid into the car seat and waited for Cam to get in.

"Oh, Cam, this has been the happiest time of my life."

"Me, too. I don't want to wait. Let's get married right away," Cam pulled the car from Sandy's driveway. "Unless a big wedding is really important to you."

"Right away? What does that mean in time?"

He smiled. "It sounds like you're asking me the equivalent in dog years. I'm thinking a month. Can you pull it together in thirty days? How big will your guest list run?"

Sandy's heartbeat kicked up a notch. "A month? Okay. I don't need a big wedding. As for guests, I can't think of many people to invite. My roomies and Mrs. Vreeland, of course, and the people at the two libraries, I guess. My grandmother is gone. I have no idea where my mother is or my sister and brother."

"I thought you were an only child?"

"I was four when Mom gave me to Grandma Noonie, my dad's mother, when he left.

I was the youngest, and my mother couldn't cope. I hardly remember him. Or them. My grandmother didn't want me, but she took me. I rarely heard from my father. Never heard from Mom. I don't know if she's alive."

"Oh, honey, I'm sorry about that, and sorry I hadn't asked about your history before. The firm's private detective agency could search for your family. They're good."

She looked out the car window and shook her head against the offer. "What if you found them and they didn't want to come? That would hurt worse than not seeing them all these years. Mom knew where I was; she could have found me easily. After Grandma died, the neighbors knew what college I attended. I send Christmas cards to three of Grandma's friends in Albany so they know where I am now. If my family wanted to find me, they could. Thanks, but no thanks."

"Don't be sad, honey."

"I'm okay. What about your guest list?"

"I'll try to keep it small. Liam, my brother, is in Oregon. I've asked him to be an attendant. We aren't close, but I think he'll come. I don't know if my parents can come. Wally will be my best man."

"Does Liam own half of the house?"

"No, he took his part of the estate in cash. I took the house." Cam put his arm up over the back of her seat and ran his fingers through her hair. "I love you. It's so easy to say."

"I know!" She leaned to kiss his shoulder. "A month isn't much time to arrange a wedding. We should look at invitations very soon."

"I've asked a wedding planner to talk with us tomorrow night at my place," he said. "Tonight, we go to Herman's. Then afterward," he raised his eyebrows a few times and smiled.

Sandy shook her head. "Afterward, I'm going home. No more sex until the vows."

I want it to be special."

"No sex? Sandy! Are you trying to kill me? You must have heard by nefarious means that I listed you as my beneficiary on my life insurance today."

"You did? Already?"

"The agent happened to come into the office this morning. It was the perfect time to change beneficiaries.

"Change? Who was the previous beneficiary?"

"Uh, Carter." He shrank down and closed one eye as if

waiting for Sandy's evil glare.

Sandy's glare was evil. "Why did you wait so long to take her off? Were you thinking she would change her mind and move back with you?"

"No. I didn't want her to change her mind. I didn't and don't want her in my life. I just didn't get around to it and wasn't planning my demise any time soon. It's done now. Relax."

The car slowed to a stop in the heavy traffic. He drummed the steering wheel. "How does a two-week trip to the West Indies on the Queen Mary II sound as a honeymoon?"

It took a second for Cam's question to alleviate Sandy's annoyance about the beneficiary. "The Queen Mary? Two weeks?"

"A balcony suite. Does that sound good?"

"Oh, Cam. I've dreamed about going on a luxury cruise since I started college. I never thought it would happen. The Queen Mary. Can it really be true?"

"The QMII. I booked it this morning."

"When is the cruise?"

"In thirty-one days. Works out good, huh?"

"You were pretty sure I would agree to the one-month time allowance."

"Uh, yeah, I was. Here we are, and a parking space right out in front. This is my lucky day." He smiled again. "Maybe my lucky night, too."

Herman sat at his post in front of the bar. The long mirror on the length of one side made the place look bigger than it was. Streetlights reflected oddly into the dark rooms as the liquor bottles cast colorful shadows against the wall. Herman put his finger to his forehead in his usual salute.

Cam paused at the bar. "Herman, remember when I introduced you to Sandy?" He turned to her then back to Herman. Miss Gray is soon to be Sandy Morgan."

Herman slid off the high-back stool. "Mighty glad to see you again, Miss Gray. My warmest regards on the nuptials. Good for you, Morgan."

As they made their way toward the back of the room, Cam stopped at various tables to introduce Sandy.

Wally and Marion, in their regular spot, stood to greet them. Wally patted Cam's back with large swings of his hand. "Hey, pal! Marion has been pie-eyed since I told her the news."

Marion kissed Cam's cheek and then hugged Sandy. "I knew there was something between you when we met last time. I knew! I'm glad Cam saw how great you are."

Unaccustomed to praise, Sandy flushed. "Thanks." Her humility merged with embarrassed pleasure.

Marion hugged her again. "Cam said the ceremony will be in a month. Let me know if I can help. My mother and I did all the planning for my wedding, so take advantage of my hard-gained experience. Maybe I can help to get things done quicker."

"I guess you knew when it would be before I did." Sandy struggled to hold back the glare daggers forming.

"Cam moves fast," Wally said. "You must know that about him by now."

Sandy looked at Cam, letting small daggers fly. "I'm learning."

Cam ordered Prosecco for four. Sandy listened to a few of Marion's wedding horror stories while Cam asked Wally about his work as NYPD Liaison with the Federal agencies. When the drinks came, they toasted to the wedding.

Chatting as couples provided a new experience. She had worked through college and had not been involved in dating. Her unease with this new social experience waned, but after a few more rounds of Prosecco and continuous chatting, Sandy checked her watch. "I have the early shift tomorrow. Sorry, but I need to get back home."

They said their goodbyes then walked to the car parked in Cam's lucky spot. On the way to Astoria, Sandy repeated the wedding problems Marion spoke of.

"Put all of those worries away," Cam said. "Everything will be smooth as silk." When he stopped at a red light, he reached over, took her hand, and kissed her fingertips. "Everything's good. You'll see. I walked into a library and found the most amazing woman in the world. What special thing did I do in my former life to get you?"

She wanted to revel in his love and affection. The temptation to put all of her hopes and dreams in this new situation beckoned. As far back as she could remember, she had depended on herself. Her grandmother had been the closest thing to a loving parent, but Grandma Noonie took minimal care of the little girl left on her doorstep. Mrs. Vreeland exhibited more concern for Sandy than anyone had, and Mrs. Vreeland was only a neighbor.

"Honey? You don't look happy."

Sandy pulled her hand away from him and searched his face, selecting words. "I'm as happy as I *can* be."

"What does that mean?" The light turned green.

"It means this is all new to me, and I get confused."

The car picked up speed. "Are you having second thoughts about marrying me?"

"No second thoughts. I want to get married. I know how to love. I just don't know how to trust."

"I will do what I can to help you learn to trust me. Now, smile. We're in love, and your life from this minute on will be wonderful. Okay?"

She nodded. "Thank you for being patient."

"Thank you for just being you."

As they rode, she crystallized her resolve to float along the trust pathway Cam offered her. He walked her to the front door. "I'll pick you up tomorrow at work so we can negotiate with the wedding planner."

"Negotiate? Is this like a big business transaction?"

"Everything is business, my sweet."

She put her arms around his neck and rubbed her lips against his ear. "Everything?"

"No. Some things are a pleasure." He pressed his hips against hers at the door jamb.

A jolt of energy surged through her body. Being near him sent quivers in all directions.

He kissed her, touching his tongue with hers for a second. "I'll see you tomorrow. I love you. God, that feels good to say."

"I love you, too. It does feel good." Sandy sniffed her hand, breathing in the smell of Cam's cologne. "Smells wonderful. See you at five tomorrow." She waited outside the door, watching the Lexus pull out of the drive, needing the time to dissipate the adrenaline pinging in her bloodstream brought on by his goodnight kisses.

She had given her heart, her virginity, and now her trust. Although she had dated a few times, there had been no one else who had attracted her. Except for Oggie. That relationship could have gone somewhere. But it didn't matter now.

CHAPTER 14

The next morning, at her desk, Sandy tried to email Oggie. She needed to let him know about the wedding. He had told her he could get in touch with her, but since he would be moving around so much, she wouldn't be able to email him. She tried the last address listed on his message, but her email bounced back. She regretted not being able to contact him. Eventually, he would write. Sandy knew how Oggie felt about her, even if he hadn't said it outright. But what happened, happened, and Og was a big boy. She chided herself for being dismissive. He was a good guy to whom she felt deeply attached, and he deserved to be informed.

At five that afternoon, Cam waited for her in the car at the rear of the library. He brought Chinese take-out, and when he opened the car door for Sandy, the smell made her hungry.

"We have just enough time to get to my place and eat before Mrs. Lovejoy, the wedding planner, is supposed to arrive."

Sandy laughed. "Mrs. Lovejoy? Is that her real name? It's perfect for a person who handles weddings."

"I don't know if it's an alias, but you're right. Makes you think everything will turn out happy. Love and joy. She was recommended to me by the office manager. I'm sure she'll be efficient."

As he turned into his drive, Cam pressed the button on the headliner to raise the garage door in the back of the house. The garage was connected to the house by an enclosed hall that led directly into the kitchen.

This time, Sandy noted how much she liked the house.

Most of the walls had heavy wood paneling, giving the place a comforting but elegant feel. Some of the Persian-type carpets were worn, but that added to the charm of the place. However, the rug in the dining room should be replaced. *I'm already making changes! Will this house really be mine?*

They sat at a small kitchen table and dug into the warmed-up white cartons decorated with red pagodas.

"This orange chicken is delicious," Sandy said.

"Here," Cam selected another, pushed away the thin metal bale, and opened a carton. "Try this. It's shrimp with lobster sauce. This place makes the best."

She agreed and traded the chicken for the shrimp. They shared the containers and enjoyed the assortment of foods. Sampling the varieties, sharing, and making jokes with Cam—all new experiences for Sandy, warmed her soul.

They just finished the meal and cleaned up when Mrs. Lovejoy rang the doorbell. The lady was barely five feet tall and appeared to be almost as wide as high. She wore her dark hair short, and the front locks curved sharply toward her heart-shaped face. Obviously, the wedding planner didn't realize, or perhaps didn't care, that the loud colors and crazy pattern of her pantsuit called attention to her large body.

The woman gave them samples of invitations, brochures for catering, five bridal magazines, and suggestions for ceremony styles. "I know this is a lot of information hurled at you all at once, but if we are going to get this party together in your time frame, we need to move on it." She smiled at Sandy. "Such a pretty bride." Mrs. Lovejoy handed Sandy two business cards. "These are bridal shops I recommend. They have a large selection and will treat you as a priority if you need alterations or special requests."

Cam took the cards and read them. He put them back in Sandy's hand. "Spare no expense, honey. I want you to be happy."

"Ah," Mrs. Lovejoy said. "That's the perfect way to start a marriage." She winked at Sandy. "You have already trained him to give you the upper hand."

The comment set off a buzzer in Sandy's mind. *Will I ever have the upper hand with Cameron Morgan?* She put the cards in her purse. "Maybe Lorraine and Paula can take time off and help me select a dress."

Mrs. Lovejoy directed her words to Cam. "These bridal shops will open after hours to accommodate the bride by appointment. No one needs to take time off from their jobs. Make an appointment, and they will work with you." She turned to Sandy. "I would try to do this as soon as possible. Time is the adversary here. I'll get back to you in a few days to see what invitations you've chosen, and maybe you will have other things ready for me to get the ball rolling. The ball needs to roll if we want everything in place for your wedding date."

After Cam walked Mrs. Lovejoy to the front stoop, he returned to the couch, where Sandy read a brochure on catering. Cam brushed all of the paperwork to the floor and pushed her down on the couch. Self-control came easily for Sandy due to her upbringing, but her instant reaction to arousal surprised her. Sticking to her wish to wait to have sex after the wedding would challenge her self-restraint.

"Cam, we should wait. I want to make the honeymoon special. Give us something to look forward to."

Pressing his cheek against her breast, he unfastened the top button on her blouse. "Are you sure?" He unbuttoned the second and third so fast she hardly had time to answer. He reached into the back of her blouse and undid her bra. "God, I love you."

Sandy thought she must have power switches connected to her nipples because when Cam touched them, she was definitely *on*. It reminded her of the gas fireplace in the house in Astoria. Push the button, and the fire ignited. And that ignition fired her like launching a rocket. If she had known earlier in her life how great sex would be, she would have given up a few hours of study and made some friends, and attended more college events.

She quivered when he pressed his groin against her. The little voice inside chided her for not holding to her vow to wait until the wedding. Then the voice said it was a good thing she had skin because all of the inner stuff had just turned to electrified jelly.

"You don't want to go home now, do you?" Cam pulled off her blouse, and the bra came with it. He kicked off his shoes and undid his fly. Within a few seconds, he had the rest of his clothes off.

Sandy could barely get her words out between shallow breaths. "Oh. Just tonight."

"Yeah, yeah, okay," he said into her ear. "Just tonight."

CHAPTER 15

In the days that followed, the wedding took on a personality of its own. Sandy had little to decide about the arrangements. Her life rearranged into something she couldn't control. Since she couldn't decide on one Maid of Honor, she selected two, Lorraine and Paula.

One evening, when Mrs. Vreeland came to their house, Sandy and the roommates talked about dresses. "Look, I think of you girls as the daughters I didn't have. I want to be part of this happy event in any way I can. So, Sandy, would you consider wearing my wedding dress? It's in a box in my closet. Can I bring it to you right now and let you look at it?"

A flush of warmth ran through Sandy's body. She never had this kind of closeness before. Her two best friends became like sisters, and now Mrs. Vreeland had stepped into a slot much like a mother would be.

"Yes, I'd love to see it. Do you want me to help you?"

The smile on the older woman's face almost obscured her answer. "No need. I have it right behind the closet door. I hoped you would say yes." She scurried out to get the box.

Within a few minutes, Mrs. Vreeland returned with a box and an album, filling her arms. She beamed when she lifted the lid and took out the dress, a fifties-era wedding gown. Mrs. Vreeland draped the satin gown over the back of the couch.

Sandy touched the shiny fabric, running her finger over the surface. "I love it. Thank you so much. I hope it fits."

Mrs. Vreeland's face became serene as if she saw a movie inside her mind. After a moment, she snapped out of her memory.

"I think it will fit. I was about your size when I wore it. Look at my wedding photos. You'll get an idea of how it will look on you."

In the album, the black and white photos showed Mrs. Vreeland as a slender young girl and a handsome mustachioed man standing between two pillars decked with flowers. A long train wound around the skirt and flowed down the steps between the columns. The dress in the pictures was white, but now the years had turned it to a mellow beige. It was beautiful, perfect for Sandy's taste.

Typical of the fashion of that time, the shimmering satin gown had a dropped waist and lace overskirt. Tulle covered the strapless bodice and the sleeve ending in a pointed cuff. The back closed with twenty covered buttons, each with a loop for a closure that went down past her hips. The matching tulle veil attached to a cap of silk flowers. The headpiece had been lovely in its day, but it now had rust marks from the metal stems of the silk flowers.

Lorraine examined the veil. "The dress is beautiful, but you can't wear this. We need to get a new one. Let's go shopping on Friday. We'll go to the ones your wedding planner suggested."

Sandy called the first store on the list and made an appointment for seven pm. They agreed to stay open for them.

"Wow. You must be important if they will let you shop off-hours," Mrs. Vreeland said. "Can I come, too?"

"Of course. We are all in this together." The feeling of being in a family took a little time to assimilate. Sandy had found a family and now a husband. Or had it been the other way around? No matter. She reveled in the sensations of closeness and caring.

During her break the next day, when Cam called, he offered to help her shop, but Sandy reminded him of the bad luck associated with seeing the bridal clothes. "But I'll let you meet us for dinner afterward."

"Yeah," he said, "but I'm not making reservations. I'm not sure you will be finished before midnight."

"Well, that's too bad. You might get hungry." She laughed after saying that to him. Was she growing a spine all of a sudden?

"Let me know when and where. I'll be there."

"Right." She rang off. Cam could be controlling, but he was patient with her, too.

Friday evening, Lorraine, Paula, and Mrs. Vreeland accompanied Sandy for a flurry of intense wedding shopping. After finding a headpiece that suited the dress, Mrs. Vreeland said, "I'm paying for it. I can afford it and want to do it. Actually, I'm having a lot of fun being part of your wedding."

"While we are shopping, why don't we select bridesmaid dresses?" Sandy asked. "All three of you will be in my party, so choose what you like as long as they don't clash and make a spectacle."

Lorraine chose a lavender silk sheath with a matching bolero jacket. The top of the dress and jacket sported glass beads and small lavender pearls embedded in matching embroidery. The dress set off her almost-lavender eyes and light brown hair.

Paula chose a lime-sherbet green dress with an empire waist. The color enhanced her pale green eyes. Her curly dark hair made a striking contrast to the light colors.

And Mrs. Vreeland chose a red damask dress that made her gray-streaked hair stand out. After the elderly lady insisted on paying for the veil, the magic word at the bridal stores was *Mrs. Lovejoy*, meaning no other payment was discussed. Cam had told Sandy not to concern herself about the cost, and she took him at his word.

At ten, after the shopping, Cam met them for dinner in a small French restaurant near the bridal store. Sandy ordered a salad but was so excited she could hardly eat. Mrs. Vreeland ordered crepes, and the other ladies wanted Croque Monsieur.

Cam ordered escargot and Caesar salads, plus wine for everyone.

A strolling violinist came over to their table, and after a few serenades, Cam gave him a twenty-dollar bill to play somewhere else so they could talk.

After dinner, Cam ordered a car service to take the three ladies back so he and Sandy could talk privately. He paid the check and walked her back to his car. He kissed her before opening the car door, then got in his side but didn't start the ignition.

Sandy put her hand on Cam's. "I have money saved. It's not much, but I can help pay for some of the expenses."

"Don't worry about a single thing. I just settled a lawsuit out of court, and my client, Robert Ross, did so well that I'm getting a bonus. And, when he heard I was getting married, he offered his penthouse terrace for the ceremony. How does that sound?"

"Maybe it's terrific, but everything is falling into place without me. Other than the dresses, I hardly need to make any choices." She tried to keep the frustration out of her voice. "Mrs. Lovejoy called and said she had a calligrapher for the invitations, and I had to give her my list in two days."

"Yeah, I already gave her mine."

"Your bonus, is it enough to pay for everything?"

"If it isn't, I'll use my savings account, and the rest we can put on the card. I'll just put it all on the card and pay it off." He winked. "I get airline miles."

The next day, Sandy and the roommates had the day off, and she enjoyed the excitement buzzing around the house. Lorraine and Paula went about their chores humming tunes and, every so often, would hum the Wedding March.

That night, she and Cam went to a local theatre to see a double-feature film noir, *Casablanca* and *the Maltese Falcon*. Afterward, they had pizza and beer. Sandy declined to stay overnight with him. He agreed and didn't pressure her. Somewhere between the warmth of love and the feeling she didn't have control over her life, she had to find order, balance.

The next morning, as the three roommates had breakfast, Lorraine cleared her throat and asked, "Uhm, sorry to be nosy, but have you thought about birth control?"

Sandy wrinkled her nose at her friend. "I know you are concerned about me. I've only *been* with Cam a few times. He took precautions. I have an appointment on Tuesday to get an IUD. Truthfully, I can hardly say no to him. I'm trying to wait until our honeymoon."

"That's got to be hard," Paula snickered at the double entendre. "I mean difficult."

"It's very difficult. He really makes me crazy, and I want to do it. But I don't want to disappoint my grandmother. We weren't close and didn't talk much about love or sex, but the one thing she told me was never to give your husband a reason to doubt why he married you. If you have a baby soon after you say vows, even if you didn't know you were pregnant, a man at some time during his life will wonder if you trapped him. I promised her I wouldn't give my husband a reason for doubt."

"Interesting advice," Paula said.

"I know Grandma Noonie would rather not have been responsible for me, but she took me in anyway." Sandy looked to the ceiling. "Thanks, Grandma Noonie."

CHAPTER 16

The days flew by, and the wedding plans slipped into place like pieces of a beautiful puzzle. Every day, Sandy hoped to hear from Oggie. She pictured him showing up at the library and her having to tell him she got married while he was gone. The dread of telling Oggie, however, was minor compared to the trouble she knew she would face trying to get time off for her honeymoon. With no vacation left, she would have to take a personal leave, and based on what she had heard from other employees, getting that corresponded to pulling teeth.

One afternoon, a few minutes before her shift ended, Sandy saw Cam leave her supervisor's office. By the time the three patrons waiting to check out books were served, her shift had ended.

Cam waited in the back lot of the library. He held the car door for her. "Hi."

"Hi." She pecked his cheek. "You were in Dolores's office for almost an hour. What's going on?"

He pushed the ignition button and put his hand on the gearshift. "I hoped I could talk her into giving you paid leave even though you have no more vacation time left for this year. She said you could take unpaid leave, but I think you should quit. You don't need to work. I make enough money. You could do lots of things with your spare time."

"Cam! Quit?"

"Come on, Sandy. Most women would jump at it. It will take you an hour to get there from our home. That's two hours a day for travel. Even if I get you a car, it will take too long to travel."

"Cam, the more I think about this wedding, the more pissed I get."

"Pissed? Why? Where do you want to go for dinner tonight?"

Sandy gritted her teeth. "Queens. Take me home right now. Look, this has gone too far. Why am I pissed? You made cruise plans without my knowledge, announced our wedding date before I knew about it, picked a wedding planner, and who knows what else I'll discover. You want me to quit my job. I've had enough. Don't do another thing unless you run it by me first."

"Sandy."

She narrowed her eyes. "Coordinated decisions. Mutually, or it's all off."

Cam pulled over into a parking lot and cut the engine. "You'd call off the wedding?"

Sandy stiffened. "I've tried to go along with you so it would be seamless, but you have pushed me into a corner." She crossed her arms over her chest. "I'm not going to marry a tyrant."

Cam scratched his nose. Then he touched her hand. "I'm sorry. I know I can be a steamroller sometimes. Does my report card say *not a good team player*?"

She knew he wanted her to smile at his humor, but she wouldn't let him off so easily. Her nostrils flared.

He nodded. "It's hard for me to understand that other people can do things as well as I do. I hope you can learn to deal with that as much as I will try to change. No more solitary decisions. God, Sandy, losing you... I couldn't stand it. Everything needs to be perfect. That's why—"

"Okay," she said. "I'll straighten it out with Delores tomorrow. But, take me back to Astoria. I need a night to myself to do some thinking."

Cam threw her a panicked, questioning look.

Sandy sighed. "We'll get through this. Consult me, okay?"

"Okay. Sorry," he said and started the car. He took her home.

The next morning, Sandy knocked on Dolores Reed's office door and peeked in.

"Come in," Dolores said.

Sandy closed the door and took a seat in front of the desk.

Dolores hit the save button on her computer and turned her attention to Sandy. "Are you going to resign?"

"No. I don't know what to say about Cam talking with you yesterday. He shouldn't have done that. I hope you aren't angry."

"Angry? Absolutely not. He's adorable. I'll bet he wins all of his cases. We had a lovely chat. You know, you are my best staff member. You're friendly, knowledgeable, eager to help, prompt, and dependable. I would hate to lose you, but I have to agree with Prince Charming: if you don't need to work, why would you? I would tell my own daughter that."

"I'll resign when *I* decide. How's that?"

Dolores smiled wide. "Good. When *you* are ready. Never let a man think he has the upper hand." She cocked her head a bit and smiled again. "Even when he does. In fact, don't *let* a man take charge. It won't go well for you. It's plain to see that Mr. Morgan is accustomed to taking charge. And I see why. Heck, I would have given you paid leave if I could just to please *him.* And that's the first time I met him. What a catch, by the way, good work."

Sandy thanked Dolores for the compliment. *I don't think I was the fisherman.* "Oh, Dolores, I sent you an invitation. I hope you will come to the wedding."

The woman put on her glasses, indicating the interview was over. "Of course. I'll bet he's even cuter in formal wear."

On the following Sunday, Sandy boxed a few of her

belongings, and Cam put them in his car. During the ride to his house, she asked about his part of the guest list. Most of the RSVPs had arrived, but nothing from his parents.

"They aren't coming," Cam said.

"Why wouldn't they come? Are you on bad terms with them?"

"Of course not. But we rarely see each other, and they dislike New York. My brother, Liam, is trying to arrange his schedule so he can be there. My dad sent me a lot of money for a wedding present. I cashed the check and put the money in the house safe. Later tonight, I'll show you how to open it."

"Wow, a safe. A lot of money? What does that mean exactly?"

"Five hundred thousand dollars. Several stacks of hundreds. My folks live in Switzerland. I'll tell you the story of how they moved there sometime. What about your parents? If you have changed your mind, we can find them. I'll arrange for them to come and stay in a hotel."

"I don't know where my mother is and don't care to. I was never sure the man I took my name from was my biological father. When my mother left, that man took me to his mother's house and dumped me off. If my parents are still alive, I don't know it and wouldn't invite them to anything if I did, especially my wedding."

Cam reached for her hand. "I'm sorry, honey. You won't ever feel abandoned again."

"Thank you," she said and stifled the tears forming in her eyes.

When they arrived at Cam's house, Sandy was astonished to find Mrs. Lovejoy had arranged a bridal shower. What astonished her further were the people waiting there. Her roommates, Mrs. Vreeland, Marion Wallensky, a number of coworkers, and Dolores gave her gifts and wished her well. In addition, Cam's secretary and office manager attended. Cam made a hasty exit and spent the afternoon in the study.

Before Sandy knew it, it was the eve of the wedding. She and her attendants dressed in the master suite of Robert Ross's garden penthouse. The three bridesmaids lined up outside the French doors that faced the terrace. A string quartet played Vivaldi and typical wedding selections. Then, the Wedding March began, and the bride's maids preceded Sandy. As she waited at the closed doors, listening for the *Here Comes the Bride* music, she pulled back the lace curtain to make sure Cam was outside. He was there, and in spite of the scheduling difficulties, Liam stood next to him. Liam was a slightly older, slightly darker version of Cam. Wally, standing a head taller, looked dashing in his tuxedo.

Sandy heard the musical cue.

Mrs. Lovejoy opened the doors and whispered, "Good luck" as the bride walked out onto the garden terrace. Sandy could hardly believe it and silently searched for a sense of setting. She breathed deeply, smelling the roses planted around the terrace. This was her day. Her wedding, an event that would change her life. A smile hovered somewhere within her.

Mr. Ross's rooftop terrace radiated with soft twinkle lights. Mrs. Lovejoy came through with a dream setting, an arbor draped with tulle and covered with pale roses. Sprays of baby's breath curved out of the folds amid pink lights. Cam said, "I do," loud and clear, and slipped a thick platinum band on her finger, its plainness setting off the beauty of the engagement ring.

After the ceremony, the catered dinner set up in the Ross's living room offered filet and lobster for the forty people attending. Mr. Ross generously provided bottles of Perrier champagne and toasted to "The best-damned lawyer in Manhattan and his lovely bride."

Sandy met Michelle, Liam's wife, and immediately liked her. She found it amusing that Michelle resembled her, except for Michelle's large bosom. The internal voice speculated a bit on the natural state of the bustline, taking into consideration that Liam was Dr. Liam Morgan, a well-known plastic surgeon from Portland. Couples danced on the rooftop garden until the early hours. Afterward, Cam and Sandy returned to the brownstone. He carried her over the threshold.

"Welcome home, Mrs. Morgan," he said and kicked the door shut.

CHAPTER 17

The Mellow Café had been a favorite place for the roomies to dine. Sunday, the day after she returned from her honeymoon, Sandy invited Paula and Lorraine to meet her there for lunch. Paula and Lorraine waited at a table by the window.

Paula kissed Sandy's cheek. "You look great."

"Radiant," Lorraine said.

Sandy smiled. "Thanks. I feel wonderful."

The waiter took their order.

"Well?" Paula said, thudding her fingers on the white linen. "Tell us all about it."

Sandy shrugged. "What's to tell? It was an average, everyday, garden variety honeymoon." She stifled her laugh.

"Shee-yeah," Lorraine countered.

"So," Paula said. "Do you have *any brains* left?"

"Uhm, maybe." Sandy tapped her forehead above her left eyebrow. "A little one, right here." She waited for the laughter to die down. "Cam is…uhm…quite energetic." She waited again for them to quiet. "Anything important happen while I was basking in sunshine?"

"Yeah, actually." Paula took a roll from the basket. "While we shivered in the Ice Age and you enjoyed the tropical warmth, I had some dates with Josh."

"Really? I thought it was your policy not to date your coworkers?"

"Ah, it still is. Josh's father is retiring and gave his two print shops to his sons. Jake is managing the one I'm at, and Josh has the one in the Bronx. He's a businessman!"

"That's wonderful, Paula."

Lorraine helped herself to a roll. "And me, same ole, same ole." She made a face as if she were about to cry. "I want to find someone to love. But, until then, I have enrolled in college to complete my teacher's certificate. If I don't find true love, at least I'll get a good job. I only need a few more hours for the bachelor's degree."

Sandy held up her water glass. "Here's to us. May we always get what we need."

Paula stopped her glass before clinking. "Uh uh. May we get what we want!"

They clinked glasses.

Before she drank, Sandy ran her finger around the rim of the glass.

Lorraine stopped sipping. "What's wrong?"

Sandy bit her lip. "While I was gone, did Oggie call the house?"

The other ladies looked at each other and then at Sandy. "No," they said together.

Sandy put down her glass. "He's been on my mind. When I go to work tomorrow, I'm going to see if Delores knows where he is."

"Work on Monday, what a let-down from a cruise," Paula said.

"I like my job. I'd be bored staying home."

They chatted until the waiter brought their food. Just as Lorraine took the first bite, her cell phone rang.

"Sorry, girls. I meant to turn it off. Let's see who it is. I don't recognize the number. Hello?"

Lorraine's face paled. "Police? What? All right. I'll be right there." She clutched the phone. "It's Mrs. Vreeland. She's at the hospital. They think she's had a stroke." Lorraine dabbed her mouth with the napkin and choked on the words. "She's listed us as her next of kin."

Paula pushed her plate away. "Is she…"

"Not dead, but bad. We'd better go."

"I have the car," Sandy said. "It's parked around the block."

The three women rushed to the hospital and found the room where Mrs. Vreeland, looking old and frail, lay in bed, hooked up to beeping machines. After an hour, the nurse told them to come back later. Sandy dropped off her friends and drove to the brownstone.

That evening, Sandy gave Cam the details. "Mrs. Vee had a stroke. We could barely understand her, and she has trouble moving her left side. Poor lady. Lorraine is quitting the beauty salon and will care for her during the day when the old gal is discharged. While Lorraine is taking classes at night, Paula will take care of her."

Cam took Sandy's hand. "They are wonderful friends. You are lucky to have them. Mrs. Vreeland is double lucky."

Sandy swallowed hard. "I know. If I ever need them, they'll be there for me." She bit her lip. "And I'll be there for them, too."

"That's how I feel about Wally," Cam said. "I've never thought about it before, but he's closer to me than my brother. He's not the kind to say it, but I know he'd do anything for me. You and I are both fortunate to have good friends."

"I'll need to go to see Mrs. Vee tomorrow after work. I'll be late getting back."

"Of course," Cam said.

The following morning, Sandy stuck her head into Delores Reed's office.

"Come in!" Dolores said. "Your tan looks fabulous. I'm sure you had a great time. What can I do for you?"

Sandy sat in the chair next to the big desk. "Do you know

anything about Oggie?"

"Who?"

"Ogburn G. Edwards, the computer tech guy."

"Oh, yeah, him. Not since he left. Why?"

"I need to talk to him. I don't have a phone number or an email address for him. I really should tell him I'm married."

"That was a mystery to me, Sandy. Why a cute girl like you, dating Mr. Wonderful, would look at, yet go out with, that creepy guy."

"Oggie wasn't creepy. He was fun. And smart. I enjoyed his company, his unique unpredictability."

"But, so ugly. Sandy, yech."

"Ugly? I thought he was rather attractive."

"Attractive? Oh, God. That scrawny nerd? With his greasy, kinky black hair, acne-scarred face, and yellow teeth? And those nasty black-rimmed glasses?"

"Delores? He isn't thin. Oggie has straight dark brown hair and smooth skin. I guarantee his teeth were clean and white. He did wear black glasses." Sandy leaned forward toward her supervisor. "Are we talking about the same man?"

"It doesn't sound like it." A woman passed the open door. "Hey, Sue! Can you come in here a minute?"

Susan Harper, a library clerk, parked the book cart. "Okay."

Delores motioned her to sit in the second chair. "Remember that guy who worked here for a couple of months who was really good with the computers?"

"Ogburn? Yeah."

"What did he look like?"

"Uhm, short, wore a white shirt with a thin black tie every day. Had medium brown hair, and a spare tire that flopped over his belt. Oh, and black glasses."

Sandy made a short snorting sound. "No way."

Dismissing Sue with her waving hand, Delores called to her secretary. "Grace?"

When Grace appeared, Delores asked, "Remember Ogburn, the computer guy? What did he look like?"

Grace thought for a moment. "I dunno. I remember him, but not much of what he looked like. Light brown hair, white shirt, black tie, and thick black-rimmed glasses."

Delores folded her hands on the desk. "Thanks, Grace." Grace left. "Hmm. What do you know? Oh, well. It doesn't make any difference. Anything else?"

It was the *you are dismissed* phrase that supervisors use.

Sandy stood up. "At least we all agree on the color of his glasses. But I don't care what anyone thinks he looks like. Can you get me a phone number?"

Delores nodded. "I'll call Personnel. I know someone there." She smiled. "We've had enough fun for the morning. Get to work, slacker."

During lunch in the backroom, Delores sat down with Sandy. "Oddest thing. Your Mr. Ogburn Edwards was not an employee of the New York City Library system. Nor the temp pool we get techs from, nor is there any record of him working here. I called up the ladder, but no one knew anything about him. You and I know he existed, but as far as employment data, he doesn't. Sorry I couldn't help you."

Sandy tried to process that information without success. After work, she visited Mrs. Vreeland for a few hours and then went home.

Cam wasn't there and got home after eight. "I tried to get home earlier, but they hit me with a wham-damn criminal case first thing this morning. I'm probably going to be late sometimes for a few weeks. So, how was your first day back?"

"Interesting," Sandy said. "Very interesting."

CHAPTER 18

Four weeks after returning from the honeymoon, Sandy had an abdominal cramp, the kind that bent her over, wincing and groaning. Following several bouts with the same pain and a day of vaginal bleeding, she made an appointment with her doctor.

The doctor said, "I'm terribly sorry, Mrs. Morgan. It is rare, but your copper IUD has expelled. I have to remove it. We can't wait. My staff is setting up for the procedure now."

Following the procedure, Sandy met with the doctor in her private office.

"I have good news and other news," the doctor said.

Sandy sat back in the chair. "That's an odd thing to say. It's usually good news, bad news."

"True, and it may well turn out to be that or different." The doctor half-smiled. "The good news is that there is no damage left from the copper IUD, and everything looks okay."

Sandy looked at her sideways. "And…the other news?"

"You are pregnant. Very rare, I might add, since the copper affects the uterine lining, preventing the implantation of a fertilized egg, but someone has to be the million-to-one, right?"

A flush swept over Sandy, warm and tranquil. "A miracle. I have always wanted a family."

The doctor nodded. "You are happy about this and not going to sue me? I know you are married to a lawyer."

"Don't worry."

"Thank you, Mrs. Morgan. I hope you will continue to be my patient."

"Of course." A smile formed inside her and then worked

its way to her lips. "I'm going to be a mother!" The smile faded. *I wonder if Cam is ready to be a father.*

On the way home, a man in the street stopped and watched her go by. Except for his light-colored hair, he resembled Oggie. She sighed and felt the familiar pang of regret for not communicating with him.

That evening, Cam reacted to the news with raised eyebrows. His expression continued for a few seconds. His eyes softened, and his face took on an agreeable quality. "Wow. Things are happening fast. I'm on board. Whatever you want. You did say that the little room next to ours would be a good nursery. Why don't you call a decorator and do it up? Maybe in shades of blue. It will be a boy." Then he laughed. "I almost always get what I want. And if we have to redo it in pink, I'll want that, too." His face dropped into seriousness. "I think you should quit working."

"I'll think about it," she said.

On some of her days off, Sandy brought lunch to Lorraine and Paula at the home in Astoria so Mrs. Vreeland could visit with them.

And now that Sandy was pregnant, she made a closer connection with Marion Wallensky, whose baby was close to delivery.

When the Wallenskys brought their baby home from the hospital, Cam and Sandy met them with roses. Wally surprised them when he said the child's name was Cameron.

On their way home from visiting Wally and his family, they talked in the car.

"We haven't selected a name for our baby, Cam." She made a silent plea with her face. "I hope you're not thinking of Dennis or Walter."

Cam chuckled. "No. If you don't mind. I would like to honor the uncle who raised me and Liam when my parents moved to Switzerland."

"Uncle Wesley? I like that. Would you mind if we use Allan as the middle? My grandma's name was Runetta Allan. We could honor the people who raised us." Sandy patted her slightly protruding belly. "I hope our son is as adorable as Cameron Wallensky.

Cam snorted a laugh. "When Wally held him, it reminded me of a watermelon holding a pea. But Wally didn't get huge like he is until his late teens. You're right. That baby is cute." With one hand on the wheel, Cam reached over and rubbed Sandy's shoulder. "You know a lot of men aren't good with words. I *am* good with words. But it is impossible for me to describe how I feel right now. I didn't know what love was like. Now I have you, and pretty soon a kid. I just can't put it in words."

"You don't need to say anything more. That was perfect, Cam. Thank you." Sandy relaxed into the seat. There had been no nausea for weeks, she felt good, and Cam was happy. All was well with the world around her. So why did Oggie's face pop into her memory? She couldn't reach him, and he hadn't tried to get in touch with her. Maybe she should just forget him. A voice inside her said he would never forget her, and she would see him again. Sometime. On Sandy's birthday, Paula called and said she got a card with no return address. Sandy asked her to open the card and read it.

Paula did so. "Dear Sandy. Happy Birthday. I'm thinking about you as always. Love Oggie. Still." The word *still,* was underlined.

The thought of Oggie being lonely ruined her birthday. She needed to contact him. She sometimes thought about Oggie as her life transformed into being Cam's wife. His career rocketed. He had the reputation of being dedicated, confident, knowledgeable, and charismatic. Many days, he was already in his office when the early secretary arrived. He was often the last one to depart, making certain nothing was left hanging. Clients began asking for him over the other attorneys. Aaron Feldman was one of those clients.

Carter Feldman occasionally came into the law firm, and one morning, she stuck her head into Cam's office. "I heard Sarah is pregnant. It's awful quick since you got hitched, you know. How much does DNA testing cost?"

"Her name is Sandy. The baby is mine, Carter. Give me a break."

"Are you absolutely sure?"

"Absolutely and positively. She isn't like you, Carter."

Carter smiled. "You got that right, Cammy-kins. I just can't imagine—"

Cam held up his hand to stop her. "You can't imagine, understand, or be like the woman I have married." He stood up. "Look, Carter, don't start trouble. I'm happy. Leave us alone."

Carter stuck her nose in the air. "Aaron is an important client. If you're mean to me, I'll tell him to complain to your bosses."

"Aaron is a better man than that. Maybe you don't know him as well as you should. I don't want to lose him as my client, but I'll take my chances."

She scowled, then left.

***

Paula and Josh's relationship blossomed. A few months later, the couple announced their engagement and moved up the wedding so Sandy could be a bridesmaid before the baby came.

As the bridesmaids waited in the vestibule of the church, Lorraine pointed at Sandy. "We look like a bunch of vegetables in these matching crimson dresses. I am the rhubarb, and you are the tomato. But let me rub that belly for luck. Maybe I can find someone, too." She ran her hand over the satin in a circular motion. "Oh, genie in the belly! Let me find love."

"Lord, I hope the genie doesn't pop out and answer you," Sandy teased.

Mrs. Vreeland, one hand on a metal walker, was the third bridesmaid. She said, fingering her red satin dress, "If you two are rhubarb and tomato, I must be the dried-up chili pepper!" With her free hand, she held up a white envelope, pointing it to Lorraine. "I can't find true love for you, but take this for now. You have to wait until after the reception is over to open it." The old lady handed Lorraine the small white paper. "Not until later, okay?"

Lorraine shoved the envelope hidden under her bra strap just as the wedding march played.

At the end of the ceremony, the attendees adjourned to the American Veterans' Hall. When the newlyweds opened their presents, one of the gifts, a card from Mrs. Vreeland, held the deed to the house the three girls rented. When the crowd began to disperse, Lorraine opened her envelope. It was the deed to the house next door. Lorraine, wiping tears away, promised to always care for the elderly woman.

A month later, Wesley was born. Sandy had enjoyed her pregnancy, but she delighted in motherhood. An easy delivery by most first-baby standards, Sandy thought she had found her *raison d'être*.

Cam's workload had increased. "I will try to get home early," he said one morning. "I know I have been working late almost since you brought Wessie home."

Sandy held the baby to her neck. "That is your punishment for being such a good attorney. They keep throwing work at you. But don't stress. I'm fine. I love taking care of him, and I know you love what you do. Go," she said, kissing his cheek and handing him a bag to put in his briefcase. "I don't like you skipping meals."

"You've packed me a lunch?" He put the bag in his case.

"Thanks, Superwife."

***

That morning in Cam's office, the secretary put phone messages on his desk. The one on top of the pile read *important,* and the number rang in the home of Aaron Feldman.

"Oh, Cam," Carter's voice had a touch of anxiety. "I am so glad you called. I have a problem. Can you meet me for lunch? Anthony's, one o'clock?"

She hung up before Cam could negotiate or refuse. When Cam arrived, Carter sat at a booth sipping a martini. Her face brightened when she saw him. "I've ordered for us. Look, Cammy." Their crab salads and tomato bisque came. "Oh, I'll tell you after we eat."

They dined quietly, and Cam waved off dessert. "Okay, what's your problem?"

"I'm bored. Aaron is a fine man. I actually like him, maybe it's close to love, but I am going crazy. I would imagine by now you must be bored with little Miss Plain Vanilla, and since I have nothing to do, no current interest, I remembered how wonderful you were in bed, so I thought maybe you and I—"

"Hey! Stop right there. Are you nuts? You have a truly nice husband. Shame on you, Carter. I have the best woman there is, and now a baby. I am *not* interested in messing around."

"Hel-lo-o. I know a thing or two about men. You must be getting antsy keeping to one woman for over a year. And you were in love with me, remember?"

"I am in love with my wife. Go home to your man." He got up and left.

CHAPTER 19

"Sandy," Cam came up behind her and put his arms around her shoulder. "We've been invited to a dinner party. What do you think?" He kept her in the circle of his arms and turned her to face him. He tilted her head and made eye contact. "There'll be a couple of billionaires there. I wouldn't mind having a shot at them for the firm. It's next Saturday night. Wessie is eight weeks old, and it's been months since we've gone out. Are you ready to do some socializing? Are you okay with a babysitter?"

Seconds passed while her mind swiss-checked assessments and decisions. She had not left the baby's side since his birth. *Maybe I should get away. For a few hours.* "All right. Beatrice next door said if I ever needed help, their nanny, Kasti, is excellent. I'll call and see if she is available."

Kasti agreed and showed up on time on Saturday night. While Cam gave the sitter information about the baby and a written information list, Sandy slipped into her favorite ruby silk dress. Looking in the full-length mirror, she beamed, pleased that the dress still fit mostly. She had great cleavage from nursing, but her still-soft belly required a tight girdle to look flat. The voice inside teased her about wearing the *old lady's* garment.

The party, with its soft piano background music, was elegant. They enjoyed the food and the talk. No champagne for Sandy, but okay for the salty delight of caviar, which dotted a number of crackers on her plate. Pacing her snacking, she leaned back in a soft chair, admiring Cam's skillful chatting with the local notables, several politicians, a film director, and a diplomat. He charmed the people around him. A few clients would be added to his list from this evening. Breaking Sandy's focus on Cam's magnetic abilities, golden-haired Carter breezed over, hard-faced and sporting a feral smile. She took a seat next to Sandy.

"Hi, Sarah. How are things? How's the kid?"

Sandy wasn't about to let the water churn. "Wonderful, Carol. We are so happy." Before she became too confident of her newfound smuggery, a dampness in her bra took her attention. Looking down at her dress, a small spot appeared on the left side of her top. "Crap-o-rama." She checked to see if anyone but Carter would notice. All clear, Sandy slipped a napkin into her deep-vee bodice.

Carter scrunched up her face. "What's wrong?"

"Nothing wrong. It's feeding time. I'm leaking. I have to get home before it gets worse."

Carter paled. "You mean breastfeeding? Eiew. You *like* that?"

Sandy nodded gently. "Very much. I didn't think I could enjoy more love than what I feel for Cam. But when I hold little Wes and feed him, the same feeling is there. It's not love split. It's love doubled and pretty much beyond description. Have you thought about having a baby?"

Carter wrinkled her nose and crossed her arms over her bountiful chest. She sniffed with a puff, something akin to a snort. "No."

Sandy caught Cam's attention and hailed him. He came immediately. He and Carter exchanged glances. Concern altered his face. "You girls okay?"

Sandy stood. "We need to go. Nice seeing you again, Carol."

"Right," the woman said, nodding with a movement that said it wasn't nice. As Sandy stood, Carter shot her an envious glance.

When they arrived home, Sandy took over, and Cam paid

Kasti. An hour later, the three members of the Morgan family slept peacefully through the night.

On the following Monday morning, Cam called Sandy from his office. "What did you say to Carter Saturday night? Aaron Feldman phoned me in a snit. He said you talked to her. She acted weird on Sunday, and this morning, she left him. He was really upset."

"Honestly, Cam, all I said was how much I loved you and the baby."

"Yeah. Carter has some problems she needs to work out," Cam said. "Don't worry about it. I was just curious."

Six weeks later, Cam came home early, grinning. "Aaron Feldman said Carter is back."

Sandy raised her eyebrows. "Is she okay?"

"You judge. She spent the whole time with her half-brother, who is a preacher in rural Alabama. He took her to his church, where she got *saved*. Carter. Saved!"

"That sounds like a good thing to me, Cam."

"Wait, there's more. She returned to Aaron and told him she wanted to be a good wife *and* a mother. She said Jesus talked to her."

"Wow," Sandy said.

"Not done with the story. Aaron has agreed to go to church with her."

"Wait. Aaron Feldman is Jewish."

"He's still Jewish. He doesn't argue with success. If going to church gets miracles like turning Carter into a good wife and mother, he's on board with that. He said to give you a big kiss. You did it."

"Carter was ready, Cam. I was just in the right place at the right time. I hope she's serious. No one should miss out on the joys of parenthood." She chucked him under the chin. "And the love of her man!"

CHAPTER 20

By the time Wes was a year and a half, Sandy found out she was pregnant again. Cam laughed and claimed fatherhood felt good to him.

When Marion called and asked Sandy to meet her for lunch, Sandy couldn't wait to share the news. Marion was far along in her second pregnancy. Both couples would have two children.

The rainy weather dimmed the small restaurant, already dark from heavy curtains and carpeting. The gold signage on the door boasted its fifty years in business, and the deep-rooted food smell from the furnishings attested to the age.

"Sandy, over here." Marion Wallensky's face reflected the outdoor gloom.

The waiter held Sandy's chair and handed her the large tasseled menu. Sandy smiled her thanks to the waiter, who gave a slight bow as he departed.

"Hi," Sandy said. "It's good to see you. I have a nanny today for Wessie. Cam and Wally play handball regularly, but we haven't lunched for six months. Everything all right?"

"Not really," Marion sighed. She patted her pregnant belly. "Only a few weeks to go. How are you?"

Sandy withheld her news to hear about what bothered her friend. "I'm fine, but I can see you are worried about something. Will you tell me?"

Marion picked up the menu, blocking her face. "Nothing about the baby."

Sandy waited for further explanation, but none came. She

looked at the menu. "What's good here?" After a moment, she said, "Marion?"

Marion Wallensky sniffed. "Onion soup," she stumbled over her words. "That's good."

Sandy reached across the table, pulled away the menu, and took the woman's hand. "Tell me what's wrong."

Before the conversation could start, the waiter returned with water. Sandy placed twin orders with succinctness to dispatch the server.

With the menus gone, Marion had nothing to hide behind. She wiped her nose with the cloth napkin and fidgeted with the bulging red maternity blouse whose bold white lettering proclaimed *Under Construction*. "We're not getting along, me and Dennis. He is almost impossible to live with. He hates his job, and he takes it out on us."

"Wally? He loves being a cop. I don't understand."

"He loved being a cop, then a detective, but things have changed since he was promoted to NYPD Intelligence. He's an excellent operative, smart and quick, and his hunches turn out right almost every time. But when he works with the Feds, he becomes furious. They don't cooperate or communicate. Last week, they messed up a stakeout, which was just about to break. He is coordinating something now with them and comes home foul. I've never known Wally to have a temper, but I'm afraid he might hurt someone."

"You don't mean you?"

"I don't know. He's irritable and brooding at home. I'm afraid he'll punch out someone from the FBI or whatever, or really hurt an agent the next time they take credit for his collar." Marion toyed with the paper cylinders of sugar in the holder. "I've asked him to get a transfer. He could find pleasure again doing what he's good at. I'm sure they'd take him back as a detective in a hot second. But he won't do it. It's a pride thing. He says he needs to succeed where he's at." She put a Splenda packet back into the holder. "I thought buying the house in Queens would make us happy. That backfired because the long ride home gives him a chance to stew. By the time he comes home, he can be vile."

"Is there anything we can do?"

"I'm going to take little Cameron and visit my folks after lunch. Maybe Cam could talk to Wally?"

"Of course. Try not to worry. Cam is good at negotiating. He has a way of helping people deal with their problems." She gave a quick laugh. "Too bad he can't deal with *his* problem of coming home on time." She would wait to tell Marion her news.

That evening, the grandfather clock chimed nine when Cam came through the back door.

Sandy took his dinner from the microwave. "You're really late tonight."

"Sorry, this case is unbelievable, so many details. How was your day?"

"Disturbing. I had lunch with Marion. Wally is having problems at work."

Cam pulled his chair up to the small kitchen table. "Yeah, I know."

Two days later, at dinner, Cam picked at his food. "I tried to call Wally all day. He had his phone off and didn't go to work."

"Oh, maybe that's good," Sandy said. "You think he went to Albany to get Marion and their boy?"

Before she could say any more, the doorbell rang in doubles. Cam and Sandy hurried to the door. It was Wally. Liquor reeked around him. Cam grabbed his friend's arm, pulling him inside. "We're having dinner. Eat with us."

Wally scowled. "Only if you leave me alone about what I'm going to do about my marriage. I need time to think."

They escorted Wally to the dining room. Halfway through dinner, Wally's cell rang. He took the call, and as he listened, the color drained from his face. He squeezed the phone. His knuckles turned white. "Okay," he sputtered. His hand shook as he disconnected.

It took a few seconds before he could speak. "It's Marion and our son," he mumbled. His eyes welled. "There was an accident on the highway in the rain. They were on their way home." His voice cracked. "They're dead."

CHAPTER 21

Like a robot, Wally stood and left the table. Cam and Sandy followed his heavy strides toward the front door.

"Where are you going?" They asked him together. Wally did not respond, continuing his Frankenstein tread outside.

While Cam and Sandy stood on the front porch, the big man marched to his car and left.

Sandy turned to Cam. "What should we do?"

Cam shook his head. "Nothing. He needs to work this out himself. He knows we are here for him."

A week later, Cam and Sandy attended the funeral in an expansive room perfumed by a multitude of floral arrangements. One large coffin and two smaller ones lined the back wall.

At the gravesite, Cam shook Wally's hand and then led Sandy to the car. "That was the saddest funeral I've ever seen. Poor Wally." Cam opened the passenger door. "There's no consolation for him. He told me he's leaving his post at NYPD Intelligence."

"He is going back to being a detective?"

"No." Cam slid into the driver's seat. "He's quitting altogether. I don't know his plans. He's so good at what he does, I can't imagine him working out of law enforcement."

The day after the funeral, Wally visited to say goodbye. "I put the house in Queens up for sale and, in two hours, got a contract. I need to get away from New York. Find myself. I'll keep in touch with you to let you know I'm okay. Don't worry. I'm a big guy."

Over the next few months, they heard from Wally. The

emails and phone calls were brief, sketchy, but positive.

After Wally's last phone call, Cam said, "I think he is finding his path out of mourning, and maybe he can find some peace from blaming himself. Maybe he can find satisfaction if he gets another job."

Sandy agreed. "I'm glad he has your support. A good friend can help someone heal from a tragedy. You've been there for him."

"That's what friends are for," Cam said.

"True. And I am lucky to have Paula and Lorraine. I never really connected with anyone at work."

Her connection to her roommates surfaced the next day when Lorraine called with bad news.

"Mrs. Vreeland has passed away. There won't be a funeral, per Mrs. Vee's request, but there will be a memorial luncheon. Since she outlived all of her friends, it boils down to us. She's had this in mind for a while now and set the memorial up herself. The lunch will be held at the Red Star, the place where Mr. Vreeland proposed."

"I'm getting goosey," Sandy said, rubbing her arm.

"I know, me, too. She must have known her end was near."

"I will miss her," Sandy said.

"We were the kids she never had."

"Especially you, Lorrie. You were with her after the stroke."

"It was a wonderful relationship. She paid for my college and I stayed with her. Even though she gave me the house, she paid the expenses. Our arrangement was unspoken, but we both knew she would be my roommate until the end. We looked after each other. But she wouldn't want us to mourn. She'd want us to meet, eat, and be happy."

"Right," Sandy said.

"Oh, and one more thing," Lorraine's voice went up, a

little lighter, with a perceptible smile. "I'm bringing my fiancé for you to meet. I think it's time."

"Lorrie! Oh, my God! When did this happen? I didn't even know you were seeing anyone. Who is he? How did you meet?"

"Calm down," Lorrie said, the smile in her voice increasing. "All will be revealed. I've scheduled the luncheon for noon next Saturday."

On the day of the lunch, Cam found a parking space right in front of the Red Star, which was the first in a string of surprises for that day. The sign on the restaurant's door proclaimed it closed, serving dinner only. But as Cam and Sandy stood outside, a squeak, like the groaning portal in a bad horror movie, heralded the heavy oak door swinging open.

From the gloom, a thickly accented voice spoke, reminiscent of Count Dracula.

Cam said, "Vreeland memorial lunch. Mr. and Mrs. Cameron Morgan.

"Welcome," the tuxedoed man said. "Proceed to the back."

As their eyes became accustomed to the low light, rich maroon and gold tapestries swathed on the walls materialized. The gentleman who greeted them swayed his arm towards a side hall. Deep velvety carpeting woven with a royal motif led them to the back room, decorated in Victorian fashion, where a quartet played soft music. Josh and Paula, already seated, enjoyed a silver dish of dark caviar.

The count in the tuxedo followed them and pulled the chair for Sandy. He snapped his finger, and a waiter brought a new bottle of champagne, Dom Perignon. "Please enjoy the appetizers while we wait for the other guests."

It wasn't long before Lorraine stepped in and pulled the hand of her companion into the room. "My dearest friends," she said. "Please meet Mel."

Mel came into the room. Melanie, mid-twenties, with

short brunette hair, smiled at the gawkers. "Hi. I am so glad to meet you."

Sandy stood up. "Welcome, Mel. Come, sit down."

Mel and Lorraine were married two weeks later in a small ceremony held in Mrs. Vreeland's backyard. With the help of a florist, Sandy and Paula spent a day decorating the lawn. The fall colors and crisp temperatures set a soft mood. The two brides wore suits. Lorraine wore a rust-colored jacket and aqua slacks. Mel wore an aqua jacket and rust-colored slacks. They both had bouquets and exchanged diamond rings. The couple took up housekeeping in the house Mrs. Vreeland left to Lorraine, located next door to Josh and Paula.

Sandy's life had changed in so many ways. Deaths, but also happiness in the form of marriages and babies. The Morgans named their next baby, a boy, Miles Edward. Cam chose Miles for his grandfather. Sandy chose Edward because she liked the name, but she felt a bit of guilt because Oggie's last name was Edwards. The birth had been a breeze, and the child an angel, so quiet and easy to care for. When he looked up at her, Sandy saw a reflection of herself, unlike Wes, who came into the world looking like a mini-clone of Cam.

A few months after Miles was born, Wally contacted Cam and Sandy and invited them to dinner. The restaurant was in New Jersey, a little Polish place that smelled of kielbasa and spices. They sat by a window where the fluffy white eyelet curtains clashed with the beer steins lined up like soldiers on a high shelf above it.

As Wally poured the wine, he cleared his throat for an announcement. "I have a new job in the Washington D.C. area."

"Uhm, congratulations," Cam said. "Tell us about the job."

"It's a job. A desk thing. Not much to tell."

Cam nodded and drew out the word. "Oh-kay."

Wally shoved the cork into the bottle. "Later on, I'll tell

you what I can. I'm in town just to visit you and Marion's folks. I don't know when I'll see you next." He took a sip and considered the glass. "I'll be in training for a long while."

Cam nodded again. "Yeah, desk jobs need a lot of training these days."

"Yep." Wally looked directly at Cam. "Some do."

CHAPTER 22

It was a year before Cam and Sandy got to see Wally. After that, their only contact was a few short emails. Over the years, he kept in touch with phone calls and a few brief visits.

When Miles was six, they got a message that Wally was coming to Manhattan and wanted to spend time with them.

Two days later, Sandy cooked a Thanksgiving-type meal with all of the trimmings. After dinner, "Uncle Wally," looking fitter and trimmer, played with Wes and Miles until bedtime, then the three adults sat in the den, the men enjoying hot buttered rum.

"How's work going?" Sandy asked. "You know, your desk job in Washington?"

Wally looked into his glass and smiled. "Fine, as desk jobs go."

Sandy leaned toward him and put her arm alongside his. Her fair skin made a significant comparison to his darkened arm. "You mean the desk job with the sunlamp?"

"Yeah." He cocked his head. "That desk job, the one with the sun lamp." He took a drink. "Come on, guys. You have an idea of what I'm doing, and you also know I can't discuss it."

Sandy pulled her arm away from his and slapped his hand. "So, you leave it to our imaginations?"

"'Fraid so."

"If he tells us," Cam added, "he has to kill us."

Sandy gave a thumbs-up. "Mmm, hmmm. It sounds exciting. Can't you tell us *anything*?"

"How about this? I'm on my way out of the country."

Now, Wally really got her attention. "A mission?"

Wally took a deliberately slow sip. "You could call it that if you want."

Cam leaned in toward his friend. "Is it dangerous?"

Wally took another drink. "Living is dangerous for everyone nowadays." His eyes turned to slits. "I should know so well." He stared at the glass for a few seconds, hurt playing on his face. Then he put his drink down and looked at Cam and Sandy. "I hope I can help keep our world a little safer."

Sandy patted his wrist. "If anyone can make a difference, it's you."

"So," Wally said, changing the tone of his voice in an obvious attempt to change the subject, "anything new for you?"

Cam nodded. "Wes will be starting at Saint Andrews Prep in September."

Sandy put her cup down sharply on the coffee table. "What? That's news to me. When did this happen?"

Cam pulled back in surprise. "When he was born. I enrolled him right then. Miles, too."

A warm flash of anger swept over her. "Without my input? I don't understand."

"What's to understand? I went there. My children will, too."

Wally unbuttoned his shirt collar. "Would you two like to talk about this alone? I can step out for a while."

"No way," Cam said. "I don't know why she's going off like this." He turned to Sandy. "What's the problem?"

"There are several problems. One, we didn't discuss it. Two, I know it has to cost a fortune. Three, there's a wonderful public school a half mile away. And, well, I guess it's number four, but those high-brow schools make people stuffy."

"Stuffy?" Cam sat up straighter. "I went there from kindergarten to senior, and I'm not stuffy."

Wally bit his lip. Sandy put her hand over her mouth.

"Wait a minute. I'm *not* stuffy." He paused. "And we have no worries about the tuition. You know our bank balances." He looked at her. "Plus, I keep cash in the safe. A lot." He cast her an apologetic look. "I'll teach you the combination and how to open it." He forced a smile. "You can get to it whenever you want." He sipped his drink. "Once you can get to the safe, I'd better make sure we get along."

"Cam," Sandy said. "You and I get along, but it doesn't mean we always agree. You have to stop steamrolling."

"I know, Sweetheart." He kissed her forehead. "Sorry about that. You won't give me a hard time about the school, right?" He spoke in his soothe-the-irate-client voice. "It's important to me."

Sandy looked over at Wally, shaking her head.

Wally scratched his nose. "Hey, you've been married to him for a bunch of years. You should understand him better than anyone. Why fight it? You know Wes will go to Saint Andrews, and so will Miles, and so will any kids that follow."

"Yes, I suppose so," Sandy muttered low, annoyed. She caught Cam's gaze. "One of these days, something will come up, and my reaction will surprise you. You won't get your own way forever."

"Yeah, yeah, yeah, my darling, woman who owns my soul. But this time, you'll go along…right?"

The room stayed quiet, and within a few minutes, Wally stood, kissed Sandy's cheek, and shook Cam's hand. "Gotta go. Don't know when I'll see you next. By the way, keeping a lot of cash in your safe is a good idea. Double the amount, Triple it. Trust me. So long and think good thoughts for me."

Three months later, Sandy dressed Wes for his first day of school. "He looks so grown-up in his little navy-blue blazer." She folded a child-sized handkerchief and stuck it into the breast pocket emblazoned with the school's pretentious heraldic shield.

Cam patted the boy on the head. "My dad said this to me on my first day. 'Go get'em, Tiger.' So that's what I'm saying to you."

On the weekdays, Sandy took Miles with her and walked Wes to the bus stop, where they waited for the jaunty light blue bus, proudly displaying the affected shield. The bus stop was an easy walk two blocks away in front of a few stores. One of the stores sold and repaired vacuum cleaners and sewing machines. If the weather was bad, Sandy waited under the shop's roof overhang. The store's windows revealed vacuum cleaners, a few sewing machines, and cleaning products lining the shelves. The shop at the end, the one that used to sell men's shoes, was empty, and its windows were covered with newspapers. Oddly, the newspapers covering the windows of the closed shop had something about them that reminded her of Oggie. His memory popped into her mind each time she saw them.

Sometimes, Wes would entertain himself by trying to read the words or peek through the cracks of the paper into the dark rooms. When the bus arrived, Sandy would squat, check her son over, and kiss his cheek.

Two years later, Miles donned his blue blazer and joined his brother at the snobby school. A year after that, Jeanette was born. Early each school day, Sandy walked the boys to the bus stop and brought Jeanette in the stroller.

On a brisk Thursday, the routine for morning transportation completed, Sandy returned home for her daily routines. She watered her big fern and put it back into its place atop the line of dark wooden cabinets. The sun shone brightly through the stained-glass windows in the kitchen.

The phone rang.

"Hi, Sandy."

"Wally?"

"Yeah. I just finished a meeting here in the city. I'm about twenty minutes from your house. I'd love to stop by and see you, Cam, and the kids."

"Can you stay for dinner? It's pizza night."

"Can't wait."

"Great. Come over whenever. I'll be here."

Wally arrived right away and accepted the cocktail Sandy offered. He walked to the mantle where family pictures occupied the space. Picking up two school photos, he held one in each hand. "The uniforms haven't changed in thirty years. Miles looks like you. He held two photos. "These two look like twins. Except for the slight fading of the paper, I wouldn't be able to tell which one was Cam at eight and which one is Wes."

"Scary, huh?" Sandy said. "And Wessie acts just like Cam. The perfect boy for Saint Andrews Preparatory School. Stuffy and arrogant. Miles isn't quite so uppity. He'll be okay."

Wally laughed and returned the pictures to the mantle. "Too bad you can't do something to save Wes."

Sandy pulled in her breath. "I hear that. If only we could move to a cattle farm or something before it's too late." She was kidding, agreeing with Wally's jest, but as soon as she said it, the idea sounded good.

At three that afternoon, Wally walked to the bus stop with Sandy. He pushed Jeanette in the stroller. They waited for the boys.

"You know," she said, "I could use some laundry detergent. I'll just pop into this store and get some."

The man behind the counter was friendly but had to look up the price of the merchandise. He struggled to find a bag to fit the box.

He looks familiar. It feels like I know him. But I've never been in the store before.

When Sandy joined Wally at the curb, he took the box of detergent.

"How does a store that repairs vacuums and sewing machines stay in business?" she asked. "I've never noticed anyone in there, and the box of detergent had dust on the top."

Wally scrunched his eyebrows together. "Really? Are there a lot of vacuums and sewing machines in this neighborhood?"

"I'm not sure. The store has been there since I've walked the boys to this corner. The shoe store never reopened."

Sandy paused a beat. "You know, I thought there was something familiar about the sales clerk, and something just hit me. He was wearing a shirt-pocket protector. I didn't think anyone still used them. There was a guy I knew years ago. Oggie. We worked together at the library. He had something to do with computers. I even went out on dates with him. He always wore a pocket protector."

Sandy's brow furrowed. "I can still picture what Oggie's pocket protector looked like. White with blue lettering."

Sandy's hand flew to her mouth. "Oh, my God. I just remembered. His was printed with the same name that was on the clerk's protector. *North Atlantic Aviation Corporation.*

"Is that where this Oggie works now?" Wally asked.

"I don't know. One day, Oggie just disappeared. It was the strangest thing. My boss tried to track him down. He didn't exist in the library's employee databases. Matter of fact, he didn't exist in any of the *city's* employee databases. Every year, he sends a birthday card to my old address."

Before they could continue the chit-chat, the little blue bus with the impressive logo dropped Wes and Miles off.

Cam came home early, which was unusual for him, but a visit from Wally was special. At dinner, Cam uncorked the Chianti and poured the glasses set on the table. Cam picked up his glass of wine to salute. "So, here's to seeing Wally again, safe and sound."

Sandy held up her glass. "Here's to Wally's happiness."

Wally held his glass to theirs and, in solemn words, said, "Here's to down with terrorists."

They touched glasses. Cam frowned. "That was ominous."

Wally raised his eyebrows. "But true."

Cam stared at his friend. "Are you leaving the country again?"

Wally sighed and nodded.

CHAPTER 23

The alarm rang. Sandy moved to the side of the bed, but before she could sit up, Cam rolled on top of her.

He kissed her. "Wanna fuck? You can stay with me for five more minutes."

"Five minutes?"

"A quickie," he said, kissing her neck.

Even after ten years, Sandy responded to his touch. "Jeanette will be awake, and the boys need to get up for school. I haven't brushed my teeth."

"You have never had bad breath in your life," he said, pulling at her pajama bottoms.

With little resistance, she melted when he rubbed her shoulders and neck with his stubbly chin. She could never resist that stimulation. Even a quickie would be enjoyable.

When he finished, he leaned back on his knees over her. "Do you have any idea how much I love you?"

"Of course. It's the same as how I feel about you."

He extended his hand to help her up. "I'm a lucky man."

"Get the boys up. I'll change Jeanette and start breakfast," she said.

Her busy morning had started happily, and she hummed to herself as she worked. Cam kissed her at the door and said she was the perfect wife. She continued her humming song as she ushered the boys outside. Miles was entertained by the newspaper taped onto the windows of the vacant shoe store while they waited for the Saint Andrews Preparatory School van. While the boys were at school, Sandy enjoyed playing with

Jeanette. She was such a happy baby. When Wally walked to the bus stop with her and the kids three months ago and saw Miles trying to peek through the newspapers, he said Miles had the makings of a good spy.

Cam returned later than usual that evening. "Sit down," he said as he went into the den.

The look of concern got her attention. "What's wrong?"

"A man visited me as I was getting ready to leave work. He showed me his credentials and told me Wally was in deep trouble. He asked me to help. He said I was their only hope. I didn't recognize the agency on his badge, but I think it's part of the CIA.

"How do you know he was genuine? What has that got to do with Wally?"

"He never said so, but you know Wally is working with one of the agencies. Evidently, as a failsafe, he disclosed something only he and I knew about in case something like this ever happened. I believe the man. I need to help."

"Cam?"

"It requires travel to a foreign country, and there might be some danger."

"No, Cam, don't. It doesn't sound right. You have a family, you aren't experienced, you can't—"

"It's for Wally. I already agreed to go. You know he would do it for me."

Sandy let out a slow breath. "He would. Where are you going? What is the danger?"

Cam paced about the room. "I don't know. The guy couldn't give the details. He said I would learn what I need when I'm en route. I don't know anything, Sandy, not where I'm going or how long I'll be gone."

"When are you going to leave?"

He put his arms around her. "Tonight."

After dinner, Cam went upstairs to pack a bag with enough clothing for a few days. As he came downstairs with a small duffle bag, a cab outside honked its horn. He pulled Sandy into a strong embrace. "I love you," he whispered and left the house.

A few hours later, Cam settled into his seat on a well-appointed Lear jet and ordered a drink from the flight attendant, a young man in a white uniform.

An attractive blonde lady in a business suit sat next to him. Nodding at the half-filled glass on Cam's arm tray, she said, "Myers Rum? That's the only rum you like, and you never could convince Ralph to carry it in his bar." Cam turned his head and gave her a once-over. *Only Wally would know that.*

"I'm Heda Blakely." She slipped a small leather wallet from her pocket, and before putting it in her purse, she flipped it open for Cam to see. "I'll be with you at Ste. Eunice Island."

"Is that where Wally is?"

In low tones, Heda explained the mission. She gave Cam a passport with his photo in the name of Allen Patterson. With few details, she told him Wally, a government agent, was currently staying at Ste. Eunice, a small island owned by a Venezuelan drug lord. The island featured an all-inclusive resort catering to wealthy clients who enjoyed nude bathing, heavy drinking, fine dining, and wild parties.

"Ste. Eunice is the nerve center for a well-organized cartel specializing in world-class drug deals, especially opium, and uses the island's resort as a cover. Wallensky came to get information." She sipped her Bloody Mary. "Other agents had been sent before him, and after they were able to dispatch some data, they disappeared. The heavies suspect Wallensky, and he's being closely monitored. Recently, his communications with us have broken down. He doesn't know whom to trust."

Heda stirred her drink with a celery stick. She licked the

stalk and let it return to the glass. "Your presence would let Wallensky know I am authentic. I will help him complete the mission or at least get out safely. It could get sticky."

Cam sat without responding to her report, holding his drink with a grip of iron.

"You are Alan Patterson. We are booked at the resort as an engaged couple. Stow that wedding band in your wallet." Heda said.

Cam found his words. "Couple? Look, I'm forty-one, been married ten years, and have three children."

Heda tapped his ring. "No. You are wealthy, single, and staying at the El Toro Azul for a swinging vacation with your ditzy girlfriend. Is that clear? This is serious stuff, Alan Patterson. Don't mess up."

Cam struggled with the band. He drizzled some ice on his finger to ease his wedding ring off. "A swinging vacation?"

"That's right, Al, sweet-cheeks. Give me your wallet." She held out her hand.

Cam put his band in with the dollar bills and passed his wallet to her.

She gave him a new one, complete with a driver's license, credit cards, and cash. "We are typical Americans and will eagerly participate in beach volleyball, three-legged races, and other recreational sports, mostly naked, by the way. The resort encourages nudity on the beach. The night pool parties are wild. Rest to make sure you are up for it."

What the hell did I get myself into? Cam, in Alan Patterson's persona, chugged the remainder of his Myers and Coke.

CHAPTER 24

Heda Blakely and Alan Patterson arrived at the resort El Toro Azul early in the morning and slept until dinner time. The island décor of the dining room matched the smoky perfume of searing steaks.

They found a table not far from Wally, who sat with an Asian lady. A young island woman clad in a flowery sarong brought them tall glasses of the resort's signature drink, Plantation Punch, served throughout the day.

Heda bent forward slightly toward him. "Don't you need to use the men's room, Alan?"

Alan paused and then bobbed his head. He picked up his drink and walked in the direction of the men's room past Wally's table. He tripped. Contents spewed from the glass, and the liquid was spraying on Wally.

"So sorry, sir and ma'am," Alan said. "I guess I am still tired from my plane ride."

"It's all right," Wally grumbled. He made no sign of recognition.

Later that evening, at the mixer around the pool, gentle breezes made the wispy potted palms sway. Ocean smells blended with the soft, low music, and the only illumination was the glow from the blue-green bulbs coloring the water in the pool. Heda asked several men to dance, including Wallensky.

When she returned to Alan, she whispered that Wally had warned about the rooms having multiple cameras and listening devices. Most areas of the hotel were bugged. The pool area and beach were the only places where conversations could not be overheard.

When Heda danced with Alan, she kissed his ear, saying they needed to put on a show for the watchers and listeners in their suite. That night in the room, Heda acted like a nymphomaniac to give them a conspicuous cover. Their act continued most of the night. Alan Patterson hated the faked passion and longed for Sandy, but performed his best with Heda.

Each afternoon, the couple took long nude swims in the crystal ocean. Heda wore a simple gold pendant, which was a satellite beacon impervious to salt water. The gadget functioned as a locator and was also a limited transmitter for short messages.

The first week at the resort produced little results. What was a paradise for other swinging couples became monotonous toil for Alan. The hotel provided a new supply of condoms beside the bed each day when the room was cleaned. Every morning, they ordered room service for breakfast and ate it on their balcony. With the door closed, the noisy television blasting inside muffled their al fresco conversation.

"Another one of us is here," Heda said, picking at the bacon on her plate.

Alan flicked a fly with his linen napkin. "How do you know?"

"I've been able to get a few words with Wallensky. He got a coded message from a communications expert working here. I wasn't aware of the sleeper. He is trying to find out how the agency's plans are leaking to the cartel." Heda stabbed a chunk of melon. "But here is some interesting news for you. Wallensky heard gossip about some fine films being made of one of the couples. Guess who? We should receive an Academy Award after this."

Bile gathered in Cam's throat. "Great."

CHAPTER 25

The next day, Alan and Heda entered their hotel room. She turned and pointed to the white paper he held and raised her eyebrows. "What's that?"

"Someone's luggage tag," he explained, letting it fall from his hand into the trash. "I found it outside the door on the carpet."

Turning toward the closet, she fell, uttering a small cry, and knocked over the can.

Alan helped her up. "Are you okay?"

"Sure. Trick ankle. Does that now and again." She put the spilled contents back into the righted container. "Alan, take a shower with me."

He removed his briefs. "Aren't you waterlogged after all the swimming today?"

Heda smiled. "Always an excuse to get naked with you, babe." She stripped off her clothes and headed to the bathroom.

The bathroom included an oval Jacuzzi-type tub elevated three steps up on a pedestal in the middle of a square marble room. The spacious shower fit on one side, fully exposed by two glass walls and a door. Stylish, but not private. The toilet sat in a tiny corner enclosure the size of an old-fashioned phone booth.

Heda leaned into the shower and turned on the water. Then she removed her diamond stud earrings. Before putting the second with its mate, she gave the backing a little twist and threw a bath towel over the glass door.

Alan stepped into the transparent enclosure as Heda adjusted the ornate shower head to pulse. She moved to allow the water to splash over her head and pulled Alan close. "We can talk in the shower for exactly five minutes. That earring prevents recording and sends out shower sounds. A summit meeting with ISIS connections will begin here in a few days. We need to stay until then."

"Then can I go home?"

"You can go when we say you can. Tariq Shisoltin will attend that conference. Interpol and everyone else want that bastard. Teflon Tariq, we call him. He has slipped away every time we've tried to catch him."

Alan soaped his arms. "How do you know this?"

"Remember the luggage tag? I had to trip to fetch it out of the trash when you so hastily tossed that message."

"Message? No way. It didn't say anything but a name, just someone's lost tag."

"Trust me. The name on the tag said, Robert Steele. It's a code."

"Remember the room service bill under the door?" Heda continued.

"The charge for laundry services?"

"Did we get any laundry services?"

"No."

"The bill was the coded message. Just do what I tell you."

"You got all that from a luggage tag and a room service slip. Impressive."

"Your tax dollars at work."

Heda rinsed in the flow of warmth gushing from a metal swan's mouth. "The heat is off Wallensky because that Asian chick he hangs with reports his every move. The Venezuelans figure he's just a big, dumb gringo. They haven't detected any transmitted messages, so they think since they got rid of the previous agents, they are in the clear. Now, dry me, and we'll give the cameras a show." She pulled the towel from the glass door, rendering her full image to the cameras, and excessively shook her breasts as Alan dried her back.

The night the summit group arrived, Heda whispered to Alan that she used her gold pendant to summon an immediate takedown. "Get dressed." She hurried into her underclothes and pulled on a knit dress. Sorting through her purse, she grabbed a few items and stuffed them into her bra and panties. "Move, or you may find yourself naked when you won't want to be."

Alan was dressed and waiting when the door burst open. Military types flicked the barrels of their guns toward the door, indicating that the pair should leave the room. The place was swarmed with armed agents who seized the resort. Gunshots, loudspeaker orders, and screams of the surprised, combined with blaring helicopters illuminating the ground with spotlights, made the place appear like a scene out of a movie.

Everyone, staff and guests, some clothed and some without, marched with their hands in the air to the beach where a line of black-clad guards awaited with M-16 rifles. After thorough body searches, the prisoners waited to board the rigid hull inflatable boats, which were beached on the sand.

CHAPTER 26

Spurred by men in dark uniforms wearing berets, the captives filled the boats to capacity and rocketed over the waves to a mid-sized cruise ship waiting offshore. Hours passed as the captives were interviewed and sorted. Alan Patterson found himself shoved into a small room with bunks along each wall. The thin pillows and rolled olive drab blankets gave the cabin a barracks feel. Three other men, one in pajamas, two in boxer shorts, sat with eyes downcast and shoulders sagging on their bunks. Canned music played, and no one spoke. Alan lay down on an empty cot. At daybreak, a khaki-uniformed man escorted him to an office. Cam's dark mood turned to anger.

"You are?" the man at the desk asked without looking up.

"Alan Patterson."

"Also known as?"

Cam pressed his lips together. "Cameron Morgan. Look, I'm done with all of this. I want to go home."

"All in good time," the man said. He pushed a button on an intercom. Two different men in khaki outfits entered. "Take him back," the desk man said.

"Wait a minute," Cam demanded. "Who the hell are you?"

"One of the good guys," he said, without looking up.

"I'm one of the good guys, too. Where are Dennis Wallensky and Heda Blakely?"

"My advice to you, Mr. Morgan, is to keep your mouth shut and your head low. It will take a while to sort all this out. It's best not to talk to anyone you don't know."

The two uniformed men grabbed Cam's arms and ushered

him back to the cramped cabin. One by one, the room's occupants left and returned. Obviously, they had been given the same advice because no one said anything. Cam spent the rest of the day on his bunk, except to use the narrow head or eat the MREs and bottled water served by the uniforms.

The next day, the ship pulled into a port. Voices from the hallways spoke Spanish and English. Armed guards marched the roommates out of the cabin, through hallways, down stairways, and eventually over a gangplank.

On the dock, a man with a black and white uniform, an A-K 47, and a shiny billed military cap tapped Cam on the shoulder. "Come with me, *Señor* Morgan. No questions, *por favor*."

They walked around warehouses and cargo cars until they reached a clearing. A helicopter waited, its rotor making the *wop wop* sound. The man pointed to the chopper, and two khaki uniforms escorted Cam into the craft. He was the only passenger.

After a few hours in the air, they landed in a clearing in a rainforest.

A woman wearing a white shirt and navy blue pants walked up to the helicopter. "Mr. Morgan?" She checked a clipboard. "This way, please." Her name bar said *N. Hannette*.

Cam followed her on a path to a small steel hangar. Ms. Hannette held the door for him and offered him his choice from a tray of sandwiches and canned sodas on a low table.

"Am I going home? I need to talk to my wife."

"Not right now," Hannette said. "You need to be debriefed. Relax. A plane will come for you shortly."

Cam finished his Coke and chicken sandwich, and ten minutes later, Hannette guided him to a short runway where a twin-engine aircraft with *North Atlantic Aviation Corporation* painted on its tail waited. To his surprise, he felt sleepy and drifted off until the plane landed. At the next stop, three soldiers led him to a building that looked like a medical complex. He noted American cars in the parking lot.

Inside the front entrance, one of the soldiers handed a folder to a woman in a white lab coat and a badge that said *V. Fanizzi. R.N.* She smiled and said, "Good afternoon." After a brief glance into the folder, she nodded to the soldiers. They left, and she locked the door. "Mr. Morgan. Please come with me."

"Where am I?" Cam asked as he followed the woman.

"A government medical facility."

"Why?"

She leafed through the papers in the folder. "Says here medical exam and debriefing."

"Okay, but *where* are we? In the U.S.?"

"I'll show you to your room. Sorry, I can't give you any information. Be patient." At the end of a hallway, she stopped at a wide door and swiped her badge through a slot in the handle. "Ah, your suite at the Ritz."

"I need a phone. I have to call my wife."

"Your things are there," she said, pointing to a plastic bag on the floor sitting next to a bed.

Cam took in the spacious but undeniable hospital quarters, with its bright, happy wallpaper and pale tile floors. He picked up the bag and rifled through it. "My things from the resort. Good. Here's my real wallet." He pulled out his driver's license. "Thank God, I'm me again." Tipping out the rest of the contents from the bag onto the bed, his cell phone tumbled out.

"You must be hungry," the nurse said. "I'll get your dinner."

He fumbled through the bag and found his watch. It indicated six o'clock.

Nurse Fanizzi put her badge through the inside slot. The lock clicked and opened.

"Hey," Cam said to her as the door released. "When do I get my badge-opener thing?"

"I will be right back with your supper."

Cam grumbled at the dark screen of the phone. Dead battery. No charger in the bag. He walked around the room. No handles in the windows. No window in the bathroom. He opened the blinds by turning one slat. No attached cords. The room faced a parking lot and beyond that, a low hill. Neatly lined Italian cypress blocked the view past the hill. He tried the white phone on a dresser. No dial tone.

A soft hum from the door lock heralded the nurse's return. She put a plate of roast beef and mashed potatoes on an over-bed rolling table.

Cam shook his head. "I don't know if I should eat this. I'm sure those sandwiches they gave me for lunch contained drugs. I never slept like that before. I don't want to be drugged again."

"Mr. Morgan, this is a medical facility. If I wanted to drug you, I would call an orderly and give you an injection."

"Fine!" Cam sat on the bed, pulled the table toward him, and picked up the tiny packages of salt and pepper.

Fanizzi handed him a remote and pointed at a flat screen mounted to a metal arm on the wall. "We have 180 channels. *Bon Appetit.* I'll check on you later."

"How does the phone work?"

"The phone is for calling within the complex only. If you need me, dial three."

"How do I call out? I need to get in touch with my wife and children."

Using her badge, she opened the door without an answer.

"Hey, wait!" Cam said, but she was gone.

The meal was surprisingly good, and he ate it all, including the contents of a plastic container of chocolate pudding. He put the tray on the sink counter and played with the remote, checking most of the 180 channels. He settled on the History Channel and learned about Hadrian's Wall.

When the nurse came in for the tray, he asked for a phone.

She pulled a hospital gown out of a drawer and held it open for him. "No calls to the outside right now. Shower tomorrow. Time to go nighty-night. Take everything off."

"I've really had enough of stripping for my country. It's been like a damn roller coaster ride."

"The ride is over," Nurse Fanizzi said and shook the gown to hurry Cam's cooperation. He undressed while she watched, and he allowed her to fasten the flat ties in the back. She got a pair of cloth slippers wrapped in cellophane from the dresser drawer and put them in front of his feet. "Wear these when you go potty." As she hoisted the tray, she turned to him. "Get some rest. Someone will be here for you early tomorrow morning to assist you."

"Assist me? With what?"

She withdrew before Cam could ask another question.

In the morning, Cam received a full examination, including an examination of all orifices, blood, and urine.

The next day, a large, serious man with a thick mop of silver hair sat across from Cam at a wooden desk. "I am Agent Steinmetz. Please tell me what happened to you from the time you boarded the jet going to the island until you came here on this ship. Take your time. I have all day."

"Well, I don't." Cam's fist came down on the desktop. "This isn't right, detaining me like this. I want to go home."

"Then I suggest you cooperate."

Cam recited the chronology of the assignment and added a mention of his dedication to Wallensky. "I put my life on the line. I just about screwed myself to death for my country."

Steinmetz made notes. He spoke no words while Cam whined about dedication and sacrifice. Then the man said, "We in the trenches give our best daily. Most of the country doesn't know what awful things go on behind the scenes to keep the U.S.

safe."

"Am I done with this interrogation?" Cam asked in a hostile tone.

"This isn't an interrogation, Mr. Morgan. It's an interview. We don't employ civilians very often, and we must be careful gathering information."

"You know my physical status, and I've told you everything I could possibly think of. Now I have questions for you."

"Mr. Morgan, we ask the questions. You do the answering. Understand?"

"I'm not answering anymore. I'm done with your questions."

"You will answer, and you will do it when I tell you to."

"Or what? You'll torture me? You'll kill me?"

A little red light flickered on a console sitting between Cam and the interviewer.

"I'll be right back," Steinmetz said.

In less than five minutes, he returned. His countenance differed. He came into the room with an easy step and a smile. "Mr. Morgan, I will answer your questions. You've had a difficult time. What would you like to know?"

"Those films, the ones from the resort, are they on the internet?"

"No, the agency took possession of them."

"Good." Cam sighed. He closed his eyes and inhaled. "I just want to go home."

CHAPTER 27

In Manhattan, after Cam had been gone a week, a large orange envelope slid from the mail slot onto the floor. Wessie grabbed it and the other mail and brought it into the kitchen. He took an apple from the fruit basket and went upstairs.

Sandy looked through the few bills, glossed over the junk mail, and turned the package over. Addressed to her, it had no return information. The fiber-reinforced paper didn't open easily. She slit the end with a knife and pulled out a sheaf of computer-printed photographs. She blushed. The pictures showed a man and woman making love in low lighting. Each page showed a new position and at different angles. Disgusted, she pulled the trash bin from its concealed place in the lower cabinets. As she tossed the items in the trash, she noticed the man's chest-hair pattern. She snatched the up pile and took them back to the table. Using a magnifying glass, she examined the photos and put her hand to her mouth to hold back the cry. The man was Cam.

It took her a few minutes to compose. She told herself it was an ugly prank. Someone had obviously used porn pictures and photoshopped Cam's face. But after seeing all the photos, some of them close-ups, she knew this was no prank. The images displayed him in his favorite positions and glassy-eyed, receiving the attention he liked from a beautiful, chesty blonde.

After that, Sandy took the mail chore away from Wessie. For the next four days, a new envelope came dated chronologically. Some of the daytime photos had been shot poolside, where everyone was nude. In one group, she recognized Wally. Her eyes scanned his body past the tan line to the pale part. A shock of dark hair contrasted with his member. Each day, she didn't want to open the package, but she could not resist.

Insomnia dominated Sandy. Lying awake in the dark brought visions, some from the past, good memories, but also visions of the photographs vividly engraved in her mind. She couldn't stop wondering what Cam was doing while she grieved. His cheating tortured her. Hadn't he told her how lucky he felt having her, the perfect wife? He seemed so happy, so devoted. None of it made sense. Cam could spin the truth legally, but he was not a liar. She dreaded his return, doubting he was aware of the photos. What could he possibly *say* to her? But— why did she need to see him at all?

The outside cover of the fifth day's package of photos was hand-marked *Last*. Relieved that the photographic nightmare had ended, she made up her mind to leave New York.

A new, improved Sandy made plans to start a different life far away with her children. She never wanted to see Cam again and needed to make sure they left without a trace. Odd that he had shown her how to open the safe a few days before he left. Odd, but good. In the safe, she left the jewelry, including her wedding rings, but cleaned out the cash, which she stuffed into a kid-sized Batman rolling suitcase. Her own personal *Bat-cash-mobile*.

As she packed, memories invaded her mind and flipped like pages in an album. She remembered their time together the night of the engagement. They were so hungry for each other. Cam became excited that he was her first lover. He was physically attractive — perfect the way his body was shaped in classical proportions, his muscles taut and developed just enough. His chest hair grew in a triangle as if it had been arranged and precisely trimmed. Over the years, their lovemaking had been tender and satisfying, sometimes a bit rough just for spice. Sandy believed life had been wonderful with Cam. That blissful life was shattered.

Making sure the valuables were locked in the safe, she left the entire packet of photos on top of the kitchen table and left. With everything stowed and belted into her Lexus SUV and Jeanette in her car seat, Sandy backed out of the drive. She stared back at the house. "For the last time," she whispered, then swallowed the acid that crept up her throat. Marbles, the cat, squirmed in his carrying bag on the floor of the front seat. She left her cell phone behind so she couldn't be tracked.

"We are going on a trip," she told the kids.

"A vacation? Are we joining Dad on a vacation?" Miles asked.

"No." She wondered when she would tell the kids they weren't coming back. She drove to a Target store and bought an atlas of the United States, and decided to drive to Minnesota.

They spent a few days in Rochester. In a grocery store, she saw a lady who looked somewhat like her and also had three small children. The haggard lady pushed a grocery cart to a sad-looking, dented, and peeling sedan. The kids shadowing the woman looked like they could use a few meals and a bath. She wore thick-framed glasses, and her hair hung in strands. With the same hairstyle and spectacles, Sandy could pass for her.

Sandy approached the disheveled lady. "Excuse me. Would you help me?"

The lady responded with a questioning look. "What do you think *I* could do for *you*?"

"I am running away from my abusive husband. We resemble one another. Would you sell me your driver's license for a thousand dollars?"

The woman took a few seconds' pause and then nodded.

Sandy added, "Please don't get a new one for two weeks to give me time to get away."

"Two weeks," the woman said. "I can do that. You really

have money?"

Sandy pulled her wallet from her purse, where she kept a little over a thousand dollars in it at a time. She counted ten one-hundred-dollar bills from the slot. "Yes." She had never been so bold, but now she was deep in it and pushed forward. "Your license?"

The woman pulled out her wallet and fished through the worn leather. Keeping the card firmly in her grasp, she held it for Sandy to examine. The name on the plastic-coated card, Wanda Gwendolyn Parker, glistened in the sunlight. The picture on the license, luckily somewhat blurry, could look like Sandy with glasses. They made the exchange.

The real Wanda Parker stuffed the bills into her leather wallet and turned to load her groceries. As Sandy left with the license, the woman called after her. "Good luck. I hope you get away. I never could."

Sandy went to a Walmart and bought a no-contract phone using Wanda's identity. With her roller bag of cash, she hoped to buy enough cell phones to confuse any attempt at tracking.

She drove the car to the Mayo Clinic. After parking at a lot attached to the clinic, Sandy and the kids entered the maze of the hospital buildings. Using the hospital's WIFI, she looked up Craigslist for a car. She arranged to meet the owner at a restaurant parking area not far from the hospital. An hour later, a man in an older Mercury Villager waited for her. His price was right, and she had the cash. For an extra three hundred dollars, he left the tag on the car. They made the trade—cash for the car, title, and tag. With a tear in her eye, she abandoned the Lexus at the Mayo Clinic and drove the Mercury van out of Minnesota.

The Villager van coughed all the way to Fargo, South Dakota, where the new Wanda Parker left it at a mall parking lot and walked with the kids to a nearby used car lot. Sandy-Wanda bought a Saturn Vue, which was a little better than the Mercury, and she paid the salesman an extra five hundred to get the tag that afternoon.

From Fargo, she drove to Lincoln, Nebraska. They stayed for a week. At a used car lot, Sandy traded the Vue in for a newer Chrysler Town and Country van. When she got the tag, she offered the salesman a thousand dollars to trade another car's plates with hers, explaining she was fleeing an abusive husband. He accepted that explanation. Not batting an eye, he pocketed her money, saying it would be a logical mistake to mix up tags when there had been five sales done that day.

Sandy headed southeast, stopping at attractions to keep the kids contented. She told the boys they didn't have to go to school for a while. They stayed in motels at night. In North Carolina, the cold weather was more tolerable than in the north, and Sandy liked the mountain environment. She thought about settling there, but noticed a lot of police officers. She headed West again, only using country roads where there would be no tolls or cameras.

The kids enjoyed what they thought was a vacation. One night, while eating at a Memphis buffet, Wessie asked, "When will we go home, Mom?"

Should I tell them? No. I'm not ready for that. Sandy dreaded this day. She had rehearsed how she would respond almost from the moment she left Manhattan. Trying to sound casual, she explained, "Maybe we'll buy a place in the country, and we'll all have new names."

Wes stopped eating and wiped his mouth. "Will Dad have another name, too?"

"He's still Cameron Morgan."

Wes eyed her for a moment. She knew that expression, a copy of Cam's disapproval glare. It looked the same on Wes.

Miles bit into a chicken wing. "I like this chicken. Are you mad at Daddy?"

I can't stall the truth forever. "I don't want to live with him anymore. I know it isn't fair to you, but I don't want you to see him again, either. Don't call him or talk about him to anyone. Do you understand?"

She had never used that tone of voice on them before, and the table quieted. Even Jeanette, who had been banging her bottle on the highchair tray, stopped.

Wes's stare intensified. She needed to be strong with Wes to keep him in line. He had a lot of his father's personality. "Do you understand, boys? If you disobey me, you won't like the consequences."

They nodded. Wes put down his barbecued rib and pushed his plate away. No one finished their meal. Sandy got them into the car and found a motel for the night.

In the dark, she listened to the whisper of the children's breathing. Her mind worked like a blender. Every so often, a thought landed and shook her memories. To keep the rough images at bay, she reminisced about a party she and Cam attended at Aaron Feldman's apartment before Cam left to find Wally. Aaron told Sandy he could never repay her for Carter's transformation.

Aaron credited Sandy for the changes, and he sang the praises of Cam's skills as an attorney. Cam was dogged about his work. The thought that Cam might apply his skills to finding them kept her up all night. When she finally fell asleep, a dark, unhappy cloud descended on her dreams.

CHAPTER 28

Cam opened the door to a quiet house. He put his bag down in the living room and went into the kitchen. There on the refrigerator was a note: *Check the table.*

He found the large envelope and dumped the contents. After seeing five of the photos, he ran into the bathroom to vomit. He took a few swallows of Pepto Bismol and then sat on the front steps for fresh air. An hour later, he summoned the nerve to examine the rest of the pictures, moaning each time he saw a new one.

When he was able to talk, he called Wally. "I know you are in D.C., but you need to get here as fast as you can. Please."

Wally came to the house the next morning. "I don't know who took these pictures or why they came here. Maybe it's blackmail, and you didn't get the message."

"I don't think it's blackmail, Wally. It doesn't make sense. Could this be retaliation from the cartel?"

Wally grimaced. "They would have just killed you. But they don't know who you are."

Cam held the note from the refrigerator. "This is Sandy's handwriting. She took a million dollars from the safe, but all of the assets and her jewelry were still there. I checked online. The bank accounts haven't been touched. Sandy has left me." He hung his head. "And I don't blame her."

"We'll find her," Wally said. "We'll make her understand."

Cam pushed his fingers through his hair. "The law firm has some good private detectives."

"We don't need them. I'll talk to some folks at the agency.

If anyone can locate her, they can. We need to relax and think."

  The next day, Wally started the ball rolling to find Sandy and the kids.

CHAPTER 29

With Memphis in the rearview mirror, Sandy headed to Nashville. The city had a lot to offer in the way of tourism. To give the kids a bit of stability, Sandy rented a pay-by-the-week suite. At first, the young fellow clerking the desk turned them down because of Marbles, their cat, but a few hundred-dollar bills gave him a blind eye to the pet. Each time Sandy used a bribe, she became more hardened to the immorality of how she could get her way using money. She considered her actions emergencies. She regretted that she had to be so morally flexible, but she did what she had to do.

As the week at the suite hotel ended, she took their dirty clothes to the laundry area. Outside the laundry room of the hotel, she overheard the room maid talking to the janitor.

"I don't know what I'm gonna do. My car broke down, and I don't have enough money for the rent, let alone fix my car. I don't suppose you could float me a loan?"

"A loan?" the male voice said. "Hell's bells, I don't have as much as you do."

Sandy waited with the laundry basket until the janitor exited, leaving the maid in the room. Sandy hurried inside and stopped in front of the maid, who folded towels onto a cart. The woman was Sandy's size and had brown hair. With the right type of hairstyle, Sandy might be able to pass for the woman. Could she employ the same story she used in Minnesota?

"Excuse me," Sandy said.

"What can I do for you, ma'am?"

"Would you sell your driver's license for $1,000?"

"You shittin' me, lady?"

"I am fleeing an abusive husband, and I need to cover my trail. Are you interested?"

"Would I get into trouble?"

"You can say you lost your wallet. But, please, give me a few weeks before you get a duplicate."

"Heck, my car don't run anyhow, and I can't afford to take the time off here at the motel, so, yeah, sure. Cash?"

"Yes." Sandy didn't want to sound like she had a lot of cash. "It will take me some time to get it, but I think I can have it tomorrow afternoon."

"Okay, I'll be here. Just ask for Sarah Green." The name Sarah Green provided a bit of irony. How many times had Carter called her Sarah?

She got a different hotel room but returned to the one where Sarah Green worked to buy the woman's driver's license. Nashville offered many places to visit and enjoy. They went to the aquarium and saw a few of the famous attractions. Sandy-Sarah kept her trail cold by paying cash for everything. The money remained stuffed in the child's rolling suitcase, which went with them everywhere.

The new Sarah Green liked the scenery and the laid-back attitude. Tennessee called to her. She was surprised at how readily people talked to her as if they knew her. New Yorkers had never acted that friendly.

The daytime sightseeing kept her occupied, but at night, after she tucked her children into their motel beds, she had time to think. She dreaded the hours before she fell asleep. And she was tired of the travel. It wasn't right for the kids. They deserved a home. The time had come to find a place to live. She met with a real estate agent who showed her a few properties out in the country.

One sunny afternoon, months after Sandy left Manhattan,

the real estate agent brought them to a brick house that sat on a two-hundred-acre hay farm. In addition to the modern house, it had a huge barn, an old bunkhouse, and a garage housing two tractors and farm equipment. The elderly owners had died a few months apart from each other. The heirs lived in cities across the country and wanted to sell it quickly. Sandy-Sarah wasn't sure how to buy the house and not bring attention to her identity. She called her old roommate Paula.

Paula answered on the first ring. "If you are selling car warranties, stop right there."

Sandy swallowed an imagined lump of coal. "It's me, Sandy. Please don't ask questions." When Paula promised, Sandy cleared her mind and chose the easiest way to ask a favor. "Two questions. Does your uncle still work as a financial liaison for that casino in Atlantic City? And does your grandmother still live near Paducah, Kentucky? You said your uncle was a genius with money, and your grandma would never cheat or lie, right? If so, I need their help. I left Cam, and I don't want to explain why. Please! I took a lot of money from our home safe and fled with the kids. I'm not telling you where I am. But I want to stay under the radar and buy a house."

Paula cleared her own throat. "My uncle can figure out something, and my grandmother can be trusted with your money. I know you well enough that if you don't want to give information right now, you have a good reason. I'll honor your requests. If I can call you on this phone number that you are using, I'll get back to you in the next few hours. Oh, honey. I don't know what to say except be careful. Cam is not one who would let things go easily."

Of that, Sandy-Sarah knew for sure.

Paula called back. Uncle Clark said Sandy should drive to the grandmother's house in Paducah, Kentucky. There, she gave the woman enough cash to cover the cost of the property.

After a few days, Sandy called the real estate agent. The agent said the house had been purchased. That bit of information let Sandy know the first part of the plan worked. Later, the agent called, saying the buyer had gifted the estate to her, Sarah Green. The heirs left everything, including the farm animals and the furnishings.

When all the paperwork had been done, Sarah Green signed the documents. The farm belonged to her. She gulped at the thought that she had committed fraud. *Let the chips fall.* Sarah Green was the owner of a hay farm.

With their few possessions, they moved in. The boys loved the freedom to run. They also enjoyed feeding the chickens, ducks, and guinea fowl.

"Mom, the baby goat cries like a little kid when it can't see its mother goat."

"Maybe that is why they call them kids, Wes," Sarah said.

After a few days on the farm, they were visited by a neighbor, tall and husky. "I'm Henry MacDonald. I live around the bend, and I was wondering if you want me to keep working here like the old Nolans did."

Sarah stood in the doorway. "What did you do for the Nolans?"

"I been taking care of the animals and such. When hay time come, I mowed, baled, and sold it for them. I keep half the profit in trade for the work."

"I guess that's okay. I don't know anything about hay or farming things."

The freckled man pushed his bill hat back and scratched his thatch of reddish hair. "Hmmm. Pretty green, huh?"

Sarah didn't know what to say regarding the odd introduction from her neighbor.

"Green, like your name?" Henry added.

"Oh!" Sarah hadn't recognized the joke referring to her

new identity. "Yes. That's funny. Um, please continue what you did for the Nolans."

"Do you have someone else to take care of the cows?"

"Honestly, Mr. MacDonald. I didn't expect to have the animals. I don't know what to do. When I get my computer hooked up, I figured I'd do some research, and —"

"Computers don't feed or water cattle. I been doing it. You ain't seen me 'cause I ain't been by the house. But I heard there's a new owner named Sarah Green, so I wanted to know if I should keep on working." He wiped the sweat from his forehead with a paisley kerchief.

The boys came from the back and stood next to Sarah.

"You boys are about the age of Eddie, my boy," Mr. MacDonald said. "I bring him with me sometimes." The man had a seriousness about him that resembled sadness. "The school ain't so close. Eddie don't hardly go, so the bus won't come out. It'll probably come for your kids, though."

"I will be homeschooling my boys," Sarah said.

"Well, that's good too, I guess. I'll just check on the water out in the pasture right now. And I'll be going into town for feed. Do you want me to bring the feed like I did for the Nolans?"

"Yes. Please. Do everything like you did. Just let me know what to pay. I really appreciate it."

"I'll work it out in hay like I did before."

"Thank you so much." Sara stopped him before he left. "Mr. Macdonald, can I have your cell phone in case I need to get in touch with you?"

Macdonald scowled. "Nope. Don't have one. Don't believe in them new-fangled things. They cause brain cancer when you hold 'em up to your head."

CHAPTER 30

In New York, Wally called Cam. "In light of your help on Ste. Eunice, the agency has authorized me to search for Sandy using all of our resources. And because they're afraid I might be suffering from mild shock, which I am not, they said to take off as much time as I need. Paid leave. Go figure. Anyway, we'll find her."

They started by visiting Paula.

"I have no information for you, Cam," Paula said. "Sandy called, said she left you without telling me why, and didn't want me to know where she is. That way, I don't have to lie to you."

Cam pushed for information, but after twenty minutes, they left, convinced Paula could not help them locate Sandy.

Wally used his resources but had no leads. Cam went back to work and waited for Wally to find more information. One afternoon, as Cam went over his phone messages, he found one saying his son had called. Cam flew into the secretary's office demanding details.

The secretary tensed at Cam's wild tone of voice. "I'm sorry, Mr. Morgan. When you were out at lunch, I picked up the phone, and it was a little boy who asked for you. He told me to say he called. He didn't leave a number."

Cam had Wally search the phone records. The call came from a North Carolina cell phone located at a Lake Toxaway gas station. Wally and Cam drove there immediately and interviewed the owner.

"I don't really remember, but a lady came in with a couple kids, and while she, I think, went to the head, the boy asked if he could use my phone and offered me a dollar. He said he had to call his dad, so I let him use my phone. That's all I can tell you."

It happened again a month later. This time, the secretary notified Cam. The caller ID installed in the office gave him the number. Cam called the owner of the phone, Mr. Owen Thomas from Arkansas, who, while in a diner in Nashville, loaned his cell to a boy while the kid's mother paid the bill. Mr. Thomas had to get the phone back because they were ready to head home and couldn't wait for the return call the boy wanted. The man described the children and the mother perfectly. It was Sandy and the kids. Cam took off from work. He and Wally traveled to Nashville.

CHAPTER 31

Henry MacDonald worked mornings at the farm. His son Eddie helped him until Wes and Miles finished their schoolwork. In a few weeks, the three boys became close friends. Once in a while, Henry took all the boys fishing or hiking. The boys were delighted the night they camped in the cedar forest located at the far end of Sarah's property.

One morning, before heading to the pasture, Henry waved to Sarah. "Ms. Green, would you trade a few of my Angus steers to let Eddie sit with your younguns while they get their lessons?"

The home-schooling was new to her. Did she want the responsibility for another child as she learned how to teach her own? On the other hand, Sarah didn't want to disappoint Henry and possibly lose the farm services. A good worker, he mended fences, fed the animals, and did all of the things she had no idea about.

Why not let Eddie learn with the boys? The kid wasn't getting any education at all right now. Sarah should help a neighbor, especially when Henry had been so helpful to her. "We could try. I just got the books in the mail. Let me see what Eddie needs, and I'll order more."

The next morning, Eddie, cleaned and combed, joined Wes and Miles at the dining room table. He was a year older than Wes, but was behind in what Sarah thought he should know. Within a week, Eddie showed promise, and Sarah ordered supplies for the boy.

The three boys studied from eight until noon. After that, they played outside and learned about life on the farm. Eddie offered a wealth of information to the two city boys.

Sarah stayed busy homeschooling in the morning while caring for eighteen-month-old Jeanette. She tried to limit trips into town and kept her head down. Gone from New York for almost six months, she began to adjust to her new life.

One afternoon, Wes came to Sandy out of breath. "Mommy! Come with me! Please!" He grabbed Sarah's hand. "We found a hurt dog. Hurry."

Sarah kept pace with Wes as he ran to the tractor shed. A white, shaggy dog, bleeding, cowered under the larger tractor.

She squatted to observe the animal closer. "Oh, the poor thing. We'll take it into Gainesboro. I remember seeing a vet's office. I'll bring the car as close to here as possible. Stay here, but don't touch it."

Sarah ran back to the house. She pulled Jeanette out of her crib and grabbed the diaper bag. Then she seized two blankets from the linen closet, rushing to get the car. She worried about driving the car on the field, but Henry had recently mowed, leveling the surface like paved gravel. She pulled the van up to the shed and hit the button to open the back.

Holding the blankets, she gave orders to the boys. "Wes and Miles, when I wrap this blanket around the dog's head, the two of you put the blanket around the dog's body, and we'll put it in the car."

The three of them carried the dog into the back of the car. Sarah drove fast on the river road leading to town. A jeep in front of the vet's office indicated someone was there. She parked the car. "Boys, stay here with Jeanette." She touched the back window to check on the dog. The animal looked up at her with soft brown eyes. "Okay, doggie, hang on there." She tried the office door. Lights in the windows and the sound of a radio contrasted with the *closed* sign on the door. She banged several times before the lock turned.

An older man, fiftyish with a ragged haircut and needing a shave, answered with a mild Southern drawl. "We're closed."

Sarah narrowed her eyes at him. "It's an emergency. Is the vet in?"

"I'm a veterinarian, retired. I'm here alone. They're on vacation."

Sarah pushed in. "I have an injured dog. It is an *emergency*. Please! I'll help."

He made a sucking noise in his cheek. "Okay, let's get it in."

The man followed her to the back of the car, lifted the dog, and motioned with his head for Sandy to follow him into the office. He laid the dog down on a steel table.

"I'll be right back," Sarah said. "My kids are in the car."

He angled his head and shot her a sideways glare. "Make sure you come back, lady."

"I'm not going anywhere."

She returned with the kids and gave orders. "Wessie, you hold Jeanette, and Miles, you keep checking on her. If she cries, give her the bottle. Spread the baby blanket on the floor and sit, in case she squirms away from you."

The man snapped rubber gloves from a box on the wall. "Here." He handed her two.

She took them. "Could she have rabies?"

"Doubt it. We don't have rabies around here. But wear 'em for general protection."

Sarah struggled with the gloves and came to the steel table.

The vet gave the animal an injection. "What happened to this dog?"

She forced herself to look at the bloody fur. "I'm not sure. We're new to this area, but I think coyotes attacked her. I heard them this morning."

He spread the fur away along the dog's stomach. "She has

pups. Where are they?"

"There weren't any puppies."

"Hmm. The coyotes got the babies. That's how she got messed up, defending her pups."

"Oh, that's awful. Can you help her?"

"I gave her a sedative. I don't feel any broken bones. No signs of internal trauma. She needs stitches."

"Is she going to be all right?"

"I think so." He rooted around in the cabinets, pulling out bottles, packages with instruments, and bandages. "Shit, I don't know where he's moved the supplies." He found a metal basin under the sink. "This used to be my practice, but I sold it to my son. I came to check on the office while they were all on vacation. Here, hand these things to me as I ask for them."

Sarah passed the supplies, kept the instruments lined up on the counter, and threw the soiled pads into the basin as the doctor tossed them aside. He asked her a few questions about the farm and her animals as he worked. She recognized the smell from his breath. The senior partner of Cam's law firm had that same whiskey smell. An hour later, he breathed heavily and washed his hands. Sarah sat in a chair in the lobby next to the kids.

"Thank you," Sarah said. "Uhm, Doctor...?"

"Vance Chambers."

"How much do I owe you, Doctor Chambers?"

"Hell, I don't know. I'll leave a note for the office manager. I guess you can write your name and address, and they'll bill you."

"Okay. I appreciate your work, Doctor."

"You did pretty good yourself. And...um, your kids were well-behaved, not like the brats that come in here. I can barely stand kids anymore."

"Thanks, I guess. Do I leave the dog here?"

"No, there's no one here to take care of her. Take her home and keep her quiet." He searched another cabinet. "Give her one of these pills every six hours for a week. And one of these twice a day for three days. Put this ointment on the stitches. Bring her back in," he looked at the calendar, "ten days. Gene'll be back then. The dog probably needs worming. If she's better, he can do all the other stuff."

Sarah picked up Jeanette, who actively sucked her pacifier. "Maybe I'll bring in Marbles, our old cat. He needs shots. Will you carry the dog to the car?"

"Sure." He looked her over for a lingering moment, then grabbed a notepad from the front desk. "What's your name?"

She adjusted Jeanette over her shoulder to take the paper and pen. The voice inside reminded her name was Sarah. "Sarah Green." She wrote on the pad. "Here's my address."

"Mrs. Green?"

"Ms. Green." She dismissed the inner gloom about her status as Ms. and refused to allow the feelings of loneliness or grief to take over. It was getting easier to deal with those notions.

Doctor Chambers went into the surgery room and returned with the sleeping dog. "You should get Mr. Green to carry the dog into the house."

"I'll have to move her. There's no Mister Green."

The veterinarian placed Scrubby, the name the boys had decided for the dog, their new pet, onto the blanket in the back of the car.

Two days later, Sarah pushed back the lace curtain in the living room at the sound of someone coming up the gravel driveway. A van with *Chambers Animal Clinic* painted on the side stopped. Sarah stepped out to the front porch.

Doctor Chambers, his hair neatly cut, came out of the van and pulled on his smoothly shaved chin. "How's the dog?"

Sarah opened the door. "She's in the living room. Is there

a problem?"

"No, I thought I would see how she is doing."

"Please come in, Doctor Chambers. We're keeping her as quiet as possible. I've given her the medications just as you said." The dog reclined on a blanket in the living room.

He squatted and petted the dog. "She looks good. And, um, I will take a look at your farm animals since I'm around. Did you say you had a donkey? And a few goats?"

"We have ten Angus cows, one bull, and four Dutch Belted heifers, along with five goats and Jethro, the donkey. Oh, and a lot of chickens. I haven't counted them, but we also have three peacocks, some ducks, and twenty guineas."

"Don't do birds," he said. "But I'll look at the equine and bovines, that is, the donkey, cows, and goats. I mean, since I'm in the area."

Sarah led the veterinarian past the barn. "The cows are all spread out. But the goats and Jethro, our donkey, are over there." She pointed at the inclined pasture.

A truck drove up and parked by the barn.

"It's Henry," Sarah said, turning to the vet, but he was already through the gate and out of earshot.

Henry came to the barn as she walked around its side. He pointed to the van. "Trouble?"

"No, Doctor Chambers was in the area. He checked on Scrubby. Now he's looking at the animals."

Henry scowled and mumbled, "Oh yeah?" He adjusted the oversized bag of feed on his shoulder and picked up his pace toward the gate. "Here cow! Here cow!" He called out in a high-pitched voice as he walked into the field. He dumped the grain into a feeder. The cows trotted from all parts of the pasture.

Doctor Chambers went to the feeder, patted the cows, looked at their udders, and eyed their rumps. In a few minutes, he joined Sarah and Henry at the gate.

"Henry, do you know Doctor Chambers?"

"Yeah," he said flatly and sent the vet a head nod. "Vance."

Doctor Chambers returned the one-word greeting. "MacDonald."

Henry addressed Sarah. "Sorry, we're late. I can't stay. I brought Eddie. Be back this afternoon." He folded the bag and walked to the truck.

"Animals seem fine," the vet said. He looked over her shoulder, and his gaze followed the truck backing up. "I lived near the MacDonalds as a kid."

"You did?"

The vet wiped his hands on his pants. "I know his older brother. Why is his boy here? He's supposed to be in school."

Sarah stiffened from his critical tone. "He *is* in school. I homeschool my children, and I teach Eddie in trade for farm work. Henry helps me learn the farm."

Doctor Chambers turned his head halfway and gave her a scowling glance. He checked his watch. "I'll look at your goats and the donkey, and then I guess I'll head on back to town."

"Want some coffee? It'll be lunch soon. Would you like to join us? It's just BLTs and leftover mac and cheese."

"Sounds good," he said. "You mind if I check around the barn? Have you had a tetanus shot? Your kids?"

"That's part of their inoculations."

"Are they boosted? You should check the pediatrician's records."

"Uh," Sarah mumbled as the voice inside warned about contacting the kids' doctor in Manhattan. "Would it hurt to get an inoculation if they've already had it?"

"No. It'd be okay. How about you?"

"Do I need to be inoculated?"

"Absolutely. Most farms have tetanus in the ground. Last year, one of the Nolan's goats died from the disease. It's safer to get inoculated. I can bring the vaccine the next time I'm here."

"You can do that?"

"Sure. We give it to ourselves. No problem."

"Thanks, Dr. Chambers. Come into the house when you're done in the barn."

Ten minutes later, Chambers knocked on the back door.

"It's open," Sarah called out.

When he stepped inside, she said, "Have a seat," nodding to a small table in the kitchen. He wasn't wearing his boots. "Where are your shoes?"

"Took them off outside. Told you, tetanus is in the ground. Best not take a chance of bringing into your house if you and the kids aren't inoculated."

"Oh. Thank you." Holding the coffee pot in one hand, she put a cup down on a placemat next to the sandwich.

"Black," he said and took a bite from the sandwich. "Not bad." He moved the cup to make room for the bowl of macaroni and cheese.

Sarah sat in the opposite chair with her own bowl and coffee. They ate quietly, the stillness magnifying the song playing on the radio. He looked at the black speaker and made a face.

"What's wrong?"

"That song," he said. "*Islands in the Stream.*"

She nodded. "I listen to these old songs. It helps me stay calm. But there's a downside. They can bring back memories."

"It used to be my favorite until my wife left me six years ago."

"Sorry." She was becoming accustomed to the way the people in the area disclosed their intimate details. This was *not* New York.

He looked into his cup. "Just like that. No notice, no reason."

"There's always a reason, Dr. Chambers."

He made a sour face. "Thanks."

"Look, I know because I'm the wife who left, and believe me, I had a good reason. Your wife had a reason, too." She waited for a response, but none came. "Hey, it isn't easy. A woman doesn't put her coffee cup down one morning and say, 'I think I'll split today.' It's unbelievably hard to leave. And frightening."

"Whatever," he said.

"Do you think part of the reason she left was because of your grumpiness?"

"Grumpiness?"

She refreshed his coffee. "Well, you are kind of grumpy."

His finger traced the rim of the cup.

She returned the pot to the coffee maker. "Will you add this morning's work to my bill?"

"Just give me a hundred."

"That's all? For everything? Scrubby's surgery, your trip out here? Your time to look at the animals and check the barn?"

"You gave me lunch."

"All right. Just a minute." Sarah went into the bedroom office and got a traveler's check. She held it out so he could see it. "I'll endorse it."

"Don't you have a checking account?"

"No." She signed the bottom line.

"Are you in hiding?"

"What?" A chill shot up her spine.

"You just moved in, obviously not a country gal. You don't have a checking account. And, the day I told you to have Mr. Green take the dog out of the car, you got this lost look on your face. It pretty much spelled out you had fled a bad marriage. I'm speculating on the hiding part."

Sarah swallowed a lump, and her face heated up. How did she get into this conversation?

"Look, I think you are an honorable man—"

"I thought I was grumpy."

"They're not mutually exclusive, you know. I *am* keeping a low profile. And...if anyone should ask questions, I would appreciate it—"

"What kind of questions?"

"Like where I live or what we look like. I plan to use Chamber's veterinary services, but I don't want to be found. It might be easy for someone to search the internet for animal clinics with cat patients named Marbles."

"I won't give out any information, Ms. Green. Can I call you Sarah?"

"If you promise to keep quiet about us."

"Promise." He drank the rest of his coffee while regarding her with an X-ray stare. Then he pushed back his chair and stood. He walked to the back door. "See you later."

The following week, the Chambers Veterinarian Clinic Van crunched in the driveway. Scrubby ran to the door and barked. While the boys sat at the table working on their assignments, Jeanette happily played in her playpen. "Hush, Scrubby," Sarah said, opened the door, and stepped aside to let the veterinarian in. "Hi, Dr. Chambers."

He patted the dog as it sniffed his pant leg. "Just Vance. School in session?"

"Yes, this morning is Music Appreciation."

"I hear you are appreciating Herr Beethoven. That's the *Apassionata*."

"You recognize it?"

"Don't be so surprised." He held his hands up and fingered an air keyboard. "Fifteen years of piano lessons helped put me through Vanderbilt. I played at a piano bar."

"I always wanted to learn," Sarah said, with a mild sigh. "Maybe someday."

"Never too late. You might want to put on the *Moonlight*

Sonata if you have it."

"Why, is that your favorite?"

Chambers held up a red plastic container. "Tetanus shots. Best they be calm for that." He put the box on the coffee table and pointed to Eddie with his elbow. "He needs one, too."

Sarah shook her head. "We should ask Henry's permission. He might get angry."

Chambers lowered his voice. "I doubt he'll give a damn. He doesn't take the kid to the doctor. The child probably hasn't had a checkup since his mother died."

"You don't like Henry very much, do you?"

"Nope. He married my second cousin and roughed her up occasionally."

"Henry?" Sarah looked over her shoulder to the dining room, where the boys listened to the music. She whispered to make sure they couldn't hear. "Henry hit his wife? So hard to believe."

"Be careful with MacDonald, okay?"

"I will." Sarah sent a quick glance to the boys at the table.

"And watch that kid, too," Chambers added.

"Why? What's wrong with Eddie?"

Vance Chambers gave her the sideways glance she now recognized. "Because he's MacDonald's kid, that's why. Fruit doesn't fall far from the tree."

"Grumpy *and* prejudiced," Sarah said.

Wrinkles formed between his eyebrows. "Maybe I am."

"And maybe we should do our best to help Eddie become the best person he can be."

Vance looked away for a few seconds, then caught her gaze. "Tetanus shots."

"Right," she said. "I'll go first to set an example."

Vance's face stayed stoic, but his eyes communicated admiration and longing.

Sarah went to the playpen and picked Jeanette up. Sitting at the small kitchen table, she put Jeanette in her lap and said, "Boys, be brave like soldiers. We have to get shots so we don't get tetanus, which is a very bad disease in farming areas. Come into the kitchen."

Sarah bared her arm and smiled at the children while Vance rubbed the spot with alcohol. She didn't wince. "Didn't hurt a bit. Wes, you're next."

The three boys took their shots bravely. Jeanette screamed.

Jiggling the toddler on her lap, Sarah said, "It's almost time for lunch. Interested?"

Vance ejected the last needle in his portable disposal container. "Yep. I figure if I time it just right, I can get a few free meals."

Sarah laughed. "It will always be potluck."

"Luck," he said. His tone with the word suggested a hundred meanings.

She put Jeanette in the high chair and went to the fridge. "Chicken salad sandwiches coming up."

Vance Chambers paid regular calls around lunchtime to Sarah's farm. When he visited, Sarah let the three boys stop their studies and watch him work. On one of his visits in his own car, the veterinarian opened the passenger side door and helped a dirty, thin dog hop from the Jeep.

Sarah stood on the porch holding Jeanette.

Vance pulled gently at the length of rope around the dog's neck. "I found this poor guy on the side of the road, petrified of the traffic. Someone dropped him off. If you take him, I'll provide free veterinary services for all of your animals and food for both of the dogs. Dogs should always be in pairs anyway to drive off predators in the pasture."

"That's an offer hard to refuse," Sarah said. "It's a deal."

Vance thanked her and left. The boys washed the new

dog, Scruffy. Following a large portion of dog food, the animal slept for the rest of the afternoon.

A few days later, the vet returned and brought medicines and a huge bag of dog chow. Chambers squatted and called Scruffy to him. "He looks good. I knew you'd have a heart. He's one of the lucky ones." Vance stood and brushed his pant leg. "I'll check on the farm stock."

After a while, Sarah went to the barn. "Dr. Chambers, Vance, I have something on my mind. I can't tell anyone how to behave, but you've put me in a bad spot. You treat my children very well. However, I notice you change your voice when you speak to Eddie. He's a nice boy. I won't have that. I appreciate your veterinary services, but unless you treat Eddie the same as my boys, I don't want you to visit us anymore."

The man gave her a sideways glare. "Then you *are* telling me how to behave."

"I'm giving you choices."

He let Jethro's hoof down. "I see."

Sarah returned to the kitchen. Hating confrontations, this one left her feeling lightheaded. The Jeep's tires ground slowly on the gravel as it backed out of the drive. She put extra slices back into the bread bag. Her shoulders sagged. *I just insulted one of the few acquaintances I can count on in this area. And he knows my secret.* Reflecting on her words, she didn't regret what she said to him, only the outcome. *What comes, comes.* She slammed the bag into the breadbox.

Midmorning of the following week, both of the dogs barked at the noise in the driveway. She checked out of the living room window and then went outside. Vance's Jeep pulled up. The car door squeaked open, and the vet emerged with a large canvas bag in his hands. Walking toward the porch, he opened the bag to reveal baseball equipment.

"When the boys take a break from their school work, how

about a little phys ed?"

Relieved to see him again, a bit of warmth spread through her. "They'd love it. I think we can break right now." She called to the boys. "Do you want to learn how to play baseball?"

"Learn?" Vance asked. "They don't know how?"

"My boys played soccer and lacrosse at their school."

"What the hell kind of sports is that? These are American boys. They need baseball. It's a law in Tennessee. You probably didn't know that, being a Yankee and all. Come on, boys, let's play some ball."

"Vance? Thanks."

He smiled. It was the first time she had seen him do that. He held her gaze while the boys ran outside. Then he touched his forehead in a salute.

That night, as Sarah tucked the boys into bed, they talked about learning baseball. Wes grabbed her arm after the goodnight kiss. "Mom, Eddie's dad doesn't like Dr. Chambers."

She ran her fingers across his cheek, noting his resemblance to Cam. "I know. Sometimes, one person doesn't like another person. That's how it is. It shouldn't affect anyone else."

"Eddie's dad says it looks like we have the worst sick animals in the county, the way Dr. Chambers is over here all the time."

"Really?"

"Yeah, but Eddie's dad says our animals are fine. Dr. Chambers is just trying to get in your pants. Mom, that doesn't mean he wants to wear your clothes, does it?"

"No." Sarah flushed. "It means that a man wants to get very close to a woman."

"Eddie said it means when people roll around in bed. You and Dad used to do that. Do you want to roll around in bed with Dr. Chambers?"

She banished memories before they formed. "I don't want

to roll around with anyone."

"Mom, are we ever going to see Dad again?"

"I don't know, Wessie. I don't want to."

"That means you're really mad at him. What did he do?"

"I try to answer your questions because it's best to be honest with the people you love. But there are things I won't talk about because it hurts me. Please don't ask."

"Eddie's dad says there's three reasons why a woman leaves her husband. One is another man, two is—"

"Wes! Enough. Don't speculate on why I left. Do you hear? Especially with Eddie."

As Sarah got ready for bed, she looked in the bathroom mirror. "Vance?" she asked out loud. *He's around fifty. He visits because he's retired and needs something to occupy his time, right? Still...*

CHAPTER 32

The next morning, Henry asked her to come out to the tractor shed. "You should sell these tractors. They're no good to you. Keep the small lawn tractor. I'll show you how to run it."

Wes's comments about what Eddie said echoed in her mind. But this was business. "Will you sell the big ones for me? You can keep some of the money, whatever you think is fair."

"Okay." He leaned against a fence rail. "Eddie likes schooling here. I didn't know he'd learn like he's doing. He tells me what he does every day." Henry pulled a long grass blade and chewed it. "I ain't never talked to him so much before. Um, I'm no good with words, but I want you to know it's made a real difference to us. When my wife left and then died, I guess I kinda ignored my youngest. The two older boys just lit out on their own. I hardly hear from them. At least they had a mother, enough to give them a good hold on life."

"From what I see, you are a good father," Sarah said.

Pain wrinkled Henry's brow. "Better than I was a husband." He spat the grass blade out. "I hit her a time or two. She was a good woman, went to church, did right by me and the kids. I knew I was wrong and apologized to her. Tried to get her back. Then she got sick."

"Henry, did your wife forgive you?"

"Yeah," he said, looking away.

"Then you need to forgive yourself. You're a good man and a caring parent. Eddie is a fine boy. Be proud of him. You know, he likes music. I've ordered recorders for the boys. Maybe we'll have a concert."

Henry looked at her and sighed. Mixed emotions played over his face. "I'm sure glad you came along." He turned away from her and walked to the barn. She swallowed a throat lump and went back to the house.

The recorders came a week later. Sarah set aside half an hour each morning to let the three boys practice. They loved playing the instruments and mastered the beginning book within a few days. On her next visit to Cookeville, she bought intermediate recorder books.

A few days later, while the boys broke the serene country atmosphere with their blasting pipe sounds, Vance had to knock loudly before Sarah heard him.

"Next time, I'll bring earplugs," he said and followed her into the kitchen.

Sarah pulled out the coffee canister. "I guess you won't want tickets to our concert."

"I'll pass." He sat in a chair at the table. "Nashville has a fine orchestra. Maybe we," he pointed to the dining room, "could go to a matinee performance."

Sarah hit the button on the coffee maker. "That would be wonderful. Eddie, too, right?"

"Yes. But better for you if you get a sitter for the little kid."

"Oh, I don't think I could. I don't know anyone—"

"The church my son goes to has a day nursery. They do babysitting."

"Vance, I don't know."

"Wouldn't you enjoy some classy entertainment? Might do Jeanette good to have kids her age to play with. Next time you're in Gainesboro, check out the Hope Methodist church."

"No. They'd want doctor's records, birth certificates, and all. We can't go on the net."

"What the hell are you talking about? This is rural Tennessee, Sarah. The church might want you to join, but they wouldn't require that kind of identification. No one would find you if you had your kid babysat for a day." He drummed his fingers on the tabletop. "It appears to me that you are independent enough to leave from where ever you were and set up this existence for yourself. You shouldn't deny the good things in life because you're afraid of being found."

Her apprehension sharpened. "I haven't even taken my kids to a pediatrician in fear of our information getting online."

"I can talk to Sam Peters in Gainesboro if you want. We're hunting buddies. He's a G.P. and a good doctor. He'll see to your family without disclosing anything. I guarantee it."

"I would appreciate that, Vance."

Sarah checked on the boys and returned to serve Vance coffee. They sat quietly.

"Okay," he said as he put down his empty cup. "I'll look at the farm animals and take off. I'll let you know about the concert."

Vance called later that afternoon. "I got tickets for two weeks from next Wednesday. It's a regular afternoon performance, not a kiddie matinee. I couldn't stand a thousand brats screaming while I'm trying to listen." He paused. "I don't mean your kids. They're not too bad. I mean, they're well-behaved. I don't want to offend you."

"I'm not offended. You don't enjoy kids. That makes it your loss. I'm going to look into that church daycare you spoke of. I don't believe it will scar Jeanette to be watched for one day. Thanks, Vance. Oh, and if you are driving, you must promise not to drink for twenty-four hours ahead."

Vance took a moment to answer. "You think I drink?"

"I think I've seen a bottle of Jack Daniels in your car. And the Clorette's breath gum doesn't mask alcohol."

Vance said, "Okay."

The next day, she drove into Cooksville and took the boys

to buy clothes. All three looked fine in their jackets with ties in the dressing room. She bought herself a red sheath dress. To her surprise, when she tried it on at the store, her hourglass figure reflected in the mirror. The farm work had trimmed and firmed her.

On the day of the concert, Jeanette did not cry when the lady took her to the church nursery.

The performance outshone what Sarah expected. Afterward, Vance treated them to dinner at a fancy restaurant in Nashville, with aquariums surrounding the dining room. The church nursery, prearranged, stayed open to wait for the returning group.

At the church, Vance lifted Jeanette into the car seat and gently fastened the belt. The little girl smiled at him, and he brushed a golden curl away from her face. He kissed the child on the forehead. "You're a pretty little girl." He looked at Sarah. "She looks a lot like her mother."

It had been a delightful day, and the boys talked about it for weeks.

CHAPTER 33

Each morning, Cam answered Wally's phone call and asked the same question, "Anything new about Sandy?"

This morning, Wally said, "Yes. Something promising."

Cam sat up straight and pressed the phone closer to his ear. "What?"

"So, the only thing we really had were the two calls Wes made, right? Those leads gave us a search area. First, North Carolina, which didn't pan out. The second call that came from the restaurant in Nashville led us to a guy who verified the caller was legit and that Sandy and the kids had been there. Remember when we checked the nearby hotels and interviewed the desk clerk at that weekly rental place? He remembered a woman looking like Sandy and the kids, plus a black cat. Sandy registered under a different name and paid cash. She gave him a hundred-dollar tip to ignore that they had a cat and another hundred for easy rental. Cash gets the courtesy of no questions. That's where we lost the trail."

"I remember," Cam interrupted. "And?"

"Okay," Wally said. "I instituted several searches. First, facial recognition from all highways that have cameras in the entire state of Tennessee. We got a bunch of possibles, but none that was Sandy. Then, I searched for driver's license photos with a recognition program. The computer spits out a thousand photos with similar faces. One of those faces was Sarah Green. Along with the other nine hundred plus possibilities, we cleared Green."

"So?" Cam's jaw tightened. "What did you find?"

"Nothing at first. I came to a dead end. Then, I went through the names again, checking details like where the women worked, lived, and so on. Guess what? Sarah Green was a maid for that weekly rental place where the desk clerk remembered the cat. I spoke to the clerk again by phone. He remembered something. The older kid, most likely Wes, said his mom wanted to buy a place in the boonies. The clerk thought it was funny that the boy used the term boonies."

Cam held his breath. "Then?"

I did a wide search of real estate sales around the area. I checked every sale of women who bought real estate without a man being on the title. Along with a hundred other single women who acquired property in the area, a woman named Esther Eckberg, eighty-seven, bought a farm outside the small town of Gainsboro, Tennessee. I checked all those real-estate-buying ladies out, including Esther, and nothing jumped out at me. A few days later, something did leap out. Why would a woman who is eighty-seven buy a huge farm? I looked her up. She lives in Kentucky. Rich as hell. Got her money from investing in an Atlantic City casino that her son is involved with."

"Wally! Tell me what you found," Cam demanded.

"I'm getting there. Esther never took actual possession of the farm. The sale was brokered online. Everything, including a huge money transfer, looked good. No red flags on the financials. I kept tags on the farm to see what happened next. The paperwork lagged because that is a small community, and things are slow, but I kept checking. That's when I found out that Esther deeded that property as a gift to…a woman named Sarah Green. And according to the paper trail, it looks like the recipient is the same Sarah Green who worked at that weekly motel. More research revealed that there is no apparent connection between Eckberg and Green. I'm pretty sure they *don't* know each other. However, Eckberg is the grandmother to Paula, Sandy's ex-roommate.

I called the real estate agent, but she wouldn't answer any questions over the phone."

"Wait a minute, Wally," Are you saying Sandy is posing as Sarah Green? Using another woman's driver's license? She's paid cash for everything, bought cars, and now owns a farm in Tennessee using a fraudulent name? That's too devious for Sandy. She doesn't think like that. I mean, how would she *get* a driver's license?"

"You asshole. She saw someone who looked like her and bribed the lady to sell her license. You never appreciated Sandy's intelligence. What a genius. Eluding *you* for months wouldn't be difficult, but, buddy, she has eluded *us*, an agency with the best technology *in the world*. And all of this Tennessee farm stuff is speculation on my part. We still don't know anything for sure."

Cam let out the breath he was holding. "We've got to go there."

"Right. If you can get free, let's fly to Nashville and rent a car. We can check the agent out by this afternoon."

"I can get free," Cam said in a firm tone.

"Good. I'll make the plane reservations. I'll have the airline bump passengers if I have to. I'll text you the time to be at the airport."

Cam hung up. He leaned back in his office chair. It felt right. He would see Sandy.

When they arrived in Nashville that evening, Wally located the real estate agent's office eighty miles east of Nashville, in Cookeville, who sold the farm. They made an appointment with the Realtor, Julia Unstead, for the next afternoon. They got a rental car.

Mrs. Unstead fidgeted when Wally flashed his badge and started his questions. "Excuse me," she said and went into the back room.

In less than two minutes, Sheriff Unstead, from his office

next to the realty, came in.

"Who are you?" The sheriff asked.

Wally displayed his badge and ID. "Julia," the sheriff said to his wife, "answer the agent's questions. I'll just sit here awhile."

Julia confirmed that the lady in the driver's license picture resembled the Sarah Green, who purchased the land. She remembered the three children and the cat, Marbles.

"Finally! We found her." Cam said. "I need the address for the GPS."

Sheriff Unstead left the chair and adjusted his gun belt. "Whoa, there, fella. That's private property. What've you got in mind?"

"I'm going out there to find my wife."

The sheriff moved the belt again. "You city boys think you can just do what you want when you want ta, don't cha? It don't work like that in these parts."

"Hey," Cam stood up, eye to eye with the sheriff. "She's my wife. I'm going to see her."

"Nope. Here's the deal. Since I know you aim to visit the lady and I don't know your intentions, you wait until tomorrow morning. I'll call her to get permission for you to visit."

Cam slammed Julia Unstead's desk. "No!"

Wally tapped Cam's shoulder for a chance to speak. "Look," he said to the lawman. "My friend has been searching for his wife for more than six months. He's trying to reconcile, but if the lady knows he's coming, we're afraid she'll bolt, and he won't get the chance to speak with her. I guarantee her safety."

"Where you boys staying?"

"We don't have a place right in this area right now," Wally said.

"Let's do this my way, okay? My sister has a bed and breakfast near Gainesboro. You stay there, and in the morning, I'll go out with you to the farm." He looked at Cam threateningly.

"And I *mean,* you wait until I go with you."

Wally shook his head, warning Cam not to argue. "How about this?" he said, stroking his chin. "We'll stay at the bed and breakfast tonight, and in the morning, I'll wait at your office. He," Wally indicated Cam, "goes out to the farm, and after a little while, you can call the lady and confirm she's all right. You and I will go out there after you speak with her."

The sheriff considered the proposal for a second. "Nope. *You* stay at my office. Buddy here," he pointed to Cam, "will drive out there, and I'll follow. I'll hang back a bit while he makes his appearance. When the lady gives the all-clear, I'll call you and have my deputy bring you out there. I want to see your credentials again, though. Identifications, driver's licenses, car plates, and *the badge,* got it?"

Wally nodded.

Cam crossed his arms tightly over his chest. "Fine."

CHAPTER 34

Sarah collected the morning eggs herself because Henry and Eddie wouldn't be there until later. Focusing on her chores, she didn't hear the gravel crackle in the driveway. Rounding the barn, she saw Cam slanted against the Chrysler Town and Country.

"Hello, *Sarah*."

Her hands shook. She dropped the basket and fled to the kitchen. Cam sprinted behind her.

"Daddy!" Wes banged his chair away from the breakfast table and flew into Cam's chest.

"Hey, son." Cam went to Miles, Wes still attached, and mussed the boy's hair.

Within a minute, Sheriff Unstead barreled through the back door. He walked toward Sandy. "You okay?"

She nodded her hanging head, exhaling. A cry filtered down from the upper floor.

Cam smiled. "Jeanette! I'll get her." He hit the stairs with the boys close at his heels.

The radio, perched on Unstead's shoulder, hissed. He pulled it from the cloth harness and put it to his ear. "Ten-four." He eyed Sandy. "I have to see about some shooting near the Interstate. Do you need me to send a deputy here?"

She pursed her lips. "No. It'll be all right."

"Dial 9-1-1 if something goes wrong. I'll come by later to check on you." He left.

She tilted against the counter, feeling faint. Cam and the kids returned to the kitchen. Sandy put Jeanette in the high chair while Wes and Miles clattered into their seats.

Wes waved for her attention. "Can we have more cereal, Mom?"

Mechanically, she took the jug from the fridge and then thunked the milk on the table. As Wes poured Wheat Chex into the bowls, Miles attempted to pour the milk into his bowl. The container slipped, turning over, gurgling a river of white.

Sandy uprighted the gushing jug. "Miles!" She pulled towels from a drawer and threw them on the mess. "That was almost a whole gallon. You know how far away the store is!"

Cam pressed towels into the spill. "Calm down. It's just milk. We'll get more."

Sandy put her hand on her roiling stomach. She left for the solace of the living room.

After supervising the cleanup, Cam put cereal on the tray for Jeanette. He moved to the couch next to Sandy, his voice modulated and calm. "You knew I'd find you."

She tried to see through the watery covering in her eyes. "I figured if I was gone long enough, you would take up with that...that blonde. I left the house for you and *whoever*."

"I need to talk to you about that. It isn't like you think."

Her tears dried immediately, replaced by anger. "*What's* to *think*? I *saw* the *pictures*!"

His phone rang. He answered. "Yep, it's Sandy." Cam paced with the cell to his ear.

Sandy shut down, not processing until she heard him say, "Enterprise rental is bringing you a car? Great. And bring milk."

The words snapped her to attention. "You have a lot of nerve. This is *my* house. You can't invite anyone here."

"Actually," Cam said, "this house belongs to Sarah Green. I hope she doesn't get angry when she finds *you* living here." He waited for it to sink in. "And I have legal rights to see my children. You can't go against me on that."

She glared. "This isn't Manhattan. Tennessee folks don't

cotton to abandonment by adulterous fathers."

Cam remained poised. "I know seeing me is something of a shock, but everything will be all right."

"No! Everything is not going to be all right." The moment of defiance gone, Sandy could not stifle her tears.

Cam leaned close. As his arms encircled her, Sandy's inner voice screeched, vividly recalling the photographs. One image showed his head lodged between the thighs of a shapely torso, and another, the image of him bent over a bed edge so close to the woman they were essentially one unit. Visions dashed into her mind like a strobe.

She pulled away. "Don't touch me."

"Honey," Cam said gently. "I'm sorry. Please, let me explain."

Sandy ran out to the front porch and sat on the swing. Cam left her alone and stayed with the kids. Within an hour, another car came around the hill into the drive. Wally's large frame emerged from the driver's seat. Sandy ignored his wave, racing into the house and up the stairs. From her window, she saw Wally bring in bags of groceries. Then he came out to the car and picked up two suitcases.

"Suitcases?" She washed her face and came down to the kitchen.

Wally spread his arms for a hug. "It's good to see you, Sandy. We've been worried."

She ignored the welcoming gesture. Fists on hips, she dashed in front of Cam as he put items in the pantry. "Why did Wally bring these groceries? And *why* did he bring in suitcases?"

Cam wiped his hands on a kitchen towel. "We'll be here for a while."

"I don't think so. You've found me and seen that the kids are all right. Now go home to *your* house in New York."

"Sandy," Cam said in a benign voice. "You are fair and

compassionate. I need to spend some time with the kids. Our children. You won't deny me that, will you?"

Sandy looked at the floor. "You can see them for two days. Stay in Cookeville."

"Don't do that to the kids, honey. They want to see me, too. I don't mind sleeping on the couch. I've seen two, the one here and another for Wally in your office area."

His words swirled in her mind. The kids had missed him. Their needs outweighed her wrath. She stiffened. "You can shower and eat here, but you'll sleep in the old bunkhouse. Two days only."

A truck grinding brakes in the driveway interrupted the conversation.

"That's Eddie," Wes said, jumping from his chair and thudding the front door wide.

Cam picked up Jeanette and stood in the open doorway. Sandy passed him on her way out to talk with Henry.

Eddie shut the door of the crew cab and ran to Wes. Henry leaned against the truck door. He nudged his face toward the house. "That your husband?"

"He's the father of my children. I don't consider him my husband."

Henry narrowed his eyes. "Uh-huh. If you don't want him here," his eyes flashed to the full gun rack hanging in the back seat window. "I can run him off."

"What?" It took a moment for Sandy to realize what he meant. "No. Henry! But you could help me by doing something about the water to the old farmhouse." Her words became acid. "That's where *guests* will stay."

Henry's upper lip sneered. "Yeah? I'll do it today."

Wally came out to the porch. He folded beefy arms, leering at Henry, one big man eye-threatening another.

Henry's lip curled up higher. "No problem to rid the *both*

of them. It'd be my pleasure." He looked at Sandy. "If you need me, get me."

"Thanks for your offer, but how would I get you? You work outside all day and don't have a cell phone."

"I'll have one by this afternoon when I go into town to buy the water pipes."

"I'll be all right, Henry. But I appreciate your concern."

Henry touched the brim of his bill cap and hopped in the truck.

As the truck sounds receded, Sandy took the hummingbird feeder down and brought it onto the porch to fill.

Still holding Jeanette, Cam came over to Sandy. "Trouble with your field hand?"

Sandy capped the feeder with a forceful snap. "It's none of your business."

"Does he help you with the farm? Just *how* handy is this handyman?"

She turned and glared. "Only a cheater would suspect cheating."

"We need to talk," Cam said.

"I don't want to talk," Sandy answered.

Sandy went through the day focusing on her chores, moving about stiffly, and trying to control her distress. The thought of Cam at the table made bile back up in her throat. But the kids deserved some time with their father. Grudgingly, she fixed a big dinner that evening.

During the meal, Cam picked up one of the plates. "New dishes?"

"The former owners left everything."

He turned it over to read the logo. "These aren't as nice as the ones we have in Manhattan."

Sandy traced her finger on the green plate with the incised white leaf. "I like these just fine. You and your friends can enjoy your New York china."

Cam replaced the plate and finished the meal in silence.

Following dinner, Cam put the children to bed while Sandy and Wally tidied up. With no conversation, the room echoed with the sounds of dishes and cabinet doors. When the work was done, Sandy went upstairs to her room.

After her shower, she gathered up linens and took them to the living room. Adding a flashlight on top of the pile, she shoved the things toward Cam. "It's bedtime. Here are the sheets for the two cots in the bunkhouse. The lights work, but Henry hasn't finished fixing the water pipes, so you can wash in there." She pointed to the bathroom across the hall from the small room that served as an office. "Both of you. Go."

Sandy pulled the towel off her hair and ran her fingers through the wet curls. Retying the terrycloth belt, she sat on the couch.

Cam put the linens on a chair and moved next to her. "Sandy, I want you to listen to me. I went to that island to help Wally. The woman in the photos is an agent, and we were posing as a couple. I know this is difficult to believe, but those things... what I did...it was an act. I knew we were being filmed. It was a distraction, and it worked. Please understand, we were in danger."

Sandy made a face. "Come on, Cam."

"It's true. I swear it." He motioned to Wally. "Tell her."

Wally put his hand over his heart. "Scout's honor, Sandy. Honest."

"You two used to be honorable men. But I don't care what story you use." She took a short breath. "Do you have any idea what it was like seeing those...those horrible images?"

Cam tried to put his arm around her, but she moved away. "Don't," she said without moving her lips.

Cam retracted his hands. "Oh, God, Sandy." He rubbed

his neck. "I am so sorry you saw those hideous pictures."

She looked away. "It would have been so much better for you if I hadn't seen them. You could have come back and *pretended* you were a faithful, dedicated husband."

"I love you," Cam said.

"I'm sure that was foremost in your mind as you stuck your tongue up that blonde."

"Sandy, don't do this. Let's talk it out."

Wally stood up and adjusted his belt nervously. "Do you two really want me here?"

Cam cleared his throat. "Stay, Wally. Sit down. You're my backup. Maybe she'll believe you." He turned to Sandy. "What can I do to fix this mess? Tell me, honey. I love you and want us back together."

Sandy moved over to where Wally sat. "Do you think I'm attractive?"

"You're beautiful, Sandy."

"So, when men see me, do they think of a plain motherly type or a desirable woman?"

Wally looked confused. "You're very attractive. I've always thought so."

"You want back with me, Cam? Then pay attention." Standing in front of Wally, she opened the robe, pulled off her pajama top, and put her breasts close to Wally's face. "Make love to me right here, and Cam can watch us."

Wally jumped up and backed away. "Jesus!" He ran out the door.

Cam put his head in his hands. "I'm so sorry, Sandy."

Her voice strained. "You wouldn't like to see *me* with another man, would you?"

"God, No. I think I'd better go to the bunkhouse now."

She pushed the flashlight at him. "The path is dark. It goes through a dry creek, and you might trip."

Just then, they heard Wally's far-off swear.

Cam shouted out the door. "Wait up, Wally. I'm coming with a light." He sighed.

***

On the outside path, as Cam met up with Wally, he handed him the flashlight.

Wally grunted. "Didn't go very well, did it?" He rubbed his ankle. "Damn, I think Sandy's snapped. I never expected that."

"Me neither," Cam said. "It's not going to be easy."

CHAPTER 35

Early the next morning, Eddie joined the group for breakfast. Sandy sent a bacon and egg sandwich out to Henry, who went straight to work finishing the water system for the antiquated building.

Cam stacked dishes from the table. "What can we do to help while the boys study?"

Sandy didn't hesitate. "Clean the barn. On the east side, there's an area like a kitchen. It hasn't been used for years. I think it can be restored. Mrs. Nolan did her canning out there. It needs to be working when Henry shows me how to put up produce this summer. Move the refrigerator from the tractor shed to there. I was going to ask Henry to do it, but—"

"We'll do it."

At noon, Henry came to the back door for a drink. Sandy gave him a quart jar of sweet tea chilled in the freezer to make a layer of ice on top. Henry shook it, then chugged.

"We'll have lunch in about an hour. Will you join us?"

"Nope. Hey, is everything going okay?" Henry handed her his cell phone. "Call yourself. Your cell can catch my number."

When her cell phone rang, she entered Henry as a contact. "Got it. She returned the phone. "Do you want me to send some sandwiches out to you?"

"Yeah. By the way, did those two put on bug repellent before they started to work in the barn kitchen?"

"I don't think so. Should they?"

"Yep." Henry looked at his phone for a moment. Compared to the size of his hand, the thing looked miniature. He took his time placing it in his shirt pocket. "I trimmed the weeds around that place the other day. It'll be full of chiggers. Them two'll be miserable for a week."

He turned and ambled toward the trench he had dug for the plastic pipes.

Sandy ran to the barn, fighting with the nasty little voice in her head that said Cam and Wally deserved to suffer. But she had encountered the agonizing infestation when she first moved there and could not allow it to happen to anyone, not even someone who hurt her so badly. "Cam! Wally! You have to shower right away. It might be too late already. Run!"

The men ran. Ordered to soap up every inch, Wally showered downstairs, and Cam used Sandy's bathroom. Sandy took their clothes straight to the washer. She muttered to herself how much she still had to learn about living on a farm. As she shut the top of the machine, she heard the familiar engine sound of Vance's Jeep pull into the driveway. She greeted him at the door.

"I try to schedule my visits around mealtime," he said, rubbing his shoes over the welcome mat. "Have you noticed?"

"Now that I think about it, you do eat here a lot. So, you are grumpy *and* rude. We're having leftovers today. Does it suit your palate?"

"Depends on the leftovers. I don't eat cold pizza."

"We can get pizza here? That would be great."

"Nah, just kidding. No one delivers this far out. What's the leftovers?"

"All kinds of stuff. Pot luck, take it or leave it."

"I'll think about it. What's MacDonald doing out there halfway underground?"

"He's laying water pipes to the old bunkhouse."

As Sandy pulled out cellophane-encased dishes from the refrigerator, Wally came out of the bathroom, wrapped most of the way in a towel. Cam came down the stairs at the same time, a white terry cloth around his waist.

Not introducing himself, Vance folded his arms over his belt and said, "Nice skirts."

Cam commenced a staring contest with Vance. Flinching first, he lost. "Who's he?"

Sandy took paper plates out of the pantry. "Dr. Chambers, our veterinarian. Look, I don't have time to find something for either of you to wear, so walk to the bunkhouse like that. Lunch will be ready shortly."

Having been dismissed, Cam and Wally, clad in towels, left the kitchen.

Vance twisted his lip. "I'm guessing the blond guy is the mister. He looks like Wes."

Sandy nodded grimly.

Vance peeled the cellophane from one of the leftover bowls, checking the contents. "I can take care of them for you. I keep a shotgun in the back of the jeep."

"What is it with you Tennessee men? Henry made a similar offer."

"We country bumpkins solve our problems directly. Ever hear of Occam's Razor?"

"Yes. But I don't think that applies."

"We call our solution the Redneck Razor. I'll explain it to you sometime."

"Maybe I don't want to know," Sandy said.

Vance gave her his sideways glance. "Are you going back with him?"

"*No.*" She set a dish down hard on the kitchen table. "He's only here for a few days."

Vance shoved his hands into his front pockets. "Sarah—"

"I guess the time has come for you to know my real name, Sandra Gray Morgan."

"Okay, by me." He waited a moment. "Uhm...I won't stay. I'll just go check the cows."

"Thanks," she said.

Within a few minutes, Cam returned to the kitchen. "I don't like that old guy."

"It's not necessary for you to like anyone here. This is my place. I have Henry, my hay agent, and Vance, my veterinarian. It's my business. Don't interfere."

"Please. Let's talk, Sandy. I found you. I'm here."

"I don't need to talk. *I'm* here, and I'm here to stay. We are through and were through the minute you slept with that woman. And I don't care about the circumstances."

"Sandy, listen to me."

"Go back to Manhattan. File for divorce. I took the money from the safe. That's all I need. So, I don't want anything from you, no support, no alimony, nothing. I just want you out of my life."

"No. We're going to work this out."

Sandy slammed the refrigerator closed. "Go home."

"I'm not going back until I've had a chance to make you understand."

"I already understand, Cam, and you're going back. Tomorrow."

The next morning at breakfast, Sandy rehearsed her *you have to leave today* speech with her inner self. She was ready to deliver the directive as soon as they stepped into the kitchen.

When her unwelcome guests came through the door, she knew they wouldn't be leaving that day or the next. Cam, the quintessential preppie, the man who, as long as she'd known him, had never been uncouth with a burp, fart, nose pick, or ball adjust, gouged at his crotch, cussing with each scrape. Wally, a pleading look on his face, gyrated in an attempt to relieve itching in five places with only two hands.

"I have some chigger medicine, but it doesn't help all that much," Sandy said. "I'm sorry. It's Saturday, no doctors. Do you want to go to the Emergency Room in Cookeville?"

"No way," Cam scowled. "Not for itching."

Wally held his hand up, declining the offer.

"All you can do is rub alcohol when it starts up. Try not to scratch."

"You're kidding," Cam snarled. He dug at his waistband. "Alcohol! Please!"

"Okay." Sandy put her cup down. "Help yourself to breakfast while I go upstairs."

"Breakfast?" Cam stuck his hand down his pants. "God, who could eat?"

CHAPTER 36

Cam and Wally spent the day in the farmhouse, each man bonding with rubbing alcohol.

At breakfast the next morning, Cam appeared with the almost empty bottle. He shook the container at Sandy. "We're almost out. Where can we buy a gallon?"

Sandy stacked a few dishes in front of her. "I saw gallon jugs at the beauty supply store in Cookeville."

Cam turned to Wally. "Good. I'll take my rental.",

Wally nodded, stacked his dishes, and left the kitchen.

Sandy picked up the silverware on her way to the sink. "And while you're gone, maybe don't come back."

Cam scratched at his armpit. "You know that's not going to happen. Why do I think you're enjoying our misery?" Cam dug at his beltline. "Sandy, I want to be together as a family. Put all the pieces back together. By the way...." He gathered the cereal boxes and placed them in the pantry. "I went to a lot of trouble to retrieve the Lexus. *In Minnesota*. Thanks for that. Impound fees, towing, paperwork."

"Whatever," Sandy said, keeping her back to him.

"I thought you loved that car."

"I did. So, you can see how much I wanted to get away from you."

"Look, Sandy—"

Wally ran into the kitchen. "You two *gotta see this*," he said, jerking his head toward the open door.

Everyone, kids included, moved fast to see what excited the unexcitable Wally. Sandy toted Jeanette on her hip and joined the crowd in the driveway.

The rental car's hood stood vertically. Wally thumped the fender. "The car sounded odd when it started, so I checked under the hood. Look!"

Where they should have seen a motor, on top lay a conglomeration of hay, pieces of foil, newspaper shreds, and detritus of unknown origin that obliterated the inside of the compartment.

"That's a rat's nest," Eddie commented casually. "They can build it in a day or two. Better check the wires. They love to chew the rubber and plastic." He reached for a strip of foil. "Them rats love shiny stuff."

"Great," Sandy said. "Happy birthday, me. It just gets better and better."

Cam winced. "Your birthday. I forgot. I'm sorry." He scratched furiously at his armpit. "Wes, get a garbage can." He and Wally launched into the nest's destruction.

Sandy shifted Jeanette to her other hip and went back into the house.

Miles fished something out of the tossed debris and held up a metal object. "Dad, look at this funny dime."

Cam stepped close to Miles. "What is that?"

Wally took it from the boy and palmed it. "Shit."

Cam wiped his hands on his pants and dug at his crotch. "Problem?"

Wally leaned close. "It's a tracking device," he whispered.

"From the rental?"

Wally motioned with his eyes to step away from the boys. "Look at all this crap. Stuff from the garbage, the recycling bin, and even a few silk flowers from the front porch. I don't know which car it was on. At least *one* of us is being tracked." Wally pulled his hand across his chin. "And since we found it while we were here, it means someone else knows about Sandy and this place. She could be in danger."

"You think it's the same person who sent the photos?"

"Could be. Your family needs to get out of here. Give me a few minutes to think on how we should do this." Wally went back to the farmhouse.

A half-hour later, Wally called Sandy to the picnic table in a shady spot behind the barn. "We're meeting out here in case the house is bugged."

Jeanette fidgeted as Sandy stiffened. "What?"

Cam took Jeanette on his lap and explained how they found the tracking device. "Sandy, you and the kids need to leave right now. Wally has a plan." He held up his hand to suspend her sputtering refusal. "Honey, this is serious. We need to get you to safety."

"Listen," Wally said. "Don't pack. Take I-40 east to the Walmart at this address in Knoxville." He handed her a note with instructions. "Buy the things you'll need for a few days at the store. Park your van in the lot by the automotive department. There will be a white Mercury Grand Marquis with a Zorro antenna topper. You will find the key to the trunk on top of the front driver's side tire. Act naturally, relaxed." He rubbed her hand. "Listen carefully. Open the trunk with the key and load your purchases. There's a box in there welded to the bottom with a combination keypad. Use your six-digit birthday to open it. Inside that is a second key, the proper one for the ignition. *Don't use the first key to start the car.* It will lock the doors and sound a loud alarm. Understand?"

Sandy nodded.

"There will be an envelope with two thousand dollars. Use the cash. The directions to a safe house in Knoxville will be on the front seat."

"You can arrange all of this?" Sandy asked.

"Already done. We need to split up. I've put the tracking

device in my rental and I'm going west to Nashville, then on to Washington. Cam will head north, returning to Manhattan. Leave your phone here and get another pay-as-you-go cell at Wal-Mart. I'll contact you in a few days."

Sandy recognized Wally's serious demeanor and agreed to his directions. She contacted Henry to look after the farm while she was away. Within half an hour, they were ready. The three cars convoyed down the driveway, around the bend, and upon reaching the highway, they all turned in different directions.

When Sandy and the children arrived at the store, the car and the directions were exactly where Wally had said. She got a new phone and drove the rest of the way to the address, a long-term suite rental where she was already registered. That night, after dining on fast food and putting the kids to bed, Sandy watched television. A knock on the door made her heart pound. She looked through the viewing hole and saw a young woman illuminated in the hall light.

Sandy opened the door as far as the hotel security chain allowed.

"Sandra Morgan?" the lady asked. "May I talk with you? It's important. I'm alone."

"No," Sandy said. "Go away."

"Mrs. Morgan, I know you are here because your husband and Dennis Wallensky think you are in danger. I assure you there is no threat from me." The lady held her badge up to the opening. "Mrs. Morgan? I work for the same agency as Dennis Wallensky, and I need to talk to you."

Sandy didn't respond, not knowing what to do.

"Mrs. Morgan, let me in."

Sandy peered out the crack. Folding her arms in front of her navy-blue suit, the woman tapped her foot. Blonde hair pulled back in a bun, frameless glasses, with gold button earrings. Sandy thought she looked familiar, but was certain they had never met.

"All right," Sandy said. "But I'll set my phone on nine-one-one with my finger on the send button."

"That's a good idea, Mrs. Morgan." Sandy pushed the digits. She opened the door, showing the phone as the lady entered. The woman picked up the remote and turned off the television before she sat on the couch.

Holding the phone, her finger hovering over the send button, Sandy sat on the other end of the couch. "Who are you?"

"My name is Heda Blakely. I believe you saw some pictures of me and your husband."

Sandy recoiled and jumped from her seat on the couch, the cell phone falling from her hand onto the floor. "You! What are you doing here? *Get out!* You can have him. I don't want him anymore."

"Sit down," Heda commanded. "I have something to say, and you are going to listen. I came a long way to speak with you, and I *will* speak."

Reluctantly, Sandy sat hard on a chair opposite her. "There's nothing—"

"Mrs. Morgan," Heda said, overriding Sandy's protests. "The pictures you saw were real. The situation was not. I am a federal agent. I can't give you details, but I assure you, we, your husband and I, posed as a couple to rescue your friend Dennis Wallensky. As soon as we arrived at the resort, it became apparent we were under suspicion. Our room was being filmed, and the only way we could divert the danger and rescue agent Wallensky was to *perform*. Please, believe me, I took little pleasure in those events. I was doing my job, and your husband cooperated. No more, no less."

Sandy looked away. "No way. Agents don't look like you."

Heda smiled. "You'd be surprised."

"Cam sent you here. Where did you get that badge? It's

against the law to impersonate a government agent, you know."

Heda reached into her purse and displayed the small leather holder. She unfolded the case to show a golden badge and an ID photo. She snapped it together before Sandy could see much of it."

"So, Wally sent you?"

Blakley stood and smoothed the navy skirt. "Agent Wallensky doesn't have that kind of authority to get me to travel from Washington to speak with you. Someone higher asked me, and I agreed. Your husband risked his life and his marriage. He did a noble and brave thing in offering to rescue his friend. He had no foreknowledge of what would occur. Sometimes, what happens during a mission just happens. We have to go with the circumstances to survive."

Agent Blakely walked to the door. "I've given you the facts and the truth. The ball is now in your court. Good night." She walked out of the suite.

Sandy had a bad night, taking hours to fall asleep. She woke up late in the morning when Jeanette cried. The boys sat watching television with the volume low.

They ate lunch at a restaurant across the street. The place had a dining room with a kids' arcade on the side. Sandy gave their order at the counter, and they sat at a table near the game area.

Wes leaned over the table to whisper. "Mom, that biker guy keeps watching us."

Sandy looked over Wes's shoulder at a tanned man dressed in black leather. He had a doo-rag on his head, chains hanging from his pocket, a kerchief around his neck, and laces keeping his leather Harley jacket closed. He held a white envelope and smiled at her.

"Don't stare at him, Miles. Wes, just look at me and ignore other people."

"Too late, Mommy," Miles said. "Here he comes."

The biker approached and shook the envelope at her. "Happy Birthday, Sandy."

Sandy's mouth dropped open, and then she drew it shut. "Oggie?"

Oggie pulled a chair over to the table and sat backward. He handed her the card. "Hi."

"You're a biker?"

"For today."

When the counter man called their order number, Oggie grabbed the receipt from the tabletop and scooted the chair away. "I'll get it."

Wes watched Oggie head to the counter. "You know him, Mom?"

"I did a long time ago."

Oggie paid and returned with the tray.

Miles tugged at Sandy's sleeve. "Mom, I have to go to the bathroom."

"I'll take him," Oggie said. "You should go, too, Wes."

Sandy shook her head. "No, that's all right, I'll walk them to the restrooms."

"Sandy. I won't do anything to your kids. Wes, Miles, and Jeanette. Great kids. They should have been mine, you know." He disconnected his keys from one of the chains. "Here, you can hold the keys to my chopper. Relax."

He took the boys by the hand to the restroom within sight of Sandy's table, and her observation did not waver until they came out. On the way back, Oggie stopped briefly at the game area. He slid out his wallet, attached to another chain, and removed a bill. After he brought the boys back to Sandy, he spoke to the counterman and returned with four rolls of quarters.

"Eat, guys," Oggie said to Miles and Wes. "Then I'll show you how to work the Claw Machine." He sat down and touched

Jeanette's cheek. "Adorable." He looked at Sandy. "I need to talk with you, okay?"

The boys wolfed down their burgers in a few bites to finish, eager to learn the Claw. At the machine, Oggie squatted to demonstrate how to finesse the prongs to snag the toys. In full view of their mother, quarters in hand, the boys assaulted the Claw. Oggie came to the table and sat in the chair in the normal way.

"Hey, Sandy. Been a long time, huh?'

"You live around here?"

"No. I came to talk to you." He reached for a French fry. "Sandy, I'm going to tell you some things I'm not supposed to, but I've got to try to undo some bad stuff... things I did to you. Let me get this off my chest. I have a lot to say, so I'll start at the beginning."

Sandy gave Jeanette a drink from her cup and blew on a fry to cool it. "Okay, I guess."

"When you were transferred to the library where I was, it looked like I functioned as a computer technician, but I really didn't work there. I work for a federal agency with a name you wouldn't recognize. The tech job covered my surveillance of a terrorist cell across the street. The minute I saw you, I loved you. I've never stopped. I love you right now."

A bell went off in the arcade. Oggie waited for it to abate. "After the terrorist thing, I had to leave for another assignment, but I kept coming back to New York to date you. I knew you were starting to care for me, and I was ready to quit the agency and propose when you married that stupid shit."

Sandy dropped her head. "I wanted to tell you I was engaged, but I didn't see you again."

"Yeah, well, I didn't like it, but I knew about it. I figured he would do something to make you recognize him as a viper. I couldn't believe you didn't see it."

"What?"

"That guy, the grand manipulator, owned you. You, the most creative and brilliant woman I know. You were a perfect wife, but never comprehended how you became his slave. I'll bet he told you *how* to vote. Over the years, did he listen to your opinions or appreciate even one personal idea?"

"You came to tell me that?"

"Not done. While watching you, I noticed Dennis the Pollock. When he went nuts after his wife died, I recommended him to the agency. No family, partially trained as an agent by the NYPD, *and* had a death wish. Not that we necessarily look for a death wish, but he was obviously willing to risk his life for a cause. He joined us and made a good operative."

Sandy held an onion ring close to her mouth as in a freeze frame. "Wally knows you?"

"I know him, but he doesn't know me. Sandy, I was on the mission when they sent Wallensky to that resort. Things went bad. We lost two agents, and the bad guys were beginning to look at him. His contacts were gone, and he didn't know who to trust. His lines of communication were down, so the agency sent in another agent. You know her as Heda."

"Wait," Sandy said. "She came to see me last night. Cam sent her to explain."

"Shish! Neither he nor Wally would have a clue how to contact her, let alone get her to come here. I pulled strings and had her sent to you." He touched her hand. "Listen to the rest of this while I have your attention."

The onion ring fell from her fingers.

In a blurred movement, Oggie caught it mid-air and returned it to the plate. "Because Wallensky didn't know Heda, he needed to see her with someone he trusted. That's why the agency sent in that ass you married. What a surprise, and it's hard to surprise me."

"Oggie, how did you find me? What do you want? Why are you telling me this?"

"Please, just listen. So, the jerk, Morgan, fulfilled his task, and Wallensky got the message, but things became pretty rocky, and we couldn't send Morgan home. I could get into trouble with the agency if they find out I'm talking to you, but... Nothing will happen; they need me too much. Okay, so, at the resort, I allegedly worked for the Cartel, embedded as we say. The Venezuelans, with ties to al ISIS no less, hired me to man their communications."

"You speak Spanish?"

"*Si*, and Farsi and a few other uncommon languages. Unfortunately, on that island, I shared responsibilities with another tech, a smart cookie, a Russian woman, who could have snagged me if I did anything to alert our people. Neither Heda nor Wallensky knew about me. I had charge of all the computers and monitoring devices, including the security and room cameras." He paused. "That's when I saw Morgan eagerly carrying on with Heda. In spite of his protestations, he enjoyed every moment. I knew I had the proof to convince you to leave him. And maybe I would show up at the right time, and you would start seeing me again. Bottom line? Sandy, I sent you those photos."

"Oh, Oggie." She put her hand to her cheek and closed her eyes. "How could you?"

"For love. When Heda sent her message for the takedown, the Feds arrested everyone. We, that is, Heda, Wallensky, Morgan, and I, were separated and flown to D.C. for debriefing. I asked them to detain him to give you time to start a divorce."

Sandy opened her mouth, but no sound came out.

"I saw the debriefing tapes. Of course, Morgan claimed he didn't want to be with another woman. He was afraid the Cartel would think he was a spy, so he went along with Heda and *performed*. Yeah, yeah, yeah, it made him sick because he loved his wife. Uh-huh, sacrifice for his country… Sure, he did. Even though Heda said he merely cooperated, I saw him live *in flagrante,* and you needed to know how much he enjoyed himself."

Oggie took a deep breath. "After Ste. Eunice, I was incommunicado for a while, and when I got back, I tried to find you. Jeeze, Sandy, I had no idea you would leave like that without a clue."

He tried to touch her hand, but she pulled it away. "I wanted you to be angry, not pulverized. I went to the debriefing center and told them to let Morgan go. Even though I know he's bad for you, I realized I made a big mistake. I never was any good with regular people. Please, Sandy, I beg your forgiveness."

Sandy looked at the tabletop. "So, Cam told the truth. He *had* to do those things."

"No one held a gun to his head. He could have refused."

"But he had to do it. To save Wally."

"Come on, Sandy. He could have said no and made the agent go to plan B."

Sandy pursed her lips. "There was a plan B?"

"There's always a plan B. That shit Morgan got an excuse to play, and he *played.* I wanted to make sure you knew about his choice."

She stood up. "You are worse than Cam. Worse than anyone I know."

"Sandy, don't go. Please. There's more. I wanted to explain this to you sooner, but I haven't been in the country for all this time. I went on another mission and couldn't track you myself. I wasn't sure Morgan would search for you, but in case he did, I made all of the department's services available to Wallensky, who's a first-class agent."

Sandy sat back down but wouldn't look at him.

"I was the one who had the tracker put on the Pollock's rental car. Who knew the device would be found? From his point of view, the reaction to get you away from the farm was correct, but you were never in danger. Having that car tracked backfired on me. I screwed up again and caused you more distress. I suppose I owe Morgan an apology, but I can't reveal myself for professional reasons. So, I did the next best thing, which was to let you hear Heda's statement. Then, *I* had to tell you the whole truth and personally assure you of your safety. Sandy, I regret this awful mess. I'm sorry I hurt you."

"Get away from me. I don't ever want to see or hear from you again."

Oggie leaned toward her. "Not possible." He went quiet for a moment. "You can't tell anyone you saw me or what I've told you. I know I can trust you."

Wes ran over to them. "Look what I won!" He had a handful of rubber toys. "Hey, Oggie, can I see your chopper?"

Oggie took his keys from the table. "Can he?"

Sandy narrowed her eyes instead of verbally refusing.

"Maybe some other time, Wes. It's right by the window, the big black one. I'll rev the engine for you." He patted the boy's head. "Sandy, when you need me, I'll be there." He left the restaurant.

Both boys pressed against the window to watch Oggie start the bike.

"*All right!*" Wes said when the chopper roared out of the parking lot.

CHAPTER 37

Sandy shut her eyes to think. *What just happened? I'll sort it out later. At least we can go home now.*

The boys helped her pack their few things into the car. Sitting in the driver's seat, Sandy looked around at the mountains aflame in their fall colors. "Hey, boys. Let's take our time driving back."

With Jeanette safe in the child seat and the boys buckled, Sandy started the agency's Crown Victoria. She wondered if her car would still be at the Walmart in Knoxville. *After all the hassle I've had, I will use this car. I have plenty left of the money from the lockbox in the trunk. They can come after me if they want it. Damn that agency. Damn, that woman spy. Damn, Wally and Cam. Double-ass damn, Oggie. I'm tired of moving my kids around because of all of you.*

"We're on vacation?" Wes asked as Sandy pulled out into the street.

"For a few days before we go back to the farm. We'll eat pizza and fast food, too."

"Cool, Mom."

"Yay," Miles said. "Clap your hands, baby."

Jeanette clapped her hands and exposed her lovely front teeth.

They spent five days seeing the sights near Knoxville. Sandy refused to think about the circumstances of their situation until after they went home. When she pulled into the Walmart parking lot, her car was where she left it. She returned the remainder of the cash to the Crown Vic's lock box, secured the doors, and placed the key on the top of the tire as she found it.

They drove home.

When they arrived at the farm late in the afternoon, the dogs celebrated their return with yapping and barking, happy to see the family. Sandy did a quick inspection. Henry had taken good care of the place. She let the kids split what was left of the Burger King meal bought at the drive-through on I-40 when they turned off for their exit. They all went to bed early.

After breakfast the next day, the three boys returned to their studies while Sandy brought Jeanette, the playpen, and her coffee out to the porch. She moved the swing gently with her foot. Now, she could ruminate over the past week.

Maybe I have been unfair to Cam, after all, that woman said…. But I saw the pictures. As for Oggie…he didn't have to send Heda to me or explain what he did. So why did he? Which one is lying? Are they all telling the truth?

Arguing with her internal voice, she admitted deferring regularly to Cam, but *had* she given up her own opinions for his? *Oggie was right about a few things.* Even if Cam had insisted on voting for certain candidates, she hadn't been his slave. And she willingly did all the things a good wife should. She reviewed the last eleven years. *Pretty good years. Maybe I should let Cam visit to see the kids. He has been a worthy father. But the photos. Cam and that woman, the close-up with his tongue….* She shuddered. She didn't want to think about *that.*

Sandy finished the last swig of coffee. She swept her gaze over the vista of the mown fields. Huge rolls of hay dotted the tan ground, and the trees studding the three mountains surrounding the farm blazed in magnificent colors. The crispness in the air made the hummingbirds move about in a frenzy before their southern migration.

A car came down the long road, casting a cloud of dust behind it. She didn't recognize it, and no one drove there unless destined for her farm. It pulled in. Cam and Wally stepped out.

Cam took the two steps up to the porch in one stride. He picked up Jeanette and sat down on the swing next to Sandy.

"Is there any more coffee?" Wally asked.

"Sure. It's still plugged in." She moved as an impulse to get him a cup. *Wait, I'm no one's slave.* "Help yourself."

Cam hugged the baby, who immediately grabbed his nose. He pulled Jeanette's tiny hand to his mouth and kissed it. "So," he looked at Sandy. "Why did you leave Knoxville?"

"False alarm."

"How do you know?"

She turned to him. "Remember all those times when you defended people, and you answered my questions, saying there were things you knew that you couldn't tell? Well, I'm saying that to you right now. My safety has been assured, but I can't divulge how I know. So why are you here? I thought you two went back north."

"We changed our minds."

Wally came out with two cups. He handed one to Cam. "What's happenin'?"

"We're going to stay for a while," Cam said.

"Oh really?" Sandy said, hearing Oggie's words. *That guy, the grand manipulator, owned you.* "You don't know this, Cam, but I never voted for one person you wanted."

A deep vee formed between Cam's eyebrows. "What?"

"Never mind. I'll let you stay for a few days. But you leave when I say. Am I clear?"

Cam stroked his chin. "Crystal."

Wally drank his coffee in two long pulls. He set the cup on the doorstep. "I'll put our stuff in the bunkhouse."

Cam and Sandy sat together on the swing. The clicking chirps of the hummingbirds made the only sound. Jeanette squirmed toward the playpen, and Cam rearranged her on his lap.

"Cam, I met Heda."

"Who?"

"Heda, in the photographs."

Cam's face flushed bright red. "Um, really? How did that happen?"

"She visited me at the safe house."

Cam sat up a little straighter. "What did she say? I hope she told you—"

"She confirmed what you said. I don't know what to believe." A few images appeared in her mind's eye. "But it doesn't make a difference. I can't get past those pictures."

Cam put his chin on Jeanette's head. "Well," he said, sighing. "At least you know the truth. It's a start." They sat quietly for a moment. "Sandy—"

She held her hand up to keep him from finishing. *A start? No! He's a grand manipulator.*

Before she could say anything, the boys came out on the porch.

"Dad!" Wes and Miles said in unison.

Cam put Jeanette in the playpen and hugged the boys, one on each side.

Eddie came from the house and waited for the boys to come out of the hug. He held out his recorder.

Wes turned to Sandy. "Mom, we're done with our assignments. We want to show you what we have learned. Dad, do you want to hear us play the recorders?"

Cam patted Wes's head. "Sure. Let's wait for Uncle Wally."

When Wally returned, they went inside, and Sandy stayed on the porch. The boys sounded good, playing a simplified version of Vivaldi's *The Goldfinch*, each boy playing one of three parts. She couldn't help smiling at their success.

After the mini-concert, they came back to the porch.

Wes sat in the swing. "Can we hike up the back mountain

with Dad and Uncle Wally?"

"All right," she said. "Be careful."

The men followed the three boys up the small, steep mountain marking the western boundary of the farm and came back mid-afternoon, starving. As Sandy put out sandwich items, they talked about the things they saw.

"Mom," Wes said. "We saw prints and bear poop."

"Nah," Eddie said, "the poop is called scat."

"Eddie can track animals, Dad," Wes said. "Once, we lost a little goat, and he found it."

"Impressive," Cam said. "Smart, like Uncle Wally."

Wally nodded. "Thanks." He directed his words toward Sandy. "You know, we would have found you eventually, but Wes's calls led us here."

Sandy put the mayonnaise down with a thwack. "What calls?"

Cam picked up a paper plate. "Wes called me from North Carolina and then again from Nashville. It narrowed the locale."

Sandy's eyes widened. She glared at Wes. "You called your father? After I told you not to contact anyone? You disobeyed me. We will discuss this later."

"Mom," Wes stammered. "I'm sorry, I wanted to talk to Dad." Wes winced at Sandy's glare.

"You and I will talk," Sandy said. She took a breath and turned to Cam and Wally. "You will work for your stay. Clean the gutters in the farmhouse and the old bunkhouse."

They did not refuse.

CHAPTER 38

Cam and Wally left the house to clean the gutters.

Sandy stood next to Wes and waited for him to speak.

"Mom?"

"Come with me." On the way out of the kitchen, she pulled open the utility drawer and removed a wooden ruler. Taking Wes by the hand, she led the way upstairs to her bedroom. After closing the door, she sat on the bed. "Come here."

Wes stood in front of her. "Mom, I'm sorry. I forgot what you said about not calling."

"You didn't forget. You wanted to call your father. Being a single parent means I don't have help raising you. I must have obedience and punish you when you disobey. Remember when you and Eddie left Miles in the cedar forest and snuck away to swim in the pond?"

"Mom," Wes said and tried to back away.

Sandy grabbed his arm. "I can't have this kind of behavior." She bent him over her lap.

Before she had time to bring the ruler down, he hopped away, ran to the window, and screamed. "Help! She's beating me. Dad!"

Sandy rushed to the window. Cam jumped from the ladder and threw the long brush aside. He raced into the house. His steps made loud bangs on the stairs until he reached the bedroom. Wally followed.

Cam threw open Sandy's bedroom door. "What's happening?"

Wes pointed to Sandy's hand, which still held the ruler.

"She beat me."

Cam grimaced. He grabbed the ruler, threw it into the trash can, and turned to her, his lips tight and strained. "You never hit the kids before."

His comment stabbed like a sharp knife, but Oggie's words about Cam's bullying braced her. "I wasn't alone before."

"You must be out of your mind. Wes is coming with me. Get some of your stuff, Wes." The boy ran out and headed for his room.

Cam pointed his finger at Sandy. "You are not fit. I will sue for custody of my kids. There are laws against child abuse."

Anger pulsed. Her face heated. "It's discipline."

"We'll see about that. I'm taking you to court. I don't care if this *is* Bumfuck Tennessee. Child abuse means I get the kids. And you should know that using a false name to buy this property equals fraud, a felony, *Sarah*. I'll get this house and everything. Maybe you'll even do jail time."

Sandy's volume increased. "Go for it! Remember those photos of you and that blonde? You'll be drummed out of your job. And Tennessee courts don't look favorably on wayward husbands. You violated our marriage. The pictures tell all. I've been in Tennessee long enough to know how highly esteemed mothers are. While you, you are a philanderer. Yeah, take me to court. I can't wait to see what it will do to your reputation."

Wally cleared his throat, a sign that he wanted to speak. Cam held his hand outspread, stopping any dialogue. Cam lowered his voice. "I burned those photos. I don't believe you saved any, not with kids around. If you did, it will serve me. I'll take the kids away, I promise."

Miles appeared. He grabbed Sandy by the waist. "I don't want to go with him, Mommy. Please, don't let him take me."

Cam shouted down the hall toward the boys' room. "Hurry, Wes."

Wes ran into Sandy's room, holding a canvas bag spilling with clothes. "I want to go."

Wally put his hand on Cam's shoulder. "Hey, buddy, we should talk about this."

Cam shoved Wally's hand from his shoulder. "No, we don't. Let's go," he said to Wes, grabbing the canvas bag. Nudging the boy out of the bedroom, he whirled back to Sandy. "I'll be back for the other two."

Sandy watched out her window as Cam slid into his car, backed out of the driveway, and sped to the bunkhouse across the gully. Wally and Wes walked the pathway to the old place. By the time they got there, Cam came out with their suitcases. They all got into the car that peeled out in a spray of gravel.

CHAPTER 39

Miles sat on the bed. "Is Daddy going to make us go back to the house in the city? I like it here."

"I don't know, Miles. I need some time to think. Go out and play with Eddie. His dad will be here soon to take him home."

Sandy had wanted Cam to go, but not like that. *Can he practice here in Tennessee?* Even if he couldn't, he could help a local lawyer. She reclined on her bed and ran through the things that had recently happened. Oggie had said she was brilliant and creative. She never thought of herself that way, but if she had any abilities, this would be a nice time for them to surface. *What would a brilliant, creative woman do?* Even if she headed in the right direction of being independent, she couldn't go against Cam by herself. She needed some powerful help. But from whom?

Oggie.

She was pretty sure Oggie worked for one of those government agencies that go by three letters. And, he had told her he'd been watching out for her. Did he watch now? Maybe monitoring her phone? But which one? Cell or home phone? Both?

She went downstairs and rifled through her purse for her cell. Gritting her teeth, she dialed her farm's landline. Picking up the ringing receiver, she said, "Oggie, call me."

Thirty seconds after she hung up both phones, the cell rang.

"It's me, Oggie."

"Damn it, Oggie. You *are* spying on me."

"I happen to be checking your cell, perfectly legal, cells

being radios. You wouldn't have called if you didn't need me. How can I help?"

"I lost my cool and tried to punish Wes. Cam took him back to New York. He called me a child abuser and threatened to get custody of the kids. Plus, he threatened to take me to court for fraud in using a fake name to buy this farm. I can't lose my kids. I can't lose this house."

"Calm down. What do you want me to do?"

"Any way to get a few of those photos you sent me?"

"You *want* them?"

Sandy let out her breath hard. "I want one that isn't so bad, in case Wes sees it. I told Cam I'd show them in court. I couldn't think of anything else."

"I could put my hands on a few."

"Would you send it to Wally? I think that would do. He would tell Cam I had access to the pictures. Wait, I'll have to find Wally's address."

Oggie's smile carried over the phone. "I know his address. It's as good as done. Hey, relax. Morgan can't do anything. Trust me, okay?"

"Trust you? You bugged my phone."

"And you got ahold of me because of it. Listen, I won't bug your cell if you'll call me directly when you need help. I'll give you my special phone number. Okay?"

She rested the cell against her cheek for a second and moved her jaw back and forth.

"Sandy?"

She groaned softly as she put the phone to her ear. "I'm sorry. Trying to be brilliant and creative has made me tired."

"Don't you worry. Just leave your problems to the Og. I'll handle the name problem for you. By the time Morgan tries to hang you for it, Sarah Green won't own anything. And I'll fix your Tennessee driver's license, too."

She took Oggie's number, and as she put the phone in her purse, she said, "I hate men."

Before she finished her statement, a car pulled into the driveway. The distinctive squeak of Vance's car door meant she was about to deal with one more. He knocked. She let him in.

"Damn, what happened? You look awful," Vance said.

"Bad day at Black Rock."

"What can I do?"

She spat the word out. "Nothing." *Why am I taking it out on him? He hasn't done anything wrong.* "Don't expect good company this afternoon."

"You want to tell me about it?"

She did want to talk about it. "I got mad at Wes and almost hit him. Cam took Wes with him to New York. And…" The words choked in her throat. "Wes *wanted* to go."

"Wait a minute." Vance walked with her into the kitchen and sat at the small table. "You almost smacked the kid, and the mister took him away?"

"Child abuse." Sandy sat in the opposite chair. She cocked her ear toward the stairs. "Jeanette is up from her nap. Hold on. Lord knows I need to pay close attention to my kids now."

Sandy came back with Jeanette and put her in the high chair.

"Sandy-Sarah," Vance called her that now as a joke. "Don't worry. You're a perfect mother, not capable of abuse. Some folks ought to whack their little darlings once in a while."

Vance tapped the table lightly. "Are you okay?"

"No." She held back words to prevent crying.

"Yeah, not if he took your kid."

"Cam's going to try to get custody of them. And I think I might be in trouble with the fake name."

"Hmm. I thought that might come back to bite you in the ass. Don't go off the deep end, though. Think it through and try not to worry." He sniffed a quick laugh. "I wonder how the mister will enjoy taking care of a preadolescent. It won't be easy. I'll bet you did most of the parenting."

Sandy nodded. "I hadn't thought about that. Cam will have his hands full."

"Give them a few months. He'll be calling, begging to give the kid back."

Sandy managed a brief smile.

Vance drummed his fingers again. "Well, I need to check on the cows. Last week, one of them looked like she would deliver soon. Twins. I heard double heartbeats. It might be tricky. Don't worry about that. You have enough on your mind. Everything will work out, you hear?"

"Thanks, Vance. I appreciate it." She watched out the window as Vance walked to the pasture.

***

Outside, Vance stomped to the gate. He kicked the post. "Goddamn it," he shouted. "I can't do a thing for her." He kicked the post again and yelled, "Double goddamn it." Then he opened the gate.

CHAPTER 40

The next morning, Henry brought Eddie to the farm late. He came to the back door for his tea. "Eddie told me what happened here yesterday. I suppose you're pretty broke up over it."

Sandy hung her head and took a big breath. She didn't want to bawl in front of anyone, having done enough of that the night before. She got his quart jar of tea from the freezer. He shook it to break up the crystals and drank without taking a breath.

"Henry, I need to tell you something. My name isn't Sarah Green."

"I know. The boys told Eddie." He wiped his mouth with the back of his hand. "I figured you'd tell me when it suited you."

"I'm Sandra Morgan. You might as well start calling me Sandy. Um, I might be in some trouble. I bought this place and have all of my business as Sarah Green."

"You'll get it straight. People in these parts overlook stuff as long as you had good reason. People who know you will help."

"Thank you for saying that. It makes me feel a bit better."

He handed her the empty jar. "I got enough time under my belt to know things roll theirself upright. They do, so don't get too broke up. You'll see."

Henry and Vance offered her solace and encouragement. Oggie might be able to help her. She had to think positively, like a brilliant and creative woman. *Oh, if only.*

Over the weeks, Sandy longed to hear Wes's voice. Several times, she picked up the phone and started to dial the Manhattan number, but the voice inside stopped her. It was killing her not to call, but the voice said to let Wes contact her. After six weeks, she got the call.

"Mom?"

"Hi, Wessie. I'm so happy to hear from you. Are you okay?"

"I guess. I miss the farm. I miss playing with Eddie. How is he?"

Sandy thought for a moment before she answered. "Eddie misses you, too, but he makes do playing with Miles."

"How's Jethro?"

"Henry brought a bridle to get Jethro accustomed to the boys on his back."

"They're riding Jethro! You said we couldn't do that. How come you let them ride now?"

"Henry supervises. Eddie and Miles sit on the donkey's back, not really riding. But maybe Jethro could be trained. Dr. Chambers said he'd bring tack over in a few weeks. Do you go to Saint Andrew's school again?"

"Yeah, but school isn't fun like on the farm. Can I talk to Miles?"

"He went fishing with Eddie and Henry."

"Fishing? *Mom*?"

Sandy flinched at the drop in his voice. "Are you doing your homework? Eating right?"

"Dad doesn't cook. He brings stuff home. Remember how me and Miles always wanted pizza? I'm sick of it now. I don't want any more Chinese food, either. And the new housekeeper, Clarice, is mean. I'm not doing so good in school. Clarice doesn't help me study. I don't like that place or the uniforms. I hate lacrosse."

"Try to do better in school, honey. Education is important."

"Okay. I guess. I better go. Mom, are you mad at me?"

"Yes, but I love you very much. I'll get over being mad. It hurt me when you wanted to go back to New York with your father."

"I know," he said. "I'll talk to you later. Bye, Mom."

Wes, like his father, was proud. He wouldn't say he wanted to come home. He expected her to ask him, but she wouldn't be manipulated, not by Cam and not by Wes. Oggie must have sent the photo because Cam had not contacted her. By now, he would have called to negotiate if he had made progress on a lawsuit. Could Oggie really help her with the Sarah Green thing? She had the feeling he'd fix it. Oggie, a man from the past, was now firmly in the present.

The next day, a plane, looking like the agricultural sprayers she'd seen, landed on the road in front of her house. The man who emerged from the cockpit wore an old-fashioned pilot's skull cap and goggles. By the time he reached the front porch and removed the headgear, Sandy recognized Oggie, but he did not look like the biker persona from the arcade restaurant. He appeared taller and sans ponytail. His hairline was less receded. She chalked up the difference to her state of mind that day at the restaurant.

Oggie smiled wide. "Hello. I bring good news. Did the lawyer back down?"

"I haven't heard from him, so I don't know. He's not one to back down or give up. Look, I appreciate your help, but I don't want you to get the idea that you can just come here whenever it suits you."

"I know you're miffed at me, but can't I visit once in a while? I moved to Nashville so I could be nearby. Just in case you need me."

She fiddled with her watch. *I hope I don't need you again.* Sandy groped for something to say. "First a motorcycle, and now a crop duster?"

"Yes, to the motorcycle." Oggie sat on the porch swing. "No, to the ag-plane. That," he said, pointing to the aircraft, "is SPECTRUM-UMP, an acronym for Stealth Prototype

Experimental Cloaked Transport Resource Utilizing Magnetic Propulsion." He turned his hand in a presentation. "Sandy, meet Specky, my jaunty jet."

"Jet?"

"Yes, a jet that looks like an Ag Cat. Stealth. You know, soundless."

"I heard it," Sandy argued.

"Fake propeller. The engine sound is an amplified recording. Cool, eh? I'm testing it."

Sandy stared at the aircraft. "You're kidding, right?"

"I will never lie to you. If I tell you something, you can take it to the bank." He swayed the swing by jiggling his foot. "Would you mind making me some coffee? It's my only vice."

"Okay, but give me a minute." She left him on the porch.

She came back holding Jeanette. Sandy shook the blanket and laid it down inside the playpen. She smoothed Jeanette's hair with her hand. "I'll make Coffee, and it will be ready in a few minutes. How do you like yours?"

"You'd put the cream in the coffee for me?"

"You're a guest."

"I guess the lawyer still has you trained, eh?"

"Oggie, you are rude. Do you know that?"

He put his finger under his lip. "I don't mean to be rude. I've never been able to talk to people. Machines are my friends. It's hard to aggravate machines."

"When you insult Cam like that, you insult me, too."

"No way. But, sorry. You are the last person I want to annoy. Now, *him...*"

"I'm surprised you haven't offered to remove Cam permanently. After all, this is Tennessee." *Both Vance and Henry offered their services.*

"Remove him?"

"You're a spy. Don't spies do that kind of thing?"

"I'm not that kind of spy. I don't even have a gun. I'm not wired for violence, you might say. I'm the nerdy kind who sits at a machine decoding or listening or inventing something to decode or listen."

"You don't have a gun?"

"Hey, I am one hundred percent geekmeat. The agency has a whole bunch of Dennis-the-Pollock-muscle types. They only have a few like me. See that jet on your front road? I'm working on that now. Me and the other tech. We relocated here. The move worked out good. We have an apartment near a small airport outside of Nashville."

"Another tech?"

"Yeah, who got called away this morning. I hope A.J. will be all right. I think the mission might be dangerous, but when the agency calls, the Oggies and the A.J.s go."

"How did you get to be an agent, Oggie?"

"I like my coffee heavy on cream. I know you use real cream. Can I have a few swigs first?"

Sandy brought out a cup and saucer. "Tell me your story."

He took two long sips. "Mmm, good. Hot. My story. The Feds started watching me when I was in middle school. They threw things my way, competitions, grants for summer science camps, and scholarships when I got older. They put me through M.I.T. Plus, I have a Ph.D. in biotechnology and further studies in electromagnetism and some other stuff."

"M.I.T.? Why become a spy?"

"I owed my soul to the company store, you might say. They gave me free rein in my studies, funding everything. But I didn't have time to develop a social life. I don't think I would have anyway. I'm not the kind of guy chicks dig." He sipped the coffee. "But apparently, my internal chemistry works because when I saw you, it was like being struck by a whopper lightning bolt. No fooling." He closed his eyes and sighed.

"Earlier, you said you watched me from afar. What did you mean?"

"I kept tabs on you. I rented stores down the street from your brownstone and did a lot of my research there. Do you remember a vacuum repair place and an abandoned shoe store with the newspaper in the windows? I set up camp there for a couple of years."

"You worked in those stores? I never saw you."

"I'm trained not to be seen. But I saw you. You bought cleaning solution from me."

"I did?" *Why didn't I recognize you?*

"Yeah, made my day. Year." He shook his head. "So many times I watched you walk the kids past the shoe store to their bus stop."

"The shoe store? The windows were covered with newspapers. I couldn't see in, so how could you see out?"

"Oh, that just looked like newspaper. It was a special film cooked up by yours truly. Newspaper from the outside, clear inside."

"Really?" She traced her bottom lip with her finger. "You watched us? From that place?" *I wish you wouldn't mess up my good memories of you. You were so much fun.*

"From there and other ways. You've heard of satellite surveillance. I have access to a satellite. When it's not being used, I put in your coordinates. A couple of times, I caught sight of you gardening in the backyard in Manhattan. You had a patch with carrots and radishes."

"You saw that from a satellite?"

"Yeah. There's a geosynchronous satellite hovering over this farm. For now, anyway, until they need it for something else."

"What details can you see from it?"

"I can read headlines from the rolled newspaper on your

driveway. Heck, when I turn to the infrared lens, I can see your cows farting."

Oh, Oggie, I know you mean well, but you are so weird.

CHAPTER 41

When the cow delivered, Sandy assisted Vance in the barn. While he wiped his instruments with a cleaning cloth, he said, "By the way, you've got rats."

Sandy flinched. "What?"

"All barns have them." He swept his arm to include the stalls. "But your barn has more than its share. This cow needs to stay in the pen because she's weak from delivering the twins. The rats will be all over the calves."

Sandy walked with him as he headed to the Jeep. "What should I do?"

"Cats. Seriously, it will help. I'll bring you a couple tomorrow. Don't feed them a lot." Vance opened the back hatch and switched his instrument case for a narrow bag and a small box. He motioned with his head to the picnic table, where he unsheathed a long gun. Then he put the box of ammunition next to it. "Behold, the twenty-two rifle. Have you shot a gun before?"

Sandy shook her head.

"Well, you'll learn. A twenty-two beats a cat any day. If you don't do something, you'll be overrun with rats, then snakes. We have timber rattlers around here, not to mention copperheads. And you should be able to defend yourself against other things, too."

"What things?"

"Coyotes, snakes, and skunks, to name a few. This gun won't kill a bear or a feral pig, but it'll make them leave. And, there exists a two-legged species of the family Rodentia whose attention often needs stimulation. Now watch."

Vance showed her how to load and unload. He gave her a cleaning kit and had her clean the rifle.

"Keep it loaded. You can't fire an unloaded gun."

"I have kids here. I can't have a loaded gun in the house."

"You live on a farm. You need farm implements. This," he held the gun horizontally in front of her, "is a farm implement. Most kids around here have their own guns by the time they're twelve. Kids need to learn respect for it. And they should fear it, too."

Sandy made a face and looked away. "I don't know, Vance."

"I *do* know. After I teach you how to work with the twenty-two, I'll spend some time with Miles, okay?"

"Not a good idea."

"You need to trust me. Do you?"

An internal war battled within. She and her family lived on a farm far from New York. *I trust Vance.* She nodded to him.

Vance spent most of the afternoon teaching Sandy the art of gunmanship. When she could ably handle the rifle and ping target cans at varying distances, he pronounced her qualified.

"Send Miles into the barn," he told her.

Later that afternoon, Miles came into the kitchen with his face off-color. He put his arms around Sandy's waist.

"What's wrong, honey? You look awful."

Miles wiped a tear away with the back of his hand. "Dr. Chambers showed me how to use the rifle, and I killed a rat. It was gross. There was blood and everything. I don't have to do that again, do I?"

Vance wiped his boots at the back door and peeked in.

Her nostrils flared. "Look, Vance."

"Respect and fear. Keep it loaded." He put the rifle on top of the refrigerator.

The following week, Oggie flew the SPECTRUM-P in and

landed on the lawn.

With Jeanette bobbing on her hip, Sandy strolled out to the craft. "Obviously, you don't need a proper runway for that thing."

Oggie unbuckled his vintage aviator goggles. "Nope. V-STOL. Very short take-off and landing. It's almost vertical, like the Harrier. I have flown it around here for a month, and no one has noticed. Not even the FAA in Nashville. Neat, huh? You haven't mentioned it, have you?"

"Of course not. I don't want to be killed."

Oggie laughed. "Consider yourself the safest person on the globe, Sandy. You have my personal protection. Heard from the jerk?"

A burn flamed her neck. "Nothing. And it makes me nervous because Cam likes to win. I miss Wessie so much."

"Try not to worry. I'm sure the photo I sent to the big guy had an effect. You'll get Wes back. Promise. Hey, I can only stay for a little while cause there's a meeting in Frankfort, Kentucky. I'm showing the jet to some bigwigs from the military. What's for lunch?"

Sandy believed Oggie helped her in some way with Cam, but she didn't want to get too confident. *How much can he do? I can at least give him lunch. Vance, Henry, and now Oggie help me. I feed them. How did that happen? I still hate men.* She waved Oggie into the kitchen.

A week later, Henry dropped Eddie off at the farm. "I can't work for you this morning. I have business in town."

Thirty minutes after he left, Oggie landed the crop duster fake on the newly mowed lawn in front of Sandy's house.

"You took a chance," Sandy said. "Henry usually works here in the mornings."

"Yeah?" Oggie stepped into the living room. "Farmer MacDonald has business to attend. Coffee? You don't mind making me coffee, right?"

"I don't know if I want to make you anything. I'm still mad at you for stalking me."

"And you know I'm still sorry. Come on, Sandy. Things happen for a reason."

"Your reasons."

"You get even prettier when you're annoyed."

"Cut it out, Oggie. I won't be manipulated."

"Good! See there, I already did you a valuable service. Now you are aware when people are working you."

"If I make you coffee, will you shut up?"

"Yep." Oggie ran to the window. "Hey, the kids can't get close to the jet." He went outside and talked to the boys.

"Good luck," Sandy said when he came back in. "That thing will probably be too much of an attraction."

"Not a problem." He pulled a thin black device from his shirt pocket and pushed one of the red buttons. "An anti-curiosity alarm." He sat at the kitchen table.

She shook her head.

"You don't believe me? I promised I wouldn't lie to you." He showed her the palm-sized remote. "This turns on an agitation signal from a mechanism in the cockpit. People feel uncomfortable as they approach it. They don't know why, but the closer they get to Specky, the feeling increases, and they automatically retreat. I should patent it. I'd get rich."

Sandy started the coffee maker. "But wouldn't another scientist invent a machine that neutralizes yours?"

Oggie smiled wide. "Maybe. I already have a neutralizer in case someone turns the agitation device against me. You are a very smart woman. No wonder I'm crazy for you."

Sandy rolled her eyes. "Hey, did you ever hear from A.J.? You were worried that the mission was dangerous."

"No." Oggie's expression became serious. "I do worry. No

word, not yet."

The bottom cabinet opened, and Jeanette emerged. "Her new play area," Sandy said, moving around the child.

Oggie picked Jeanette up. "You've got to be the cutest kid I've ever seen." He held her above his head and spun in circles, eliciting baby-voiced screams and cackles.

"Careful!" Sandy said.

He held the toddler by the back and stomach and dive-bombed her toward Sandy. "She loves it."

Jeanette let out a loud squeal.

"Perfect timing for the coffee. I'll trade you a cup for the kid."

Oggie transferred Jeanette to Sandy, who put the creamed coffee in front of him. As soon as the child touched the floor, she went to Oggie and hugged his leg.

"She likes me," Oggie said. "Good taste. Maybe she can influence you."

Sandy leaned to see out the living room window. The boys were circling the jet with a wider perimeter. "That device works. Wow. It won't scramble their heads, will it?"

"No. I tested it on myself. He tapped his forehead. "See? Kidneys. Intact."

Sandy laughed. They chatted for an hour or so. When Sandy invited him to stay for lunch, he declined, saying he had a lot of work to do but promised to come again.

Sandy didn't know how Oggie arranged to get rid of Henry so regularly, but when Henry announced he had business in town, Oggie landed his little jet *Specky* a few minutes after the dust on the road settled.

On one such morning, Sandy heard the fake engine. She pulled the curtain in the living room back to see Oggie and another person, short, dressed in a hooded coat, walking toward the front porch.

Oggie put his hand on his companion's shoulder as he knocked.

"Come in," Sandy said as she held the door. The individual's head went down, keeping the face out of view.

"Sandy," Oggie said with a hint of sadness in his voice, "I need your help."

"Of course, I'll do anything I can."

"I knew you would. She's had a bad time. Worse than bad."

Oggie gently removed the diminutive woman's coat. He carefully slid the garment away from the sling on her arm and adjusted the bandage wrapped around her head as the hood slipped down. "Remember when I said the mission was dangerous?"

"She's A.J.?"

"Yes. Sandy, meet April June May." He turned to his friend. "I told you she'd help."

Oggie guided April in her zombie state to the couch, where he gently helped her. He sat next to her. "They tortured her, pulled a few teeth, and broke her arm."

Sandy put her hand to her mouth. "My God!"

"The arm and the teeth can be fixed, but," Oggie put his hand to the woman's head.

April turned away and started to cry.

"They scalped her, too. She couldn't stand being in the private medical center in Maryland any longer. She called me to come get her."

Sandy pulled Oggie into the kitchen. "Oggie! You shouldn't talk about those things right in front of her. Did you see what it did to her?"

"Oh, yeah. You're right. I shouldn't have. You get that I don't know how to communicate in normal company."

He returned to April and put his arm around her. "Sorry,

A.J."

Sandy sat on the other side and patted April's hand. "What can I do to help you?"

April shook her head as if nothing could be done.

"She hated the hospital," Oggie said. "The silence and the people prodding her were too much. Can she stay with you for a while? It's so pleasant here, and you'll take care of her the way she needs."

"Of course. She can have Wes's room. Bring her stuff up to the blue bedroom across from the bathroom." She turned to April. "I hope you don't mind a twin bed. Unless you need your own bathroom, then you can have my room. I should have thought of that first."

April shook her head, meaning she didn't need Sandy's room.

"I'll get A.J.'s things from the jet," Oggie said. "She's having trouble eating and sleeping. I know you'll figure out something."

Sandy put her hand over April's. "Can you speak?"

"Yes," April said and looked away.

Sandy moved her head close to April. "Oggie has a lot of faith in me, doesn't he?"

"Yes," April said.

After Oggie put April's things upstairs, he came into the kitchen. Sandy canceled the homeschool lessons for the day.

"Oggie, how do you get rid of Henry right before you visit? I know you have something to do with it."

"Uh, yeah. It seems that a Mr. Ralph Ferraro is doing important soil research and needs Henry to collect samples in the area. Henry gets well-paid for his service and hops to it when Ralph calls. Isn't it fortunate that Farmer MacDonald now has a cell phone? And he used to be so against the new-fangled things."

"And you said Cam was a manipulator."

Oggie hung his head. "Please don't hold it against me. Sometimes, I need to do unorthodox things."

Sandy let the comment slide. She made grilled cheese sandwiches and served them with tomato soup laced heavily with butter and cream. She coaxed April to have a quarter of the sandwich and a little soup.

"See," Oggie said. "You've already made strides in A.J.'s recovery. I knew it would be good for her. Maybe she won't have so many nightmares sleeping here."

Oggie stayed long enough to make sure April would be all right in her new locale.

Sandy took her guest by the hand and led her to the porch. "Okay, April, now you have to pull your weight around here." She demonstrated how to keep the bird feeders full.

April managed to relax a little as she watched the birds do their air dance around the feeder. Later, Sandy, April, and Jeanette took tea on the front porch. Jeanette loved the chocolate mint cookies on the plate. April drank a cup and ate two cookies.

"You don't like hospitals?" Sandy said, trying to engage April in a little conversation. "That's a stupid question, isn't it?"

April teared. "Too many men," she said in a cracked voice.

"Oh, April. The people who hurt you did more than what Oggie told me."

"Yes." Tears flowed down her cheeks. Her words came in groups. "I was monitoring terrorists. When I sent the message to get picked up, somehow… they intercepted my communication… The code words were 'I have a toothache.'… But the message messed up because I hit the wrong keys and wrote I gave a toothache, and before I could correct it, they broke through the door in my apartment… and… They thought I had a transmitter in my tooth… They pulled some of my molars… but when I didn't tell them… they broke my arm. Then they…"

"I can figure it out."

"There were five... they took turns...you know. Then one of them... started to cut pieces of my scalp." April bent over and sobbed on Jeanette's blanket.

Sandy rubbed her neck. "I'm so sorry."

April wiped her face with a paper napkin. "They would have cut my whole scalp and then killed me, but the rescue team came. The team wouldn't have come at all because of the wrong message, but Oggie received my transmissions and figured it out. He saved my life."

"Thank God! What happened to the terrorists?"

"The team was supposed to take them alive for questioning, but when they saw what the men had done to me, they became so enraged that they shot every one of them."

"Too bad," Sandy said. "Maybe we could have inflicted some of the same treatment on them before they talked." She put her hand on April's arm. "Listen to me go on. I never had a thought like that before. Sorry."

April turned her head to Sandy. "I'm glad you said it. I have been wanting to talk about it, but couldn't." Her bottom lip quivered. "I hope they burn and suffer in hell."

"They will, for sure. Keep that in your mind."

They sat quietly for a few minutes. "Come with me. You can help me weed the herb garden. Jeanette loves it out there. You will, too. It smells really good." Sandy took April's hand and helped her up. "Aromatherapy. It's the best."

CHAPTER 42

The next time Oggie came, he brought a calendar with red and yellow markings on the days. "I thought it might look less medical if I used happy symbols. The star means Old MacDonald-Who-Has-a-Farm will be doing business for my Uncle Ralph, so I can visit. The flower means I need to take A.J. to the doctor. She doesn't like to go, but she needs to. You will help her get ready on the flower days, right?"

"Of course. I can tell you really care about April, Oggie. It's nice to see that side of you."

"Yeah, she's second on the list after you. So, does that make me look a little more *human*?"

"You can be a bit strange," Sandy said with a smile. "It makes you a *little* more normal."

"Thanks. Hey, where *is* A. J.?"

"With the cow that had the twins. She likes the animals. I think it's good for her."

"You are good for her. You've always been good for me."

Over the following four months, Oggie visited the farm, and on the flower days, he flew April for her medical appointments. She didn't like leaving the farm, but she went. Sometimes, she stayed away for a few days.

On the afternoon of one of those visits, when April would be away for a week, a car came to a stop in the driveway. Sandy pulled back the living room curtain. Wes jumped out and ran to where Miles and Eddie played on a tire swing.

Oh, God! It's Cam. And Wally. Are they here to take the kids? No. Sandy grabbed the rifle from the top of the refrigerator. She would be ready for them.

Cam opened the front door without knocking and stepped in. Sandy lined up the sight.

Cam stepped back quickly. "What the…? Put that down."

"You can't take the kids. I don't care what kind of writ you have or who is with you."

"I'm not here to get the kids," Cam said. "I've brought Wes back. Honest."

"Get out of my house!" *If he even mentions this house belongs to Sarah Green, I'm blowing his damned head off.* "Leave now."

Wally peeked his head around the open door. "Sandy, lower the gun, honey. It's all right. We aren't here to cause trouble." He entered slowly, his hands palm forward in front of his chest. He talked softly as he approached her. "Careful now, be careful. Come on, Sandy." In a flash, his hand shot forward, and he grasped the barrel of the rifle, pushing it to the side as his other hand grabbed her arm. The sudden movement caused her finger to pull the trigger.

The blast, the ceiling plaster bits, and the scream seemed to come together. Cam put his left hand over his right upper arm and staggered to the couch.

"Oh, no," Sandy said, putting her hand to her mouth. "Cam!" She turned to Wally, who had the rifle and was ejecting the bullets.

"Let's see," Wally said as he dropped the empty gun and hurried to Cam.

Wally pulled Cam's hand away and assessed the bleeding.

"I didn't mean it," Sandy whined.

"Neither one of us did," Wally said. "Get some towels."

Sandy ran into the kitchen and pulled out all of the dish towels from the drawer. Handing them to Wally, she wiped tears from her eyes. "We should call an ambulance."

Wally pressed a towel against Cam's arm.

"Jesus!" Cam said, slipping into a reclining position.

Wally held the back of Cam's arm and pushed the cloth over the wound. "Sorry, pal, but this has to be hard to stop the flow." He looked up at Sandy. "It will be faster if I take him to the hospital. What's closest?"

"There's a big one in Cookeville."

Wally stood, keeping his grip on the arm. "Okay. Come on, Cam. Do you need me to carry you?"

"Hell, no." Cam sat up and winced. "Shit, that hurts." He let Wally help him stand. "Son of a bitch," he said, gritting his teeth.

Sandy followed them to the car. "Should we call the sheriff?"

Wally opened the car door and eased Cam in. "You can if you want, but what would you tell him? We entered your house uninvited." He walked around to the driver's side. "It is a ricochet shot. I doubt you'll get into trouble, but it would be easier for me to say it was an accident when I cleaned your gun."

"Okay," she said in a whisper. "Cam?"

"He'll make it," Wally said. "I'll call you later."

Sandy ran close to the car window. "Cam. I'm sorry." She stiffened. "But you can't have the kids, no matter what."

Cam closed his eyes and shook his head. "We brought Wes back. I was wrong. I overreacted. I don't want to take the kids."

He's apologizing? "Why didn't you call me to let me know?"

Cam grimaced. "Wes wanted to surprise you." He shut one eye and shuddered. "I'll help you with the identity problem. Please, when this is taken care of, can we talk?"

Coming from Cam, *can we talk?* were scary words. She didn't want to talk and stepped back. The car sped down the driveway, spurting gravel and dust in all directions, and then disappeared around the bend near the river. She flinched when she felt a touch at her side.

Wes put his arms around her. "Did you shoot Dad?"

Oh, God, what did the kids see? "Uhm," she didn't know what to say.

Wes let go. "We heard a bang, and then I saw Uncle Wally helping Dad into the car. Miles said you keep a gun on the fridge. It looked like there was blood on Dad's shirt. Is he okay?"

She had a moment of dizziness. "It was an accident." *How much should I tell them?* "Uncle Wally is taking your dad to the hospital."

"Is he going to be okay?"

She nodded, hoping her assurance matched the prognosis.

Wes disengaged his arms and looked up at her.

"Of course." She stroked his hair. "He will be fine. Please don't worry."

"I missed you, Mom. I got kicked out of school."

"What? Why?"

Eddie and Miles ran to the driveway.

"What happened?" Eddie said. "Sounded like a gunshot."

"Yeah, my dad had a gun accident," Wes said. "He's going to the hospital."

Miles sighed. "He shouldn't have been touching Mom's gun. It's dangerous."

Sandy thought about what Vance said about the rifle the day he had Miles shoot the rat. *He'll learn to respect and fear it.*

No one spoke for a moment until Wes said, "Talk about dangerous. Listen to this, Eddie. I got this fat bully at my prep school in the headlock you showed me. I made him say he was a bully-pussy, and then I made him sing the alphabet song before I released him. It was so fine! I told him if he ever bullied anyone again, I would tie him to the flag pole. He peed his pants! A big ole wet spot between his legs."

"Cool," Miles and Eddie responded in unison.

Relieved that the boys weren't traumatized by the gunshot,

Sandy processed Wes's school expulsion. As she thought about it, she realized it wasn't so bad. Her distress gave way to relief. *Thank God he's not prissy like his father. That damn school. Six months on the farm saved him.* "You got into a fight? Is that why you got kicked out of Saint Andrews?"

Wes nodded with a grin. "Yeah. That and I didn't do my homework."

"Why didn't you do your work? You know how important school is."

"The housekeeper who is my nanny didn't check my homework like you used to. And Dad stayed late a lot. I didn't like doing it. It's better learning here with Eddie and Miles."

"Oh, Wes. We don't need any more problems."

"Mom, I'll be good. I want to live here. If I'm bad, you can hit me."

Sandy kissed the top of his head. "I won't hit you, honey. I'm so glad you're home. I know you'll be a good boy."

Early that afternoon, Wally called with an update. "The upper muscle near Cam's shoulder is badly damaged, but they don't think he will lose the arm."

Lose his arm!

"He'll be here in the hospital for a few days. Cam wants to recuperate on the farm. The surgeon said he shouldn't travel right away. He needs to stay close by for physical therapy and follow-up. And Cam wants to be with you and the boys. At least until he's better. He wouldn't get rest in New York. You know the hours he puts in when he's working."

"Wally?"

"The doctor just came in. I'll call later."

Sandy stood with the phone to her ear, staring at the wall. Wes came up next to her. "What's wrong, Mom? Was that Uncle Wally? Is Dad okay?"

She slipped the phone into her pocket. "Yes. He's all right.

He'll be in the hospital for a few days."

"Then he'll come here, right?"

"Here? Oh, Wes, I...." Guilt set in. She had threatened Cam with the gun. Even though the bullet had ricocheted from the ceiling, his injury was on her. She needed to establish some form of normalcy for herself and the kids.

Later that afternoon, as she held Jeanette on her lap, Sandy worked with the boys on their lessons. Eddie and Miles continued their work. Wes needed to catch up because his fancy school had not done much for him.

The three boys did chores after the school work and then played hard outside. Sandy felt content each time she heard them laugh. Until she thought about Cam. That night, everyone went to bed early.

The next day, Oggie brought April back. Sandy waited until they were alone and explained the situation.

"Not that I condone violence," Oggie said, "but, well, you did have that gun to get rid of your rat problem."

She put her hand up to cover her eyes. "Oh, God." Then she looked over to the empty refrigerator top where the gun once resided. "Rats."

CHAPTER 43

The doctors discharged Cam after four days. At the farm, Wally parked the car in front of the house and helped Cam get out of the seat.

Sandy came to them. "I've made up the bunkhouse. It has water and electricity."

Cam groaned and adjusted his sling. "I don't want to stay in the bunkhouse. It's damp and smells musty. I have to keep the bandage clean. That place isn't sanitary."

She put her hand on her hips. "There's no room in the house."

Cam slowly moved toward the front porch. "You can put the boys together. I'll stay in one of their rooms."

"I've already put the boys together. I, uh, have a guest."

Wally stepped fast, opened the front door, and held it for Cam.

Cam, Wally, and Sandy progressed to the living room, where April sat on a recliner reading *Scientific American*. She nervously adjusted the scarf around her head. Sandy went to the chair and put her hand on the back cushion. "This is April June May. April, meet Dennis Wallensky and Cameron Morgan."

"April May," Wally said. "Your parents had a sense of humor."

Not looking up, April responded, "Gee, you're the first person to say that to me."

Cam made no comment. He squatted at the playpen and spoke baby talk to Jeanette. Then he stood, wincing from the movement. "Where are the boys?"

"Outside studying leaves," Sandy answered. "They'll be back for lunch."

Cam moved closer to Sandy. "I *need* to stay in the house." He glanced at April.

Sandy flushed. *This might upset April. She will think she's causing problems.* "Okay, you can stay in Jeanette's room. But Wally has to be in the bunkhouse."

"No way," Cam said. He grimaced, flinched, and rubbed his upper arm.

"I don't mind sleeping on that couch in your office," Wally offered. "I should stay close so I can help Cam."

"Don't you have a job?" Sandy didn't hold back her annoyance.

"Yes," Wally answered with a level tone. "I can work from my computer here, and I have to go into Nashville three times a week." He didn't elaborate on what his job entailed. "We've worked it out. The days I go to Nashville, I'll bring Cam there for his physical therapy."

She turned to Cam. "Don't *you* have a job?"

"I took vacation to bring Wes back. I called and told them I needed time. It's okay with the firm."

Oh, that's just great. "All right. Until you heal. Wally?"

"I'll take care of everything."

For the first few days, Sandy tried to have as little contact as she could with Cam, and he didn't push her into conversation. Wally spent a lot of time in the office with the door closed. On Mondays, Wednesdays, and Fridays, Wally, dressed in a dark suit, left with Cam for Nashville.

After the second week, when Wally and Cam went to Nashville, she and April enjoyed tea on the porch. Sandy took a sip from her cup. "I haven't heard from Oggie. I thought he would have something to say about Cam being here."

April dunked a cookie in her tea. "Oggie must be on a

mission. I haven't heard from him since he brought me back. I guess we'll see him later."

Except for meals, Sandy kept her distance but didn't prevent Cam's interaction with the kids.

One morning, when Sandy left the kitchen after breakfast, Cam pulled the boys aside. "Do you know someone named Auggie?"

"Yeah," Wes said. "Mom's friend. He comes over."

Cam glanced at Wally. "What does he do when he comes? Do they kiss?"

"No. Oggie's really neat. He makes us laugh."

Cam took a notepad and a pencil from the holder on the fridge. He wrote *Auggie* down. "What's his last name?"

"I don't know, but he spells it O-G-G-I-E, not the way you wrote."

"How do you know?"

Miles looked at the name. "Because we saw his name on the chopper."

"Chopper?" Cam made a face. "He's a biker?"

Both boys nodded enthusiastically. Cam looked out the kitchen window as Sandy returned with a basket of herbs from her garden. She stopped to greet Henry.

Cam swore. "Look at that fucking bastard watch her walk."

"Cam," Wally said. "Don't swear like that in front of the boys. And," he added in a whisper, "his kid is right over there," pointing to the dining room where Eddie waited.

"I don't care. That asshole has the hots for Sandy," Cam lowered his voice. "Jesus, this Oggie guy is coming over, and have you seen the way that old cow doctor looks at her? Can you cancel your meeting in Nashville tomorrow? I have a plan."

"What've you got in mind?" Wally said. "I hope it's exciting."

On Tuesday, Cam asked Sandy if the boys could go with him to Nashville for the day. Shortly after they left and Henry had gone, Oggie landed the jet.

Meanwhile, parked along the nearby Cumberland River, Wally assembled the fishing gear they bought earlier and settled in to watch the road.

After several hours, Cam stood and brushed the detritus from his slacks with his good hand. "We've been here all morning. This is the only road anyone could take to get to the farm, and we haven't seen a motorcycle. Maybe that Oggie guy isn't coming."

"Oh, Dad," Wes said. "Oggie doesn't ride his motorcycle to visit Mom."

"Huh? What kind of car does he drive?"

"I don't know. Have you seen his car, Miles?"

Miles shook his head.

"You must have seen his car if he visits," Cam said.

Miles shrugged. "He doesn't drive a car. He comes in a plane."

"Sonofabitch. Why didn't you tell me?"

"You didn't ask," Wes said.

As they hastily packed, the sheriff's car pulled up. "Good afternoon. I believe we met a few months ago in my wife's real estate office. I got a call about people fishing on the river. May I see your fishing license?"

Cam held a folding chair against the tail light with his knee, ready to stow it in the trunk. "What? We need a fishing license?"

"No license? Sorry, I have to write you a citation." The lawman smiled the whole time he wrote on his flip pad. He didn't look sorry at all.

When Cam and Wally pulled up to the farm, a plane lifted and disappeared to the west.

"Fucking shit!" Cam yelled at the diminishing object in

the sky as he hurried into the house. He faced Sandy. "Did you call the sheriff about us fishing?"

"I didn't know you went fishing. Didn't you take the boys with you to Nashville?"

Cam grabbed the citation from his pocket. "And what's going on with this Oggie person?"

A wave of pleasure surged through her. "How do you know about Oggie?" She shot a glance at Wes. "Are you being a big mouth?" She tried to feel anger, but the amusement wouldn't budge. *The sheriff? That explains Og's good mood. Yep, he's been very busy lately. And he can still make me laugh.*

Cam winced and grabbed at his bandaged arm. "Is he your boyfriend?"

"Men don't interest me. No one."

Cam took a Coke from the fridge with his good arm and popped a hydrocodone. He cooled his heels on the front porch for the rest of the afternoon.

CHAPTER 44

Cam brooded for days after what Sandy secretly thought of as the *fishing debacle*. Even though Cam's arm was healing, Sandy knew he was in pain. For the years she had known him, he had considered it wimpy to complain or take any medications to ease discomfort. He even refused deadening for fillings at the dentist. Now, besides using pills, he had taken to swearing and frequently sulked, keeping his head down, mumbling to himself.

She avoided him, and he didn't pressure her about talking. For most of the day, the seven residents, four adults and three children, kept to their own routines but assembled at the evening meal.

On the weekdays that the men didn't go into Nashville, Wally worked out of the small office downstairs, and Cam worked from his computer in the upstairs bedroom he shared with Jeanette. Sandy, although feeling a little guilty, reserved her bathroom for herself. There were two other bathrooms, one upstairs and another small one on the first floor. Coming out of her room one afternoon, she encountered Cam just out of the shower. They stared at each other for a moment, but long enough for her to *once over* him.

Twelve years had been generous to him. In maturity, he was even more handsome than when she met him. A bit of gray mingled well with the ash blond, and his hairline stayed full with a hint of curl. Precise and preppy, even his chest hair looked groomed, forming a perfect triangle of golden curls on his pecs, leading to a diamond over his abs, down to a pencil-thin line at his navel. And she well knew what lay beneath the tied towel. A flicker, a pilot light, ignited inside her. It had been more than a year since she had enjoyed his touch. As they passed each other, she thought about how three babies had taken a toll on her belly and breasts. Yet, Cam still wanted her. Or was it that he didn't like to lose? She extinguished the pilot light and headed for the stairs.

The following Wednesday, after Cam and Wally left for Nashville. Sandy and April sat on the porch while the three boys worked on their studies in the dining room.

"You are feeling better, aren't you, April?"

"I am. I haven't had a nightmare since those first few days I came here. When I tried to cut an apple, I couldn't, you know, knives.... I doubt I'll ever be normal. Oggie is the only man I trust. I owe you a lot. I couldn't eat or sleep before I came here. The gardening and the animals have helped me, too."

"Stay here forever, April. Who knows what this fresh air and quiet countryside can do? You are safe here and have a place where people love you." Sandy touched the head scarf April still wore. "When are you going to take this off?"

"Never. It covers the ugly patches."

Sandy pulled the scarf aside. "Let me see." Three angry red patches raged amid the light brown hair. "Does it still hurt? Are they healed?"

"No feeling at all. It's healed as much as it can, but it will always be this color."

"Can a doctor transplant hair from other parts?"

"Oggie says so, but I can't think about that. It's easier to just wear the cover."

Sandy ran her fingers through April's hair and moved locks over the crimson skin. "Let's try something. Come with me."

Sandy took April into her bedroom and sat her down in front of the dresser. She brushed beige concealer onto the shiny red parts and gently combed her hair downward.

"See, it's hardly noticeable," Sandy said. "How about some makeup?"

"I don't wear it."

"It's time. You're a pretty woman, April. I'm not an expert, and I only wear a little, but I can show you what I know."

"Thank you. Oggie is so right about you. You know how much he loves you, don't you?"

"I don't want to deal with that. I think you and I get along so well because we both have gone sour on men."

"You're not sour. Not really."

Their conversation was interrupted by Henry, who called from the yard to announce that his work was done and he needed to leave early.

"Uncle Ralph?" Sandy asked April with a chuckle.

April nodded. "I would say so. Let's time it to see how long it takes for Uncle Ralph to get here."

In three minutes, the fake engine whirred as Oggie landed the jet he called Specky on the front lawn.

Sandy sent the boys out to play and put Jeanette down for her nap. She, Oggie, and April sat in the living room.

"Crap-for-brains put you back on his insurance," Oggie said, accepting a cup of coffee from Sandy. "I guess his little brush with the hospital made him soft."

Sandy stopped her cup mid-way to her mouth. "I didn't know that. How did you?"

April sniffed. "I'd bet Og has a watchdog on Cam's credit card."

Oggie made a gun with his thumb and forefinger and air-shot April with it. "We think alike, me and A.J. She's the female version of me."

"Heavens, no," Sandy said. "She has good manners and doesn't put her foot in her mouth when she speaks.

"Ouch, Sandy. Is that a way to talk to the guy who loves you?"

Sandy changed the subject. "You realize the kids report your visits to Cam and Wally?"

"Of course. I want them to know. I shall turn the tables and be the thorn in Morgan's side. How do you think they found out about me, to begin with? I made sure Wallensky got the agency's new cell phone monitor. I figured he would try it on you. And, of course, he did. He knows I call."

"Oggie," Sandy said with a shame-on-you sound. "Don't you feel guilty for turning them into the sheriff for fishing?"

Oggie grinned, showing all of his front teeth. "That was like a cherry on the sundae!"

Sandy took a long, thoughtful sip. "If Cam gets his hands on you, he might hurt you."

"If he can get me. Maybe. I'm pretty slippery. Oggie the eel. The oft-referred to greased pig. Like grabbing the misty fog. As elusive as the Scarlet Pimpernel. Or—"

Sandy slapped his arm. "Enough! Isn't it time for you to go?"

Oggie put down his cup. "Unfortunately, yes." He pointed to April. "Friday, my dear, you have an appointment in Maryland. I'll be here to pick you up at ten." He turned to Sandy. "Don't worry. Ralph Ferraro has work for Henry to do. He'll leave before I get here."

"Get going," Sandy said, smiling and shaking her head at Oggie. April laughed. It was the first time she had done that since she came.

Friday morning, Oggie arrived on time and had April back by four.

April held her arm close to her chest. "My broken arm is better. They'll work on my teeth later. I don't know what can be done about my hair. I'll keep the make-up on it, but I don't want any more doctoring for a while."

Sandy hugged her. "When you're ready, you will search out the right treatments."

Oggie touched Sandy's shoulder. "Thanks for inviting A. J. to stay longer. Her body hurts are healing, but she still has a long way to go on the inside hurts."

Sandy smiled at April. "I enjoy her company."

"And Me?" Oggie asked.

"All right, I'll admit I enjoy your company, too, in small amounts. But I'm still mad at you for stalking me."

"Will you ever forgive me?"

"Never. I don't know. Maybe. We'll see."

"To speed the forgiveness, I'll just have to come over more often."

"No, not more often," Sandy said. "You don't need to be harassing anyone, and I get stressed at confrontations. April doesn't need it, either."

"Aw, you're no fun at all. Okay, I'll make my visits less obtrusive."

"That sounds slippery. Is Og the Eel talking?"

"Sandy's getting good at this, isn't she, A.J.?"

"Don't aggravate her, Oggie." April's voice was a command.

Oggie grinned. "Sandy, you must be rubbing off on A.J. She's starting to boss me around."

"Cam and Wally will be back any minute. Good afternoon, Og," Sandy said, pushing him toward the door.

Before Sandy could react, Oggie kissed her cheek. "Sweet, like honey. Oh, by the way, go to your local driver's license office. They know you, Sandra Morgan, need a duplicate license, and for some reason, your image isn't available in their files, so let them take a new picture."

The driver's license is fixed! What a relief. "Thanks, Oggie."

She gave him a quick peck on the cheek.

"You're welcome," he said, and she knew he meant it.

That night at bedtime, Sandy answered the knock on her bedroom door.

Cam stood there adjusting his arm sling. "Can we talk for a little while?"

"I suppose, but only for a little while. I get up early in the morning."

Cam sat on Sandy's bed. "Here." He gave her a card. "It's a medical insurance card in case you or the kids need it. I checked on the Sarah Green name change and saw you have already taken care of it. Your lawyer must have good connections. I'm sorry I threatened you about that. I wouldn't have done anything to get you in trouble. I've missed you. Sandy, I roll over in bed and want to feel you there next to me."

Sandy knew the feeling. She didn't like being alone in her bed. She looked out the window to be distracted.

"Honey," Cam said in a quiet tone. "We need to repair our damages, you know, fix these differences. I want you to come back to New York so we can be a family again."

Sandy shook her head.

"Come on. You said you believed me about what happened at the resort. You know I had no choice."

"I'm not going to discuss it."

He put his hand on her shoulder and waited for her to make eye contact. "I have done everything I can think of to make it easy for you. I want you to know I don't even speak to other women for fear you would find out, and it would get in the way of reconciliation. You haven't been with anyone, have you?"

"Absolutely not. And you know it. I can't talk about this, Cam."

Cam leaned toward her and kissed her. Heat rushed through Sandy's body. Cam smelled good. She had always liked the scent of his skin. White noise at high volume played in her ears. Cam breathed hard through his nose and pressed against her. He slipped his tongue through her lips.

The white noise stopped. Instantly, a vision of one of the resort photos surfaced in stunning detail. It was a close-up of Cam, his tongue poised, ready to touch that woman.

Sandy shoved him away with both hands. "Get off of me."

He stood. "Honey."

She pushed him to the door. "Out of my room." Her face was hot, and the adrenaline surged through her.

Cam left the room.

CHAPTER 45

April had an affinity with the animals, especially Jethro and the cows. Vance brought her a stray puppy, and she kept *Fuzzy* with her all of the time. She had good days and bad ones, but the good times became more frequent. April helped more with the housework and did some of the cooking, including using a butter knife. The sharp ones still terrified her. The boys took their lessons in the morning, and Henry still worked for a few hours each day. April started helping Vance when he came. Vance had partnered with his son and now worked part-time, seeing the large animals.

On an evening when the four adults sat watching television with the fireplace ablaze and sending pleasant odors from the fragrant wood, a knock sounded on the door.

Sandy answered.

"Hello, there," a man with a pencil mustache stood in the doorway. He removed the white hat that matched his white wool suit. His purple shirt practically glowed. "I am Brett Fontina, your new neighbor. I bought the farm west of you. Bought the farm! Isn't that a silly expression?"

Mr. Fontina had a problem with his *essess*. He stepped into the living room.

Sandy bit her lip, trying to keep a straight face.

"I have been asking around," Fontina said.

"I know your name is Sandy. I don't know the name of these fellows, though. I understand they are a pair. Oh, my, aren't you a big one," he said to Wally.

Wally's top lip flickered.

Fontina's finger moved around the room. "Well," he sang, "I told you my name. Now you tell me yours."

Sandy closed the door as slowly as possible to provide a diversion in order to control her face. She couldn't believe Oggie would do this, but there he was.

No one spoke. Sandy moved next to the man. "Welcome, neighbor. You know my name already." She pointed, "That is April, a good friend. Over there, Cameron, and on the recliner, Dennis. Cam and Dennis are best friends." Oh, how she enjoyed saying that.

"Maybe we can all be friends," Fontina said in his soft lisp.

Wally looked away, avoiding the conversation. Cam went into the kitchen, got a drink, and took his pain pill.

"Thanks for the welcome," Bret-Oggie said. "Have you noticed an old road that goes along the creek? Years ago, it connected our farms. Now you have only one way out to the highway, and I only have one way, in the opposite direction. If that old road was paved, we would both have another way in and out. So, if you don't mind, I would like to pave it. No cost to you. I just need your permission for the part on your property."

"I don't see why not if you are willing to pay," Sandy enunciated, *"Mr. Fontina."*

"Great!" he said. "Well, I guess I'll go. Nice meeting you."

When Fontina left, Cam came back into the room. "Jesus." He shuddered. "Don't let him do anything without a legal contract, Sandy."

Wally growled. "That man gives me the creeps."

"Oh, come on," Sandy said. "He seems nice."

April let out a loud, wet snicker. "Yeth. He doeth."

Sandy bent down to the fire to check it. "We have a new neighbor. Imagine that. I thought that old house was abandoned. Maybe I should have bought it." She brought the glass safety doors together on the fireplace. "One never knows what the next day will bring."

CHAPTER 46

In the weeks that followed, Cam sulked as he healed. The injury caused him recurring pain and discomfort. Sandy knew his inability to control situations depressed him, but he still spent time with the boys and helped with Jeanette when he could.

The two men went to Nashville three times a week for Cam's physical therapy and Wally's assignments. On a Friday, four weeks after Cam returned from the hospital, Henry left after completing his work. As Henry's car made dust on the rocky road of the farm, Specky landed.

Sandy went out to the jet to greet Oggie. "Well, who are you today? The biker or Bret Fontina?"

"Just Ole Og. The one who loves you true."

Sandy ignored the comment.

Oggie thumbed toward the house. "So, how long will that whiny baby be here playing on your sympathy?"

April, carrying a basket of eggs, joined them.

Sandy shot him a narrow eye. "Cam is really injured. I feel sorry for him."

Oggie raised his lip in a dramatic sneer. "Oh, great."

April shoved Oggie's shoulder. "Come on, Og, that isn't nice. Sandy is taking care of Cam just like she did for me. She'd do the same for you."

"Maybe I should get myself shot."

April laughed. "Not unless you pose as Bret Fontina! The real Oggie wouldn't have a long shelf life with Wally and Cam here."

"Yeah, yeah, yeah," Oggie said. "Even so, maybe I'll come

back from one of my missions needing some care."

Sandy put her hand to her mouth.

"Aha! I'm getting under your skin. I do my best to keep in one piece, believe me. I want to stay whole and healthy for when you finally see my worth."

Again, Sandy let his comment pass. "Would you like some coffee?"

"No time. I just came to say hello and goodbye. I have to leave on a mission." He pushed a door key into Sandy's hand. "Would you and April check my place once in a while until I get back?"

Sandy pocketed the key. "We can do that for you." She touched his hand. "Oggie, please be careful."

"I will. Don't work too hard. And, April, take care of yourself. You have come so far."

The two women kissed Oggie's cheek, together, each on one side. He grinned and got back into Specky. Sandy and April stepped back from the jet. Then it lifted. The craft had only been gone a minute when Cam and Wally returned.

Cam rubbed his shoulder under the sling. He winced as he moved. The physical therapy gave Cam more movement and grasp, but after the workouts, he suffered from severe cramps. That night, after everyone had gone to bed, Cam paced the hallway and woke Sandy up. She peeked out her door and saw him massaging his upper arm. He winced and groaned. Sandy opened the door wider.

"Sorry I woke you," he said. "It's really bad tonight. I think I overworked it this afternoon."

"Can't you take something for the pain?"

"Pain pills don't help the spasms. The doctor said the cramps are a sign that the muscles are healing." He moved his shoulder up and down, shutting his eyes and pulling back his lips. His fingers splayed in different directions.

Sandy pushed his fingers together and massaged his arm. Cam groaned. "Oh, God, this is the worst cramp yet."

"Let's try heat. Come with me." Sandy brought him into the bedroom and told him to sit on the bed. She shut the door to keep the talking from awakening the rest of the house. She got the heating pad from the closet and wrapped it around his bicep.

After a few minutes, he relaxed. He took a deep breath and flexed his fingers in and out. "The cramp is going away. Thank you."

Sandy sat next to him and ran her fingers inside the pad to massage his muscle. His face became calm as the muscle relaxed.

Cam opened his eyes and stared at Sandy. He unwound the heating pad and, with his good arm, grabbed her, pushing her onto the pillow. He kissed her. Reflexively, she kissed him back. He pressed his lips on her neck and worked down, and without saying a word, he pulled her nightgown up.

Alarms went off in her mind. A war raged between her will to resist and her body screaming for attention. Her body won. She unsnapped his boxers, and he moved on top of her.

"You want me," he whispered. "Say you want me."

It had been so long since she had had sex. She ran her hand down to grasp him as he hardened. She guided him to her thighs.

"Say, I want you. Say it," he demanded.

"No." But she didn't push him away. Her body wouldn't let her.

He slipped inside her. It felt better than she remembered. She hadn't allowed herself to think about sex. Now she knew how much she needed it, how hungry, how starved she was for it. She put her arms around his waist and moved her hips to receive his thrusts.

It wasn't long before Sandy drove her face against his neck and moaned. Little flashes of pleasure sparked all over her body, and she reveled in every one of them. She could not remember a better finish.

He pulled out and lay next to her. After a moment of rest, he kissed her neck and breasts, then moved the kisses to her mouth, touching his tongue to hers.

"No tongue," Sandy said. "I need to get up to go to the bathroom."

Cam wrapped his legs around hers. "No. I have you, and I'm not letting go."

The internal warning clangs sounded. She had left him in New York, broken free. Now, he had her pinned. Her mind screamed to break his hold. But she couldn't force herself to struggle out of his grasp. The need for touch overwhelmed her senses. She relaxed in his grip and fell asleep.

In the morning, Sandy stretched, feeling the vigor of a night's deep rest. The sound of Cam's shallow breathing caused her to roll on her side and stare at him.

She fought the impulse to lightly stroke his chest, remembering the night of lovemaking they had shared. There was no denying he had made her feel alive, desirable, and even sexy, things she hadn't felt in a long time. *But was it worth it?*

She rolled out of bed, needing to use the bathroom. When she washed her face and reached for the toothbrush, Cam came in and stood behind her. She looked at his reflection. Cam's hair was mussed, the little ash-blond curls framing his handsome face. She closed her eyes as he kissed her neck.

"Come back to bed," he whispered in her ear.

"I have to get up. The kids will be hungry."

"I can have you for just a little longer." He pulled her back to bed and made love to her, less energetic but soft and fulfilling.

"Don't kiss me like that," she said when he forced his tongue through her lips.

He finished and held her so tight she struggled for breath. It felt good when he held her, and although she heard the internal voice screaming, she would not listen to the protests against what she did with him.

"I have to get up now." Sandy left him in her bed. She changed Jeanette and took the child with her downstairs to start breakfast.

When Cam came down to the kitchen, Sandy was turning the last pieces of bacon. Both boys clomped down the stairs. A few minutes later, Wally came out of the office bedroom. April joined and helped butter the toast. Soon, the table was covered with breakfast delicacies.

Cam, not usually a big breakfast eater, took a little of everything. He patted his stomach. "Hey, Wally, let's clean the tractor shed. Maybe we can park the cars there now that the big things are gone. And we can nail a few boards back up where the old ones have come down."

"Are you up to that?" Wally asked. "What about the pain?"

"I can do some stuff. You have to do the heavy work."

"Okay." Wally cocked his head. "Since when did you volunteer for manual labor?"

Cam glanced at Sandy. "Since now."

Out in the tractor shed, Cam swept one-handed with the broom, whistling.

Wally stood and crossed his arms on his chest. "If I didn't know better, I would say someone got laid."

Cam whistled a long, high note. "That would be me, then."

Wally slapped his back. "So, what's the plan?"

"You mean in addition to getting laid again tonight? I'll convince her to move back to New York. We can't stay here."

Wally stroked his chin. "Good luck. They have roots here. The boys love it. You know, it isn't so bad. Fresh air, nice people, quiet. Nashville has all the big-city stuff anyone could need. I'm not one for nightlife, so there's not much in New York I'd miss, except maybe a good bagel. I guess you have your job. You could practice here."

"I'd have to pass the red-neck Bar. No thanks. We're going back to the City."

At dinnertime, although crowded at the dining table, everyone seemed to be in a good mood, and after an hour of television, Sandy bid the other adults goodnight. She vowed not to let Cam into her bedroom, but when he knocked at the door, she let him in. To talk. After one long kiss, her body took over.

One-armed, Cam deftly removed her clothing and guided her to the shower. He pinned Sandy against the tile. Even a cold cascade would not stem the lust still smoldering inside her. Their activities the night before uncorked her appetite, but her ravenous hunger remained, and she needed to empty that container. During the lovemaking, Cam tried to French kiss her, and each time she refused. Even her need for his touch could not completely erase the vision of those awful photos. However, her need for sex still dominated her voice of reason.

The next morning, Cam got Jeanette dressed while Sandy made breakfast. The meal was easygoing, and things ran smoothly. April helped the boys feed the cows. Wally retired to the downstairs bedroom, and Cam helped Sandy with the kitchen work.

Once the breakfast dishes were done, Sandy took another cup of coffee out to the front porch to enjoy the birds at the feeders. She put Jeanette in the playpen next to her chair. Cam joined her, and they sat without speaking for a few minutes.

"Are you feeling happy, Sandy?"

Sandy breathed in deeply and exhaled. "I'm feeling satisfied."

"Good. You know, my arm has healed enough for me to go back to work. I have taken a lot of time off since you left me. In fact, the head partner called a few minutes ago and said, nicely, of course, I'd better get back ASAP. I told him next week."

"Well, if you have to go, you have to go."

"Yeah, well, I do have to go, and I want you to be with me. Don't wait to sell this house. You and the kids come back with me next week."

"What?"

"We're back together. We'll all return to New York."

"We are not back together. We had sex. I'm not going anywhere. This is my home."

"Get that lawyer who fixed your name problem to oversee the house. Maybe that fruit who has the farm next door will want it."

Sandy put down her cup so hard it waved up in a peak and spilled on the saucer. "First of all, I'm not going back to New York. Second of all, I didn't have a lawyer. You already know about Oggie. *He* fixed my legal problems. Third of all—"

"Oggie! What the hell? I don't want to hear that name again. I'm going to have Wally search for that guy, and then I'll take care of *him*."

Sandy picked up her cup and took a long sip through smiling lips. "You won't be able to find Oggie unless he wants to be found."

"No one is smart enough to hide for too long. We found you, remember?"

Sandy sniffed. "You found me because a ten-year-old called you… twice. And regarding Oggie, *he* runs rings around *you* intellectually."

Cam touched her shoulder. "I am returning to New York, and I've had enough separation. I've really tried to make this work. I missed you, and I know you missed me, too. It's time to get down to business. Start packing and wind up your affairs around here."

"Down to business?" *The grand manipulator.* "I have no business with you. I agree it's time for *you* to return to New York

City."

"Sandy, I know you enjoyed being in bed with me. If you don't agree to move back to New York, I won't sleep with you. I won't even come back and stay here."

"You arrogant shit. Yes, I enjoyed our time rolling around in bed, but I won't pay your price. I'll buy a vibrator so I don't get that needy again. Go back to New York. I can manage without you in my bed or in my house. In fact, don't wait until next week. Get out *now*."

Sandy realized she had shouted her response when Wally came outside and stared at them.

"Everything all right here?" he asked.

"Yes, everything is all right here. Cam is leaving."

Wally shook his head. "Damn it, Cam. Have you crapped things up again? Whatever you said, apologize because I know *you* caused the problem."

"Hey," Cam said. "Thanks for your support when you don't know what happened. She's throwing us out."

"Us?" Sandy said. "I'm throwing *you* out."

Cam left the porch.

"Wally, you don't have to go if you don't want to."

"Thanks, Sandy, but I should go. I have an apartment in D.C., and my office has been more than generous in letting me stay here. I don't understand Cam. I lost my family and would do anything to get them back."

"I know. Truth is, I don't want Cam back. I want him to go."

By mid-afternoon, Cam and Wally had their stuff packed in the car. Wally said goodbye. Cam hugged the boys, who didn't complain about their father leaving. He did not speak to Sandy or thank her for letting him stay. Later, when the boys went out to play and Jeanette took her nap, Sandy and April sat at the dining table.

"Not a good day, huh?" April said.

Sandy stared ahead toward the large front window, admiring the trees across the expansive front lawn. "I've had worse." After a moment's pause, she dropped her gaze to the table for a moment. "I slept with Cam. I told myself he had changed. My Grandma Noonie said leopards never change their spots. I guess she was right."

"It's all how you look at it, really," April said. "Ex facto or de facto. I mean, picture in your mind a leopard having yellow skin with black dots."

"Okay, black spots on a yellow field."

"Suppose then the spots stay the same, but the background changes to black. Ex facto, the spots haven't changed, but de facto, the cat appears all black, and now your leopard has become a panther. The same animal, but different."

April tapped her fingers on the tabletop. "From what you've told me of your life before coming here, I'd say some part of *you* has changed. I mean, look at you right now. You kicked Cam and Wally out. No regrets, no negative emotion."

"You're right. Thanks for that." Sandy closed her eyes. "I do have one regret. The good part only lasted for two nights. And it *was* very good." She let out a sigh. "I can't say what another man would be like, but Cam, well, he knows how to…" Sandy fluttered her eyelashes.

"Sky rockets at night?"

"Sky rockets? A full formation of flying saucers!"

April put her hand under her chin. "Flying saucers? Interesting analogy. Have you ever seen a real flying saucer?"

"*Real?* No such thing," Sandy said.

"You don't believe in extra-terrestrials?"

Sandy made a face and looked at April. "Absolutely not. And I wouldn't think someone as smart and highly trained as you could believe in them, either."

April did not respond.

Sandy leaned slightly toward her. "Come on. April? Are you one of those people who say the earth has been invaded and the aliens are already walking among us?"

April continued her silence.

"Yeah. Okay. I'll believe when I have seen and talked to E.T."

"We-ll," April said, drawing out her words. "You actually have—"

BLAM! BLAM!

"Shotgun!" April shouted. She stood and grabbed Sandy's hand. "My God! The kids!"

CHAPTER 47

Sandy ran out the back door. Henry came around the barn with the shotgun in the crook of his arm and two bloody upside-down turkeys clutched in the other.

"The kids! Are they—?" Before she could say another word, the three boys raced around from the other side of the house.

Miles pointed toward Henry. "Man, Eddie. Your daddy's been *hunting*."

The shots had not bothered the boys.

"Hey," Henry shouted and jiggled the birds. "Lookie what I got." He picked up his pace.

Sandy, relieved from her worry that the boys weren't bothered by the gunfire, sped up and met him. "You shot two turkeys? Why?"

Henry's face took on a puzzled look. "Cause there was a whole mess of them eating the corn under the cow feeder, and I could only get two before the rest flew off. Two's better'n none."

"No, why did you kill them?"

"Meat. It's hard to beat the taste of wild turkey. And these are young ones, tender. You could probably roast them. Bigger birds, you'd have to stew. It's too late to cook them today, but you can dress one and freeze the other. Cook it later."

Sandy's lip curled up. "Dress them? I don't have a clue how to do that, even if I wanted to. When I want turkey, there's plenty at the grocery store."

"Grocery store? You better come with me." He turned and walked to the barn.

Sandy shrugged. It had been an interesting day, and,

obviously, not over yet. She followed Henry into the barn kitchen, where he leaned the shotgun in a corner and put the birds in the soapstone sink.

He took down an aluminum tub that hung on the wall. "Someday, maybe we won't be able to get to the store." Then, he got a large pot from a shelf. Filling the pot with water, he put it on the old stove. Henry pointed out the barn door at the farm. "You got a huge grocery store right there. Meat, vegetables, medicines, all for the taking. I'm gonna show you."

No, no. I don't want to learn this stuff. But the other voice inside her wanted to hear the information. Maybe she should learn from him. She stepped closer.

"Get them others in here," he said as he pulled a knife sharpener from a drawer under the counter. "They need to learn, too."

For the rest of the afternoon, Sandy, April, and the boys watched Henry dress the fowl. All participated, and April, with reluctant caution, used the sharp knife. Jeanette chased the downy feathers wafting around in the dusty rays of light slanting through the cracks of the boards.

"Tomorrow," Henry said, as he dried his hands from the clean-up, "we're going for a walk in your woods, and I'll show you edible plants and how to cook them. In times of trouble, knowledge can make a difference."

Save me! But the internal adviser, the small voice, the one that told her the truth, replied, *He's right. Pay attention.*

"Okay," Sandy said. "I'll learn about the foods of the forest, but no medicines. I'm not going to poison anyone trying to cure an ill with something I picked."

Henry didn't argue. "Maybe that's a good idea. There's plenty of folks around here who know the herbal cures. I'll introduce you to a few. How's that?"

Sandy put her hand on her hip. "As long as they don't

expect me to use them instead of a real doctor."

"Your choice," he said. "Look, I may be a hayseed, but everyone has something to offer. In a disaster, some people won't survive. I will. And the people I care about will, too."

As Henry's words registered, she looked at him in a different light. He had been a farmhand, a neighbor. But she saw more. A new side of Henry emerged. Every individual had a distinctive contribution, and Henry wanted to share his specialty, survival. Like Cam, he was smart and gifted in his own way. Her respect and admiration for this man notched up several degrees.

Okay, but no wild-ass medicines. Sandy took a deep breath. If she thought today had been full of surprises, she worried that tomorrow loomed just as outrageous.

CHAPTER 48

April rarely asked questions, accepting her life on the farm without complaint or giving opinions on how to make things better. Sandy found that to be one of the woman's attributes, and enjoyed her company. Although April did not offer a lot of help in the house, she had become interested in the cattle and worked with the animals. Vance hadn't visited the farm often while Cam was there, but when he did, April accompanied him as he made his rounds. What she learned from Vance served as therapy.

Things were quiet at the farm for the few weeks since Cam and Wally left. No word from Oggie meant he must be on a mission. An absent Oggie meant Henry had no soil samples to collect for Ralph Ferraro. Henry came to the farm a lot.

One afternoon, when April went to check on the cows, she came into the kitchen out of breath. "Call the vet! Something is wrong with Lanty's leg."

"Lanty? The cow with the twins?"

"Yes, her leg is swollen, and she is lying on the grass."

Within the hour, the women met Vance's jeep at the bottom of the hill, and the three drove out to the pasture.

Vance squatted over the animal. "She's been bitten by a snake, probably a copperhead. I'll have to keep an eye on her. I'm pretty sure she'll recover, but it will be a while before she can stand upright to feed the calves. You will have to give them a supplement. I have some powdered stuff with me, enough to feed the calves until I bring more tomorrow."

April took the box of powder and ran to the house to prepare it.

"I haven't seen you for a while," Vance said.

Sandy nodded. "I've been busy." She sat wearily on the passenger side of his jeep as he reassembled his vet kit.

"You look tired. Did you overdo taking care of the Mister?"

Sandy put her head on the back of the seat. "No. Wally did most of the extra work."

"I'm glad they're gone," Vance said, sneering.

"Well, Cam's gone for good, I think."

"Oh yeah? Why do you think that?"

"He said if I didn't return to New York with him, he wouldn't come back here."

Vance gave her the sideways, half-lidded glance. "Aww," he said. "Sorry about that."

Vance came every day, sometimes for lunch, sometimes late afternoons, and sometimes stayed for dinner. He worked with the sick cow while April tended to the twin calves, feeding them warm supplement from bottles.

One afternoon, Sandy and Vance leaned against the fence rail bordering the backyard.

Vance picked a straw and sucked on the end. He pointed at Jethro. "Your donkey is one of the finest specimens I've ever seen, Sandy-Sarah. I wouldn't mind having him or one like him. Maybe you should breed him."

He pulled another long blade and chewed it. "Oh, my, I think I just broke one of the Ten Commandments."

Sandy shot him a puzzled look.

He smiled. "You know, the one where you're not supposed to covet your neighbor's ass." He darted a look at her buttocks.

"True. And don't covet your neighbor's wife, either," she said, teasing.

"Uh, oh. Two out of ten. I'll go to hell, for sure. That's okay. It can't be as bad as the hell I've been in."

"You think you're in hell?"

"Not anymore. I *was* in hell and didn't know it. Life has become pretty good. I'm gainfully employed working for Gene, and I'm not drinking. I feel a lot better now. All because of coyotes."

"What? How did coyotes change you?"

He threw the grass straw down. "Think about it."

She focused on his words. *Coyotes?* "Oh!" She remembered. She brought their dog into the animal clinic after a coyote attack. *I brought him out of hell?*

He engaged her stare.

Sandy nodded, not knowing a proper response.

He leaned back against the wooden rail. "How about a date?"

"A date?"

"All right, not exactly a date. You *and* April. How about a concert and dinner? I'll bring the gal who babysits for Gene. You'll have no excuse to refuse."

"Okay. I won't refuse."

"Saturday, then?"

"Sure. It sounds good, and I think April would like to go out."

"Great. I'll make the plans."

CHAPTER 49

Vance's Jeep pulled into the driveway on Saturday afternoon. Sandy called up the stairs to April, announcing his arrival. April came down the steps carefully, wearing a pair of low heels. She turned so Sandy could appraise her appearance.

"You look wonderful, April. You might as well keep that red silk sheath. It looks way better on you."

"Thanks. I like the blue velvet you're wearing. If Vance wears white, we may be mistaken for the flag!"

Sandy took pleasure in the enjoyment showing on April's face. The farm had been good for her.

When Sandy opened the door, Vance, dressed in a black tux, bowed slightly and introduced the young woman standing next to him. "Sandy-Sarah, this is Gail Bundig. Gene recommends her babysitting skills highly."

Temporarily speechless at Vance's formal attire, Sandy swung her arm into the living room as a silent invitation to enter.

April pointed at Vance and said, "Wow!"

Sandy introduced the children to Gail and admonished them to behave.

Offering his elbows, Vance stood between his dates. "My ladies."

They entwined their arms in his, and he led them to the car. "You two sit in the back because I'm your chauffeur. For now. And," he added, "no questions. I have a few surprises."

Vance drove for a half hour toward Nashville but turned off the highway and drove to a huge Baptist church. He pulled under its porte-cochere, parked there, and escorted them through the front entrance of the sanctuary. After seating them in the front row, he moved to the grand piano on the right side of the stage. He bowed to both of them and sat on the bench. Vance played the Moonlight Sonata, The Mad Search for a Lost Penny, and several other Beethoven melodies. When the music stopped, his hands lingered on the keyboard for a moment, then he rose and bowed again.

April stood, applauded, and shouted, "Bravo!"

Sandy stood and applauded. "Double Bravo! Vance! Magnificent!"

He took the four steps down the stage and came to where the women stood. "I've been practicing that for two months." He slid his hand into his jacket to remove his cell, keyed a phone number, and spoke. "Ready? Good." The phone went back into his pocket. "Ladies, will you please come with me?"

He led them to a dining room in the church's banquet hall where two waiters stood on either side of a finely laid table with candlelight, white linen, and sparkling dinnerware. The waiters held the chairs for Sandy and April. A chef brought in a cart with an array of food.

Vance sat down. "I promised you a concert and dinner."

Sandy hadn't seen such a selection of delicacies since the elegant dinner parties of New York. Lobster, filet mignon, tiny lamb chops, pressed duck, escargot, and more. The meal was delicious, and Sandy sampled all the offerings.

During the meal, Vance spoke of his many years of piano study and surprised them when he said he received his bachelor's degree on a music scholarship. "Music was never my passion. That was my mother's idea. It did get me a full scholarship for a bachelor's degree, and when I gained admission to Vanderbilt for Veterinary Medicine, I played in the philharmonic orchestra."

"Why the church, Vance?" April asked.

"Ah, Reverend Stephens owed me a favor. Some years

back, I stayed up for seventy-two hours straight working to save his Thoroughbred mare from foundering. I never thought I'd have occasion to take back the favor. Then I realized the church had a fine piano, good acoustics, and a reasonable stage. Plus, you see what a nice banquet hall this is. No wine, though. Stephens put his foot down. Even my Jesus-made-wine argument wouldn't hold water." Vance smiled at Sandy. "I've pretty much given up booze anyway. Who needs it?"

"None of us," Sandy said, holding her stomach. She felt so full that she became uncomfortable.

Suffering from nausea on the car ride back, she chastised herself for overeating.

At the farm, Vance opened the door, allowing April to go into the house. As Sandy slipped out of the car, he took her by the arm and asked, "Are you all right?"

"Barely. I'm being punished for my unbridled gluttony of that magnificent dinner."

He brushed a stray lock from her forehead. "Impossible for a faultless being."

"Faultless? If only." She breathed in, tilting her head to the dark sky. "We never had skies like this in New York. Look at those stars!"

Vance put her hand to his lips. "Your visage! More fair than velvet nights, dotted with the sparkle of a billion twinkling lights."

"I didn't think you could possibly top tonight's surprise, Vance. But…" She patted his hand with hers. "Thank you for a wonderful evening." She kissed his cheek and wished she could act more enthusiastically. The events of the evening had tired her out.

Later, an Alka-Seltzer eased her discomfort as she made ready for bed.

The next day, it was hard for Sandy to get up. Tiring easily, she napped when she put Jeanette down for the afternoon. She lay on the couch, resting, when she heard the phone. She dragged herself up to answer it.

"Hey, gorgeous," Oggie said. "Just checking in. I'll be back in a few days."

"Where are you?" Sandy asked.

"How's April doing? We need her."

Sandy knew when Oggie couldn't answer her questions.

"April is doing fine, but don't even think about her coming back to work."

"Seriously, Sandy, we need her."

"Forget it, Og. Why would she want to return to that kind of danger?"

"I'll talk to her."

"Don't. Not now, not next week, not ever. Leave her alone. Come see us when you're back." Sandy hung up the phone and heard a glass break in the kitchen. "Oh, no," she said quietly.

In the kitchen, Sandy found April with her head down, hanging as if in a trance.

"April, did you hear me talking with Oggie?"

April moved her head so slightly that Sandy wasn't sure it was a response. But she recognized the whine that followed.

"Oh, honey," Sandy said, taking the woman by the arm into the living room. They sat on the couch. "You don't have to go back."

April turned her head in slow motion. The look on her pale face was pitiful. She closed her eyes tightly and took a staccato breath.

"April, you can stand up to Oggie. I'll help you. It's getting easier for me to go up against the male gender. Don't worry."

April's screaming dreams returned that night. In the early hours, the shrieks brought Sandy into the woman's room. The boys came to check on them, and Jeanette cried at the sounds.

It took an hour for Sandy to quiet April with hugging and soft talking. It happened the next two nights, and Sandy dragged more each day.

In the morning, as she struggled with a bag of cracked corn, Henry rushed to help. "You don't look so good. Let me do that. Why don't you go on into the house and rest a spell?"

Sandy didn't argue with him, welcoming the assistance. Still resting later that day, she heard the fake engine sound of the little jet. Oggie pulled up on the lawn close to the house.

"Can I come in?" he asked at the door.

Sandy answered from her spot on the couch.

Oggie went to her, but instead of greeting her with a compliment, he made a face. "You look awful. What's wrong?"

Sandy let her head fall back. "I'm pregnant."

"Aw, man! Sandy?"

"I had some weak moments with Cam."

"Shit," he said. He sat next to her and touched her arm. "Did you see a doctor?"

"Don't have to. I know when I'm pregnant."

He put the back of his hand on her forehead. "Nuh-uh. Women don't run a fever from being knocked up."

"You became a doctor when?"

"I'm a certified Field Medic with advanced training, so I'm doctor-ish. Hold on."

Oggie ran out the door, leaving it open, and sailed over the porch hedge like a hurdler. He took the same track on the way back, flawlessly leaping inches above the shrubbery. He held a small metal box.

"A first-aid kit?" She asked.

"No. A field diagnostic meter. Hold still." He touched a tiny wand to her eye. "I just need a bit of lachrymal juice." The box made a soft whirr. "My precious! Negative to the pregative, but damned sick. Your white count has soared to Neverland.

We've got to get you to the emergency room." He snapped the box closed. "Come out, April. I know you're hiding. I won't harass you, promise."

April stepped from the downstairs room they used as an office and stood near the couch.

"I'm taking Sandy to Nashville. You have to take care of the kids and watch the house. April, you can do it. I'll call as soon as I know anything. Where's her purse?"

April ducked back into the office and returned with the purse. Oggie turned to Sandy, extending his arms like he was going to lift her.

"I can walk, Og," Sandy said. "Please, will you get the boys inside? I have to talk to them."

Oggie went to the door and called for the boys, who came running to where Sandy sat. She reached out to them and pulled them into an embrace. "Wes, I'm not feeling well, and Oggie is taking me to the hospital. You're the man now. I'll be okay, but both of you mind April and help her with Jeanette."

April stepped up and put one hand on each boy's shoulder. "I'll take care of them, Sandy. I owe you big time. Please get better soon. And you," she pointed, "Ogburn Goodhart Edwards, take good care of her."

Oggie nodded to April, then gently moved the boys aside to bend over Sandy. "You're sick, Babe. Save your strength." Against her protests, Oggie lifted Sandy, carried her to the parked jet, and put her in the aircraft's front seat. He ran around to the pilot's seat. Inside, he pushed the fake dashboard to its resting place, bringing up a dashboard that displayed all kinds of dials and buttons. The phony propeller started up along with its bogus sound. The craft went forward and ascended in seconds. He radioed for an ambulance to meet him at the small airport, where he kept a hangar near his previous living quarters. Within ten minutes, he touched down and headed for the open bay. The ambulance met him at the entrance.

Oggie touched Sandy's cheek. "I need to secure Specky. I'll follow on the bike."

The high-handlebar motorcycle leaned on its kickstand next to the far wall. It had only been months since she had seen him in his biker persona, but it felt like years. The EMTs closed the ambulance door, and the vehicle gave a soft lurch as they moved.

Sandy gave the nurses in Emergency her insurance card with Cam's name as the primary holder. They had questions and called him.

***

After guaranteeing the card and covering the deposit, Cam called Wes. The boys only knew that Sandy had become sick, and Oggie had flown her to the hospital in Nashville. Cam contacted Wally, who insisted on meeting him at the Nashville airport the next morning.

"Wally," Cam said, as he approached his friend, who waited at the noisy airport bar. "You didn't have to come here."

"Oh, yes, I did. You'd mess things up worse. And," Wally said, touching the rim of his drink can, "you wouldn't be in this crap if it weren't for me. Who's watching the kids?"

Cam rolled his eyes. "According to Wes, it's April. I don't know much about her."

Wally took a pull at his drink. "Yeah. I'll bet I didn't say twenty words to the woman. I know Sandy would not like it if she found out, but I ran a search on April. You can't get more plain vanilla than that lady. Born and raised in Omaha, a degree in Communications, a medical transcriber, never married. One moving violation for driving too slow in the fast lane. She is safe, if not boring. But I'll take over at the house. I've got a rental car. Do you want me to drop you off at the hospital?"

"I have a car, too. No, go on to the farm. Thanks, Wally."

Shaking hands, they went their separate ways.

Cam stopped at the hospital gift shop and bought a flower arrangement. He tiptoed into Sandy's room and saw a doctor looking over notes. Sandy drifted between consciousness and sleep. Multiple bags hung on a stand with tubes that merged into the IV line inserted in her hand.

The doctor turned away from the light. If Cam had looked closely at the man's white lab coat, he would have seen "Dr. O. G. Edwards" written over the top pocket and perhaps would have noticed a man looking like Bret Fontina.

Cam bent over Sandy and asked the doctor. "How is she? I'm her husband."

The doctor rubbed the bridge of his black glasses. "She has septicemia, a bacterial infection of the blood, and she's too sick for company. Make sure you don't stay more than five minutes every four hours."

Sandy's eyes fluttered. She put her free hand up in the air and called out, "Oggie."

Cam stroked her cheek. "No, honey, it's me, Cam." He looked up at the doctor. "Is she going to be all right?"

"She'll get the best care possible," Dr. Edwards said as he headed for the door. "I guarantee it."

Cam pulled the chair up to the bed. He took her hand and kissed it. "Please don't ask me to leave. I want to take care of you."

Sandy returned to sleep, and Cam watched her regular breathing as he held her hand. He put his head gently on her shoulder and kissed her neck. Taking note of the time, he only stayed five minutes to make sure he would be welcome back. Staying in a nearby motel, he came early the next morning for his first visit.

Waiting for his visiting time with Sandy, Cam used his cell to conduct business, plus called the farm several times a day to check on the children. Another doctor said he could come during the regular visiting hours. He set up his laptop there in the room.

While he worked by her side, a crystal vase containing a dozen long-stemmed red roses arrived with a card signed by Vance Chambers.

"Bastard, old fart," Cam muttered, crushing the card. While the nurse bathed Sandy, he walked five blocks to a florist and bought three dozen red roses arranged with huge fern leaves and baby's breath. The next day, a splendid bouquet of rare orange and white striped roses interspersed with golden orchids arrived with a card signed, "Get Well Soon, O beautiful and delightful lady. Ever your servant, Oggie."

"Sonofabitch," Cam said. He tore the card and threw it in the trash.

***

Every so often, Dr. Edwards would poke his head into the room and, when Cam wasn't watching, blow Sandy a kiss. After a week, Oggie called her from the waiting room and told her to get rid of Cam for a few minutes by sending him to get a Snickers from the candy machine.

Oggie hurried in. "The vending machine in the waiting room happens to be out of Snickers. I'm betting the ole boy will go to the next floor to find one. I need to talk to you. I have to go, Sandy." He took her hands in his. "I'm going on a mission. Gonna miss me?"

"Yes, of course. You know the doctor said the infection was so bad I could have died. You saved my life."

"In some cultures, if you save a life, you must be responsible for it forever."

"Please be careful, Oggie."

"I'll see you when I get back. Don't leave the hospital until you know you are well. You'll work too hard."

"I look forward to working hard, Og. Thanks again."

Cam's distinctive walk echoed down the tile floor. The regular tapping of his Italian leather heels came closer.

"Maybe it's time he met the real me," Oggie said.

"No! I don't need a scene. Go. Don't get hurt!"

Oggie kissed her forehead and left, passing Cam in the doorway.

After ten days, Cam drove Sandy home. A few minutes into the ride, Cam, in a matter-of-fact tone, said, "I sold the Manhattan place. I called Aaron Feldman and asked if he was interested. He jumped at it. Carter is pregnant again, number five, and they wanted a real house. Their apartment wasn't suited for all those young children. She said our house was kid-friendly. Thanks to you. I got eighteen million, two million down, and the rest when Feldman sells his place. I could have gotten twenty if I wanted to sit on it for a while, but I'm happy. I didn't pay anything but taxes for it."

"Why did you sell your house?"

"Because I bought the place next to yours on the east."

"Three hundred acres? There's just a double-wide. I didn't know it was for sale."

"Everything's for sale, Sandy. I made them an offer, and they've cleared out."

"What about your job?"

"I quit. They weren't happy with me being away so much. They got a new fair-haired boy to replace me. I don't need to work if I live here. I will have plenty from the sale. Did you know my soil is different from your farm? I can plant corn and soybeans."

"You're interested in soil?"

"Yes, I already received some information about soil samples. Things happen fast. I got the message on my cell, and it sounds interesting. Your ground only supports hay unless it is heavily fertilized like you do for your garden."

Sandy looked out the window to hide her smile. *Oggie,*

gone but not forgotten.

"Fascinating, Cam."

"I'll be close for the kids, and if you and I sort out our problems, we could have one of the largest farms in the county. Maybe that fruity guy on the west will sell to us."

"Don't bet on it," she said.

"Sandy, I'm sorry for how things have worked out between us. I'm a jerk, and I freely admit I've been too controlling. You must know how much I care for you. I don't know why I cause so much trouble."

"Gee, Cam. That's something coming from you."

"I've had a lot of time to think lately."

When their ride ended and the car stopped in the driveway, the boys ran out to meet them, followed by April and Wally.

April hugged Sandy. "Now we can take care of you. You look so much better!"

Sandy held Jeanette while Wally fussed in the kitchen, making lunch, a simple, man-type meal of canned soup and ham sandwiches. After eating, Cam and Wally drove down the road to the double-wide trailer that Cam now owned.

That afternoon, April brought coffee to Sandy outside on the porch. They sat watching the hummingbirds.

"Thank you for taking care of the kids and the house, April."

"You're welcome. I didn't have to do that much. Henry stayed longer to take care of the farm, and Vance came every day to look after the animals. The boys did a lot of the chores, and Wally helped with the house and the kids."

"I guess you don't need me at all," Sandy said.

"I guess we do, too. Bad as this was, every cloud has a silver lining."

"April! How optimistic. Good for you." Sandy squinted, examining April's face. "What's this? Makeup? Wait a minute, my good friend Paula said a woman starts wearing makeup during the day for one reason."

April smiled wide. She blushed and ran her fingers through her hair, not stopping at the bald spots.

"All right, spill. What mischief went on behind my back while I wasted away?"

"Dennis and I are getting married," April said.

"Oh, my God." Sandy swallowed her surprise and moved close, inches in front of April's face. "And just how did *that* happen?"

April's face became serious. "Nightmares. The first night he stayed here, I had a really bad one. Wally came into my room and talked to me until I calmed down. His soothing voice helped me relax. He slept on the floor. After that night, he stayed in bed with me because it kept the dreams away. He never tried a thing like a true gentleman. After a while, I knew I could trust him, and we started getting close and…well, we discovered we loved each other. I know it happened fast, but I've never been so sure of anything."

"Oh, April, do you think you could, you know…?"

"We already have! I didn't suppose I could ever let a man touch me, but Wally is wonderful."

"I hope you kept quiet so the kids didn't hear."

"They were accustomed to my screams at night. They didn't know the difference!"

"April! Screams?"

"I said he was wonderful." April pursed her lips, fighting the smile.

"Have you set a date?"

"Not yet. I have some things to work out. Wally doesn't know about my real employment. I can't tell him details until we are legally married. Of course, I'm quitting. Oggie won't like it, but I can stand up to him now. I want Wally to quit, too, but it's his decision. Amusing situation, eh? Neither of us can reveal our identities until we marry, even though I already know about him. Oh, Sandy! I'm in love and getting married!"

Sandy hugged her. "One never knows what the next day will bring, eh?"

CHAPTER 50

Henry stopped by to welcome Sandy home.

"You look good, Sandy. Your color's coming back. We all fretted over you. I come to tell you I'm going up to my sister's in Indiana 'cause her husband's got terminal cancer, and they need me. I waited until you got home from the hospital. I'm sorry to leave you with the farm work, but your boys can do some of it. I've been showing them how. I don't know when I'm coming back. I have to help my sister settle their affairs."

"Don't worry about us. Tell your sister I'm sorry about her husband. God Speed, Henry."

"God's got nothing to do with it. If He really cared, good folks wouldn't die and leave the people who love them." Henry looked down at his feet for a moment, then fixed his gaze on Sandy. He turned his head toward the boys who played on the tire swing. "Eddie! C'mon." He patted Sandy's back. "Take care of yourself, hear?"

It wasn't long after the dust stirred by Henry's truck settled on the gravel before Oggie, as Brett Fontina, made a visit.

The newer, stronger April opened the door at his knock. "We were concerned about you."

As he stepped into the house, Sandy came out of the kitchen and stood next to April.

April put her hand out, palm up. "Oggie, I'm resigning and getting married to Dennis Wallensky."

Oggie's countenance paled slightly, contrasting against his bright red and purple Hawaiian shirt and white slacks. He threw his straw hat on the coffee table. From his expression, a whirlwind of deliberation raged behind the unflappable persona. "You can't resign. We need you because of the things you know and can do. You can't be replaced. If something happens to me, you're it."

April stood on her tiptoes to get within an inch, nose to nose. "No," she said, clenching her teeth. She parted the hair on the side of her head and showed the angry patches shiny with crimson scar tissue. "Never again."

He jerked up his hat, pulled the door open with more force than necessary, and jogged across the lawn to the paved road that led to his own house.

Sandy put her hand on April's shoulders. "He'll be back. He isn't accustomed to losing. Give him some time to adapt."

April hung her head. "I love Oggie. He's my closest friend... actually, he's more than that, but.... You know he saved my life because he was the one who recognized my coded message and led the group to my rescue."

"Og loves you, too. He wants the best for you, and after he thinks about it, he'll realize getting married will make you happy. Be patient."

"I'll try. My relationship with Oggie is important to me. But I want a real life. I hope I can have kids and dogs and... everything."

Sandy slid her arm around April. "Wally is a good man, and so is Oggie. Try not to worry. It will work out. You'll see."

Later that day, Oggie, dressed in his Brett persona, knocked on the door. He opened the door, peeked in, and called out, "April, will you come here?" He added, "Please?"

Sandy stayed in the kitchen but could hear the exchange.

April came down the stairs and waited at the bottom step near the hall.

"I'm sorry I was a jerk." He came to her and hugged her. "I want to help with the wedding. Will you let me?"

"Of course," April said, sighing in relief.

"I hate to hug and run, but I have to go away. You know... I'll be back." He kissed April's cheek. "I don't have time to stay." He increased his volume. "I have to leave, Sandy."

Sandy hurried from the kitchen. Oggie kissed both women and dashed out the door. April and Sandy watched him disappear down the road that connected their properties.

Sandy looked at April. "Everything okay?"

"You were right. Oggie apologized. He's off on another mission." April sighed. "It's because I'm out of commission. He's doing my job, too. And now I will quit."

"You and Og can't be the only ones who do...whatever it is you do."

"We *are* the only ones. I can't divulge...you know. I just want to be an ordinary woman. Is that wrong?"

"Absolutely not."

"Thanks. Wally's coming over in a few minutes. I want to show him some things about the cows. Maybe we'll get a small place with some cattle. I never dreamed I would be thinking about domestic things. It's because of you, Sandy. Thank you so much."

"Ah. Things happen."

CHAPTER 51

The next day, when the mail came, Sandy found two letters for April. One envelope written by hand had large words: "Open me first."

"April," Sandy called. "You've got mail."

April looked the letter over, then took the second one from Sandy. She sat down on the couch and unsealed the *Open Me First* envelope. "It's from Oggie, telling me how to resign." April sat for a while in thought. "I'm going to do it now." She went into the room they used as an office and shut the door.

A half-hour later, while Sandy prepared lunch, the open door carried the boys' conversation from the kitchen's back step. She listened.

Wes read, "If you truly want to do this, here's your way out. Dial *the* phone number. When it answers, say 12899438221. Wait for the cue, then speak *your* number. When you get the next cue, listen carefully to the directions. Your terminal response will be 8899334. After that, you'll be released. Your work memory will slowly fade. You might lose some other memories, too. Think about this carefully. Love, Og."

Sandy called them to come inside. "What are you doing?"

"I found this on the couch in the office," Wes said. He handed her the paper.

"This is someone else's mail."

"Nuh-uh. It didn't say Dear anyone, Mom."

Sandy folded it and put it in her pocket. She found April sitting in the living room. She handed April the paper. "The boys had this. Sorry."

April blinked, glassy-eyed, before she caught Sandy's gaze. "Oh, that." She blinked again, appearing slightly dazed. "I don't need it now." Her eyebrows raised, and she looked around the room. She smiled. "Come sit. I want to tell you about my other letter."

April read the first few sentences of the second letter aloud. "Check this out. It's your wedding present if you want it. Love, from your favorite relative, Uncle Ralph." She laughed and gave Sandy four photos from the envelope. "Look at these."

Sandy examined the pictures of a dairy. An aerial photo revealed a huge piece of land with barns, fences, and cattle. Another showed an estate with a beautiful home at the end of a long white-fenced drive. A third photo displayed the interior of the home with a double staircase. The last one showed rows of cows at milking stations, the stainless-steel equipment gleaming against modern machinery, and white-clothed workers manning the stations.

April kept reading. "It's a dairy farm in Kentucky. Three hundred and sixty acres, including all of the buildings, farm machinery, staff, hands, and managers. From Uncle Ralph!"

Sandy looked at the photos again. "Uncle Ralph? The same Ralph who meddles in others' affairs?"

"Uh, yeah. The same. But Oggie *is* kind of like an *uncle* to me."

"What, they call a Dutch uncle?"

"No. I am somehow genetically related to him."

"You don't know how you are related? It shouldn't be difficult to find out."

"That's true. Uh, I'm a little more human than Oggie, you see—"

Sandy nodded emphatically. "That's for sure. Oggie is a great guy, but has his own set of nerd rules."

"That's not what I mean. You know what Oggie and I did

for the government has a lot of secrecy involved, so I can't tell you details, but there are some things you ought to know, and I'm going to tell you."

The phone rang. "Hold on," Sandy said and got up to answer the phone.

Sandy returned to April, who waited on the couch. "Your Uncle Ralph works fast. I just hung up with Derrick Downey, CEO of the D Company, a party-planning business in Nashville. Derrick wants to see us tomorrow regarding your wedding, all expenses paid by Uncle Ralph. What do you think?"

April shook her head. "Dennis said I could set the date, and I want it to be as soon as possible, but I have no idea how to plan a wedding. I've never even been to one."

"Never attended a wedding?" Sandy laughed and gave April the slip of paper where she had written Derrick's number. "You will now! That's Og's way of doing things at the speed of light. You might want to call and confirm the appointment."

April bit her lip. "Okay. You'll go with me, right?"

Sandy nodded enthusiastically. "I wouldn't miss this for the world. Plus, I'm included in the appointment. I'll see if Gail can babysit tomorrow. I need to get busy."

The next morning, D Company's address brought them to a light industrial park northwest of Nashville. The tan and brown brick Art Deco building curved where it faced two streets. The plain colors outside belied its curious interior décor. Two exterior glass doors fitted with metal flamingo cutouts opened to a small reception area in the oak-paneled lobby. The receptionist, a small older man dressed in a trim navy suit, showed the ladies into the main office by opening heavily carved wooden doors with *Darling Derrick* incised in gold leaf at eye level. The room's décor presented an eclectic mixture of styles: Art Deco, Rococo, and Victorian. Rich black and burgundy brocade draperies lavished the tall windows, interspersed with heavy gilt-framed paintings on the walls. Dark ornate furniture, overstuffed and inviting, rested upon wall-to-wall Persian rugs. What should have been an assault of the senses merged beautifully into a visual feast.

The darkest man Sandy ever saw, dressed in a cream wool suit accented by a colorful Hermes scarf, glided into the room.

"Hello, Miss Sandra and Miss April. I'm Derrick. Don't you just love it? I'm named for a tall, strong object that provides the world with black energy!"

Sandy and April laughed. Mr. Derrick Downey had the habit of drawing out many of his syllables. This person made Brett Fontina look like a macho Marine in combat.

"Yes, yes, and yes," he said.

"What?" Sandy asked.

The man steepled his fingers. "You were saying to yourself, is he really that gay? Can he possibly live here in Nashville, and will someone like that be able to handle this wedding?" His gleaming teeth contrasted against his ebony skin.

"So, yes, I *am* that gay. Tennessee is one thing, but the city of Nashville is another country where anything goes, and I handle the best and richest bashes. You probably don't have the smallest clue regarding the money spent on parties in this city. N-o-w," he said in three beats, "let's talk about the happy day. It seems your de-ar," two syllables, "Uncle Ralph has given carte blanche to the event."

The two women looked at each other.

"Ralph Ferraro?" Sandy asked.

He stood. "Ye-es, of course! Does Miss April have another Uncle Ralph?" He waited, hands on hips. "You *will* put this in my care?"

"Uhm, okay," April answered. "What did Uncle Ralph tell you?"

"Oh, I should have such a man! He said you were precious to him and that I had better create a memorable day. I'm to arrange everything, and *you* are *not* to get in my *way*." He made the last word linger. "Sooo, let's begin, shall we? Come into the dressing room. I need a look at what I'm working with."

Sandy and April followed Derrick to a room resembling a tent. In the middle, the top of the sheer material went up to a point held by a brass ball suspended from the ceiling. He pulled aside two panels and followed the ladies in.

"Okay, sweeties, take off your clothes down to your panties."

"I don't think so," Sandy said.

"Puhlease." Derrick groaned. "I need to know what kind of bra you should wear for your fabulous gown creation. Believe me, my only interest in women's breasts is professional. Oh, you did remember to bring photos of the groom and best man, right? I have to keep them in mind while I form my ideas."

April dug in her purse for the pictures.

"Oh, yes. Mmm, this big one here, the groom?" Derrick sighed. "I can't wait to see him stripped to his undies. Oh, my." He switched photos and looked at Cam's image. "Ye-es, love the blond curls." He stuck the photos in his jacket pocket. "Hurry. Step to, girls. Chop, chop. Let me see those torsos!"

April and Sandy undressed and did not look at each other.

Derrick circled them and drummed his fingers on his cheek. "Uh-huh, yes, hmmm. Okay. I've seen what I need. Put on your clothes. Actually, you should throw those drab things away. Oooh! Jeans?" He shuddered. "Let me bring you some appropriate apparel. I mean, what if you should have an accident on your way home and... I mean, you've heard the expression *I wouldn't be caught dead in those clothes*, right? The saying comes from this type of situation."

"Thanks, Derrick, but we'll manage with what we have," Sandy said, straining to withhold her laugh.

The ladies returned to his office and sat while he made

several calls. Within minutes, three people arrived.

Derrick stood and put his arm around one of them. "Ladies, this is Spike, our hair Nazi."

Spike had the perfect name because it described the way golden points stuck up and out of his brown roots. He wore all black and sported a studded collar. Spike pulled Sandy to a standing position, gave her a hand mirror, then walked around her. He ran his fingers in an upward direction through her hair. "Right. She will have five shades of blond streaks blending with the brown. The proper cut will make her look ravishing."

"Wait a minute," Sandy protested. "I don't want to be a spectacle. Nothing radical."

Derrick rolled his eyes. "Trust us."

Spike invited April to stand, handed her the mirror, and did the same narrow-eyed appraisal of her light brown hair. She cringed when she saw the bald spots in the reflection. She cast a blank look at Sandy. Spike patted her cheek.

April glared at the mirror. "I don't remember anything about those red areas."

"Your Uncle Ralph told me about your scalp condition. Burned when you were a baby, poor thing. No problem. Hair extensions will cover the scars." He put his finger to his lips, thinking. "I go now to prepare. Ciao, babies." Spike left.

Sandy stared at April for a moment. *Either she is the best liar ever, or she has forgotten what happened to her. How could she forget?*

Derrick introduced the dress designer. Val, short for Prince Valiant, a head shorter than Sandy, with short platinum hair. He looked them over. "Derry and I work together on the dresses." He took a spin around Sandy, then April, his eyes traveling up and down. "Well, then... I believe, white with tiny turquoise roses for the bride. Pale aqua for the Matron of Honor. Sweetheart necklines, you think, Derry?"

"Definitely. Get going, Val. You've seen enough."

Derrick summoned the third in the fashion triumvirate. Within a minute, a man with dark hair, olive skin, and happiness dancing in his eyes approached the women.

"My dears," Derrick said. "Meet Butchie."

Butchie did a quick bow.

Derrick gently took April's arm. "Here we have April, our lovely bride." Patting Sandy's wrist, he said, "And please meet this beauty, Sandra, our Matron of Honor."

"So glad to make your acquaintance," Butchie said. The way he said it sounded like he truly meant it. "I do the make-up. Let's see now…the first thing we'll do? Yes! Eyebrow tattoos for both of you." He traced the line over April's bone arches with his finger and stepped back.

"Hey," April said, "I don't want tattoos."

"Oh, these aren't tattoos like hearts or dragons. Ah, such exquisite arches! We'll just do a little augmentation of what you have going. I use deadening cream, and it will be done in ten minutes. Then I'm going to show you how to apply makeup that everyone will see but not notice. Trust me!"

The rest of the afternoon became a flurry of planning and descriptions of what the wedding would be like. They chose the menu and the music. Sandy and April got their tattoos.

Two weeks later, Derrick and members of the D Company visited the farm. The ladies tried their dresses on, and the seamstress made alterations. Butchie proclaimed their eyebrows healed and perfect. Derrick walked outside with April, Sandy, and the head chef for over an hour, inspecting the hay meadows, the cedar stand, the front lawn, and even the pastures.

After great deliberation, they selected the pond between the wooded hills as a place to set up the wedding canopy. Once the artist had sketched the nuptial setting for April's approval, Derrick and Prince Valiant drove to the farm on the east to measure Cam and Wally for their tuxes.

A few days later, April received a letter. "It's from Uncle Ralph. This," she held the papers up, "are the ownership papers for the dairy farm in Kentucky." April sat hard on the couch, reading and rereading the papers. She wiped a tear from her eye with her finger and sniffed. "Oh, my dear Oggie. He bought that place for me. He says I can add Dennis's name to it at my convenience. That's so like him, isn't it?" She sniffed again, stifling a full-blown cry. "Dennis is resigning from his job and is excited about having a dairy."

Sandy sat next to her and read the forms. "Where do you think Og gets the money to fund these things?"

"Probably from inventions. I don't know for sure, but not too long ago, he worked on adapting that anti-theft emission thing on the jet for driving out rodents. He told me he might patent it and call it *The Better Mousetrap*. Or maybe it's his one-sided window film. I'm sure there's mystifyingly brilliant stuff that I don't remember anymore."

"You don't remember?"

"No, and that's fine with me. I don't know what I've forgotten. That makes life easy, don't you think?"

"Yes. Easy and very Oggie-like. By the way, the day Derrick first called you were going to tell me some things about your genetic relationship to Og."

April contracted her tattooed eyebrows. "Was I?" She made a little teeth-sucking sound. "I don't know how we are related."

"That's okay," Sandy said. "I'll learn it from Og when it's the right time."

April made the *okay* symbol with her finger and thumb. "Promise me, though, what you might learn, you'll keep to yourself. I'm becoming blissfully unaware of the effects of Og-knowledge."

"Please! April! Try not to sound like him when you speak!"

CHAPTER 52

A month later, the D Company came two days ahead and set up the chapel by the pond. The trees surrounding the still water made the perfect setting. Multiple white arbors covered with flowers flanked a large central arch for the ceremony, with a stage for the musicians on the left. In front of the arch, comfortable ribbon-bedecked seating waited for one hundred guests. The large dining tent, illuminated by twinkle lighting and enhanced by candles, sat nearby in the meadow. Derrick had thought of everything.

On the day of the wedding, the house buzzed with activity. The makeup people, hairdressers, and clothiers moved about like bees in an apiary. Derrick assured Sandy the groom and best man were being treated to similar indignities in the double-wide up the street.

While Butchie served April in another bedroom, Derrick supervised Sandy's primping. "Beautiful, lovely, gorgeous," he said as the dressing progressed.

She watched in an oval cheval mirror as he did his work. "Such a happy man," she said.

"Happy and gay," he said, with a chuckle. "Life is wonderful, Sandy. We need to consider every day as a gift and be flexible to catch the joys sent our way."

"What a philosophy, Derrick."

"I suspect your virtues keep you from enjoying what's available." He put his face next to hers. Their image in the mirror looked like a photograph. "Sandy, your beauty is boundless. Knowing you in this short time has shown me the splendor of your soul. And now, with my talents, you look as good outside as inside. Seize the time. Enjoy. Taste the flavors, smell the scents, and feel the pleasure. See life in full color and hear the music of the spheres!"

"I will," she said. "Thank you."

He zipped up her long aqua silk dress, designed to enhance her figure and coloring. "I'm done here. Go face your public."

As the guests filtered into the outdoor chapel, soft music played. A harpist performed several solos followed by violins. Visitors came from all over, and their accommodations were generously provided by April's rich Uncle Ralph.

Old friends and new attended, like Sheriff Unstead and his wife, the realtor. Two members of the unrecognized agency, known to Oggie, forgotten by April, came and were introduced as *former associates*. Paula, Josh, and their baby attended, as well as Lorrie and her life-mate Mel, guests of Sandy's but welcomed by the bride.

The nuptial setting, almost as lovely as the bride and her Matron of Honor, brought sounds of "ah" and "oh" from the guests. Derrick and D Company had done their work well. The wedding began with little Jeanette, dressed in her turquoise lace dress and white leggings, throwing pink rose petals on the red carpet laid down on the canvas flooring. Sandy followed Jeanette. Strains of Wagner heralded April, beautiful in her flowing white silk gown. The dress sported hand-worked tiny blue-green flowers throughout the skirt and a simple, elegant top flecked with pearls, ending at the waistline with a point. April's veil covered her face. Vance escorted the bride and gave her away. Wally wiped his eyes as he announced, "I do."

The food, starting with Beluga caviar, on to filet mignon, lobster, and Ahi tuna, washed down with the finest champagne and served by multitudinous tuxedoed waiters, added an extra layer of class. By the glow of candlelight, the guests dined to the delicate sounds of a string quartet. After the meal, cake-cutting and bouquet-throwing entertained the guests while a rock band set up on a platform in the meadow. Then, the dancing began.

The band, so good Sandy couldn't resist the call of moving feet, gave herself up to the rhythms. After dancing with the sheriff, Cam, and even Brett Fontina, Sandy needed a short rest. As she took a breather, she listened to a few of the songs and swayed in her seat. Vance brought a chair and set it next to her.

In a few minutes, when a soft ballad commenced, Vance stopped a waiter and put his drink on the tray. "Sandy, may I have this dance?"

CHAPTER 53

Rested, she extended her hand. "I didn't know you liked to dance."

"I like being near you," he said, pulling her close. "And, how about I get all the slow dances the deejay plays?"

Sandy slid her hand up his shoulder. "I guess so. They don't play many slow dances."

His fingers surrounded her waist. "I'll take my chances."

One after another, they danced to the slow, romantic songs from past decades.

Sandy put her head on his shoulder. "I didn't think they would play all of these oldies."

"Ouch," Vance grimaced. "Oldies?"

"Lovely oldies. Wonderful. You dance so smoothly, too. Who knew? Imagine this run of good slow songs."

Gently swinging her around in a spin, he laughed. "It was worth the C-note."

"What?"

"I gave the dee jay a hundred bucks with a list of songs I wanted."

"You old coot!" Sandy whispered in his ear.

"Dirty old man?"

"Are you dirty?"

"I washed my face and hands before I come, I did," he said, imitating Eliza Doolittle.

"You are positively charming tonight." Sandy patted his abdomen. "You've lost weight."

"Yep," he turned her again. "I'm in the best shape I've been in eons." He raised his arm and flexed his bicep, the movement barely visible in the tuxedo sleeve.

Sandy pinched his muscle. "Impressive."

He eyed her up and down. "As for impressive, may I say you look ravishing? You changed your hairstyle. And that dress, hmm, hot, baby."

"Glad you noticed the new and improved me."

"Dearest Sandy, there was nothing to improve. Yet, you managed. What a woman."

When a fast song played, Vance kissed her hand. "Thus, the nirvana ends."

As Vance guided Sandy toward the seats, Cam tapped her shoulder. "My turn."

Sandy bid Vance adieu with a nod and turned into Cam's open arms. He embraced her for a few seconds, then stepped back and caught the beat of the music. She fell into the rhythm of his movements and danced until her breathing labored. They both sat in the nearest chairs.

Sandy barely had a chance to rest. Each time she sat down after a dance, one of the three men, Brett Fontina, Vance, and Cam, waited for a turn to dance with her.

Quiet generators supplied light to the darkened meadow. Champagne flowed. Black and white uniformed servers brought trays of appetizers. The celebration lasted well past midnight.

When everyone was exhausted, the event ended. Wes and Miles were so tired they almost fell asleep standing, lolling as the bridal party said goodnight to the attendees. Limos took the guests back to their hotels, and cars quietly filed down the road, which turned along the riverside. As the last limousine made its way down the road, Wally and April left for their honeymoon to the Galapagos, courtesy of Uncle Ralph. Cam picked up Miles and Wes, one over each shoulder, for the walk back to the house. Sandy carried Jeanette, who had earlier succumbed to the long hours of reveling and had slept on two chairs pushed together.

Sandy held the door with her free arm. Jeanette cried a few tired sobs, sucked her thumb, and put her head back on her mother's neck. Cam lumbered in, still holding both boys.

"Lay them in their beds. I'll change Jeanette and put her in the crib," Sandy said.

When she came into the kitchen, Cam's thumbs pushed up the cork on the champagne, followed by a soft pop. A waft of mist flew from the open bottle.

He stretched to the top cabinet for the champagne flutes. "I snagged a few bottles of the Dom while you were dancing with my competition. April's Uncle Ralph, wow, what a big spender." He held the bottle up. "At least a hundred of these, at $170 each."

Sandy took her glass, noting the fine strings of bubbles. "Mmm, nothing like Dom Perignon." She headed for the living room couch.

Cam poured into his glass. "Comparing champagnes, sure, but I can think of something better than this." He came to the couch, placed the bottle on the coffee table, and hoisted the flute toward hers. Clinking glasses, he took a long sip and sat next to her. "I never thought I would be happy living somewhere else than Manhattan, but I love this area. You chose well. I talked to a neighbor tonight who said he'll plow a garden. I think I'll get my own tractor, though. Then I can do your work, too."

Sandy didn't respond. She took a few sips and rested her head on the back of the sofa cushion.

Cam put his glass down and scooted close. "You've always been beautiful, but I've never seen you so…festive. And that dress!" He kissed her. "Drink some more." He topped her glass. "I happen to know how Dom affects you."

She tried to act insulted but couldn't pull it off. Derrick's advice sang to her about tasting life and feeling pleasure. She chuckled and took more sips of the wine. Cam took the glass away, pushed her down on the couch, and kissed her.

She stood and reached for her back zipper. He pulled it for her.

The dress fell to the floor, and Cam stepped back, giving her a head-to-toe review. His gaze returned to her torso. "Jesus, that's hot."

"It's just a strapless long line, nothing sexy."

"Wrong," he said and swung her up into his arms. "Your room?"

She took a quick breath. "Office couch."

Cam carried her into the office, deposited her on the desk chair, and pulled out the couch in a flash. Within seconds, they had their clothes off. They made eager, hungry love. After a short rest, they went at it again, then once more. Tired, the effects of the festivities and the wine took over. They fell asleep.

The morning light cast an aura around Miles in the open office doorway. "Hi, Daddy."

Cam stretched. "Hey, Squirt."

Sandy sat up, pulling the sheet over her bare breasts. "Get some cereal, Miles. I'll be along in a minute."

She clucked. "I didn't want the kids to see us."

Cam leaned over, kissed her cleavage, and then ran his finger along the edge of the sheet, brushing her nipples. "We *are* still married. That was really nice. You know, Wally got a second chance. Do you think I have one, too?"

"Cam."

"I know. I'll go slow. I don't want to mess this up for the next time."

"Look," she said. "It *was* nice, but...I don't know if there should be a next time. I already have three kids. And—"

"I'll bring latex friends next time." He picked up the empty bottle of Dom. "And my favorite monk. Not to worry. Hey, no pressure. I'm down the street. You can call me when you want me. Can I stay for breakfast?"

CHAPTER 54

The activities of the previous day and night took their toll on Sandy. After breakfast, Cam left and took the boys for the day. Worn out, she watched from her bedroom window while the D Company removed the last of the wedding things. She was too tired to supervise and hoped they would clean up respectably. They would have to return if they didn't.

That evening, she got the kids into bed early, hoping the same for herself after a few chores. As she put the last pan on the drain board, the driveway gravel crunched from footfalls. Her body gave a quick jerk. "Now, who is that?"

It was almost night, and when the movement light on the porch came on, it illuminated Brett Fontina leaning against the jamb with a canvas bag clutched to his festive shirt.

Sandy shushed the dogs. "Hi, Oggie."

"Greetings, O beautiful one. Have I told you how gorgeous you look?"

"Yes, several times at the wedding. But thanks. Come in."

He patted the bag. "I have something for us." The bag fell to the floor as he held a fat, dark bottle. Bright red wax sealed the top, and a golden medallion attached to a ring dangled from the neck. "Special. You've never had this before. Will you get two wine glasses?"

Sandy went to the dishwasher and retrieved the two glasses she and Cam had used the night before.

"Oh, my precious, you'll love it. This bottle costs, um... gobs. It isn't available to just anyone, you know. See this thing?" Oggie pinched the medallion and traced the neck ring with his fingertip. "It's fourteen karat. No kidding. These things can be jewelry." He held the bottle close to her face to show her. "It would make a nice wedding ring. But, no, for you, diamonds. Big, clear, perfect diamonds."

"What's gotten into you? Why are you spending so much money?"

"I sold one of my patents. For a bundle. I didn't want to mention it until after April and what's his name, the Pollok, got hitched."

"April knew. She told me you paid for the estate and wedding with a patent."

"Nope, different. The one I used for April was a patent Uncle Sam paid me *not* to sell. This new one brought, well, hundreds of millions. Under a different name, secretive, you know what I mean. Not only am I forbidden to sell it, I can't use it, either."

"I thought you weren't interested in money, Oggie."

"I'm not. It's what I can do with it. For you. Pick a thousand charities. I'll fund them."

"Are you getting out of the spy business and taking up philanthropy?"

Oggie scratched his head. "No." He pulled a knife from his pocket. A blade popped out of its center, and he cut the wax off the top. The cork came out with a soft pop. Filling the glasses with a rich ruby liquid, he handed one to Sandy. "I'm still in the spy business." He raised his glass to hers, tinkling the edges in a toast. "I go tomorrow."

His usual brashness slid into regret. He sipped. "Mmm, worth every thousands."

Sandy pulled the glass from her lips to look at the color. "Delicious. Absolutely. You're going away? On another mission?"

"You know I can't give you details. I need to go, though, very important."

"When will you be back?"

"I don't know. And I won't get in touch with you until I return. I hope you will miss me. This mission should cause you some worry."

"Oh, Og."

"Tell me not to go, Sandy. I'll still go, but when I get back, I'll quit, and we'll get married."

"You know I'm not divorced."

"Not a problem. I'll take care of it. I can, I promise you, practically in minutes. I have connections, Sweetpea, big connections. One phone call."

"Jeeze, Og, this wine is...I don't have a proper word. Indescribable. Did you drug it?"

"No. I wouldn't do that to you. It has been said, however, that this wine is a natural aphrodisiac. Let's see if it works. Not for me, though. I get excited breathing the air you exhale."

"Mister Fortina, you, funky cheese, you. You can be so charming."

Oggie smiled at the bottle. "Damn, this wine is worth twice its price. I've never heard you say funky before. And you think I'm charming? Oh, boy."

Sandy wiggled her empty glass. "More. I love it."

He poured for both of them. When she finished her wine, he moved closer and took the glass from her. "Want to see how rich geeks make love?" Oggie pushed her against the cushion and kissed her.

"In the office," she whispered. "So, the kids don't hear."

Ogburn Goodheart Edwards choked on his words. "Sandy, all these years. God, how I loved you when I first saw you. And now, finally...." He looked away. When he composed, he turned to her. "Do you have any idea—"

"Hush," Sandy took his hand and led him to the room. She pointed to the couch. They removed the cushions. Oggie pulled out the bed.

Sandy kicked off her shoes. Oggie sat on the edge and removed his tan loafers.

"Undress me," she whispered.

"My pleasure." He pulled her sweater over her head, then her slacks down. He stepped away, admiring her, his eyes following the lines of her bra and panties.

"Are you uncomfortable, Oggie?"

"Nope. I'm easy with your company. I love you. Will you undress me?"

"Absolutely." She unbuttoned his aloha shirt and then tossed it on the floor. The belt came next, followed by the white linen pants. "Love your undies." Small alligators cavorted on the fabric. She traced her finger over his pectorals. "I didn't know you worked out. I've never noticed how muscular you are." The single table lamp cast shadows on his torso, showing tanned hills and valleys.

"Keep watching," he said and slid the alligator briefs away. "All yours."

She sat on the bed and patted the space next to her. He took a small package from the pants on the floor and sat where her hand rested. He showed her the contents of the package—a transparent disc with a shiny rim.

"A condom? I've never seen one so fancy."

"It's fancy, all right. Human bodies produce low-grade electric currents. I have harnessed bio-currents and used an organic battery in the rim. Our body currents will harmonically match. Perfect pulsing. I call it Edward's Spanish Fly. EBRO-C, short for Erogenous Bio Rhythms Orgasmic Condom. It's a trial run. I've been waiting, hoping for an opportunity with you."

"Are you going to patent it?"

"Nope. Just for you. Based on your biorhythms."

"Mine? Wait a minute. How did you get my body data?"

"Remember when I checked you with my field meter?"

"You know a lot about me."

"I do. And it might save your life someday. But do you want to talk or—"

"Put that thing on. I want to know if our biorhythms really match."

The biorhythms matched. A lot. Wonderfully.

When she reached the point that she couldn't enjoy one more rhythm, she put her chin against his shoulder. "Oggie, that was even better than the wine. And I don't believe the EBRO-C should take the credit. You were... unbelievable. If that's how geeks do it, well..."

"Surprise, surprise, eh?"

She nodded with deep movement. "Yes, but you are constantly surprising me. Where did you learn those things?"

Oggie smiled and tapped his head. "Kidneys."

They slept in each other's arms until a rooster's call made them stir.

Oggie ran his fingers through his dark hair. "Gotta go." He dressed and sat on the mattress. "Take care of yourself." He pressed his lips to her forehead.

"Be careful, Og," she whispered.

"I will. I have more motivation now."

CHAPTER 55

Like most days, this one had been busy. Unlike most days, she felt tired from her activities, the wedding, and afterward, making love with Cam. Following that, in bed with Oggie, with all of the bio-rhythms getting in the way of sleep. Sandy, short two days of rest, and feeling physically satisfied, nonetheless, dragged. Once again, she shuffled the kids to bed early, eager to crawl into her own.

She brought Scruffy and Grubby into the kitchen and shoveled dry kibbles with a measuring cup into their metal bowls. As she set the dishes on the drying mat, the phone rang.

"Hi, Sandy-Sarah."

"Hi, Vance."

"How are your animals? Any problems?"

Derrick's admonition to enjoy life and not be held back by silly virtues surfaced. She smiled to herself. *My barnyard animals don't have any problems, but my pussy is tired.*

"You're not answering."

"I'm suppressing a nasty comment regarding barnyard animals."

"Oh yeah? Were you going to say there's something wrong with your ass?"

"Close enough."

"Man, I'll be right over."

"Are you in the area?"

"No," he said. "I'm coming to visit you."

She had time to check on the sleeping kids and shower before the dogs barked at the noise of Vance's Jeep.

She opened the door.

"Humph," Vance grunted as he held the bottle up in the open doorway for her inspection. "Brandy, good stuff. I've had it for years, waiting for a reason to enjoy it."

"Are you drinking again?"

"Not in a bad way. I don't need alcohol to feel what I'm feeling now."

"A Veterinarian-Philosopher. Interesting combination."

He shook the bottle at her. She motioned him into the living room.

Vance placed his brandy on the low wooden coffee table, the top scarred and scratched from kids and dogs.

"I'll get glasses," Sandy said, heading to the dishwasher. "I don't have snifters."

Vance sat on the couch and leaned in toward the open kitchen. "No problem, as long as they aren't paper cups."

"No paper cups." She brought the same wine glasses used by her previous lovers and placed them next to the brandy.

Vance poured a few inches for each of them. They sipped quietly. He went to the Bose system on the entertainment center against the wall and dialed the Love Channel. He pulled her from her seat, and they danced to the soft music.

"It's been a long time since I've done this," he whispered.

"We danced a few days ago," Sandy said.

"Not the dancing, the emotion. And," he added with a non-smirking laugh, "the woody." He pushed at her waist, making body contact at the hips.

"Old Coot," she teased.

"I'm fifty-four. You are, what, thirty-six? Is that too much of a difference?"

"We'll see."

CHAPTER 56

He kissed her, touching the tip of his tongue to hers. "I've wanted to do that for a long time."

"Anything else?"

"Yeah." He kissed her and slid his hands to her blouse buttons.

"Come with me," she whispered and headed for the office. The convertible couch that sat next to the filing cabinets had served as Wally's bed and, more recently, the site of Sandy's sexual pursuits. Luckily, she changed the sheets each morning.

She removed the cushions, and he pulled out the bed. When they sat on the mattress, Vance resumed working her buttons, taking his time.

"Let me show you something I learned in Vet school." He made light circles with his forefinger around her navel and lightly sucked her nipple.

"That feels good," Sandy said. "You learned that in Vet school?"

"No!" he chuckled. "I thought you'd like it."

"Oh, Vance. Don't make fun of me."

"Okay, I'll be nice."

Vance's lovemaking wasn't a mad rush, heat, or heavy breathing. He approached the passion gently, slowly, and deliberately. This was new to Sandy, and wanting him inside her added to the quiet ardor.

He pushed in, making shallow, slow thrusts.

"Vance! All the way. Please!"

"Not yet," he whispered. "You're not ready."

"I am. I am. Vance!"

He nuzzled her ear with his nose and pushed fully inside her, controlling the speed and force. When she reached her peak, she moaned. He put his hand softly over her mouth, and after she quieted, he finished for himself. They lay together in the quiet of the night.

"Oh, Vance. I don't know what to say."

"Then let me talk." He spoke in a tone she had not heard before. "I love you. Marry me."

"I'm not free. How about you?"

"We can take care of it easily. My brother is the circuit judge of the county."

"A relative who is on good speaking terms with you? Gee."

"Good enough. I can get him to expedite what we need." He turned on his side and pulled her to fit. They spooned for a few minutes. "Tomorrow, I'm going to locate Helen."

"To see if she's divorced you?"

"I think I'd know if she did. I need to apologize and set things straight. I've been a shit. I was drowning, and you sent me a life ring. I've been comatose, and you woke me up. God, how I love you."

She turned and put her nose against his. "Vance, didn't I see two of those foil thingies?"

"Yeah, BOGO at CVS in town."

She pressed against his neck and laughed, taking in the perfume sex produces on the skin. "Do you think you could…."

"I'm sure of it."

After the second session, she slept in his arms until his watch alarm awakened them.

He picked up his clothes. "I need to go. I know you don't want the kids to see me here.

I'll call you when I get back from finding Helen."

Sandy lingered in bed after Vance left, enjoying the tranquility she felt. Once she got out of bed, the morning, like most mornings, would be hectic.

CHAPTER 57

Sandy started breakfast, and when the boys came in from the chicken coop, she had the bacon draining. She counted three boys. Eddie held his share of the eggs.

"Eddie, when did you get back?"

"Yesterday," he said, eyeing the bacon.

"I guess your uncle died, then. I'm so sorry."

"Nope, the medicine worked. He's better. My dad said it's a miracle."

"That's great news. You boys wash up for breakfast."

Eddie spent the day and rode his bike home after eating supper. Sandy hustled the kids to bed early, hoping for much-needed rest, but her gut feeling said she would see Henry.

At nine-thirty, Henry's truck pulled up to the house. She waited in the open doorway as he parked and got out. Henry looked different, wearing a golf shirt and khaki pants rather than the overalls she had always seen him in. Without a bill cap, his curly, light red hair, freshly cut and combed, showed an attractiveness she had not noticed before. He smelled nice, too. Nothing fancy, the fresh smell of good soap. He showed her a mayonnaise jar.

"What's that?" She pointed to the faint pink fluid jostling about the glass.

"Shine. Flavored with peaches. It's the best I ever had." He unscrewed the lid.

"I'll get the glasses."

"Don't need no glasses. Here." He held the jar up and took a sip. He took her hand and wrapped her fingers around the jar.

She tested a bit. "My first taste of moonshine." The liquid made its warm path down her throat. Expecting the harsh tang of alcohol, a soft, fruity flavor wafted instead as she allowed the aroma to infuse her throat and nose. "It's really good." She took another swig. "Oh! I can feel it in my arms and legs."

Henry sat on the couch. He took a drink and let out a long sigh. "My brother-in-law is free of cancer."

"I heard."

"His church held vigils. They prayed for hours. It works." He took another mouthful. "I had long talks with my sister Clare. God has returned to me."

Sandy took the jar from him and placed it on the table. "Are you sure it's not the other way around?"

He thought for a moment before he spoke. "I told Clare I met a beautiful, smart, and kind woman. She said it sounded like I was in love. And, if I was in love, I should tell that woman right up front. I should take that gal into my arms. If it was right, that woman wouldn't tell me to let go."

Sandy didn't say anything.

Henry grabbed her and held her tight with a grip like iron. "You're beautiful."

"Thanks for saying that, Henry. The Nashville crew did a wonderful job."

"What are you talking about? You don't look no different. You've always been beautiful. I love you." He waited for her to reject his hold. He kissed her, and she relaxed in his embrace. Henry stood and lifted her as if she was a feather.

For the first time, Sandy realized how strong Henry was. His loose-fitting work clothes had only hinted at his physique. She pointed down the hall.

After he folded the mattress out of the sofa, he removed his shirt. Sandy quietly gasped at his tanned arms and chest. She thought about the statue of David and how it had nothing over

Henry. When he removed his pants, the white of his lower parts made a striking contrast to the rest of his tawny body.

She took an audible breath when she saw the business end of this man's groin. "My God, Henry!"

The smile on Henry's face spread, showing perfect white teeth.

The condom stretched to worrisome proportions. What the farm man lacked in suave conversation, he made up for in movement. She had never felt so filled before, and that friction helped her peak multiple times before they collapsed in each other's arms.

Henry held her fast and put his lips to her ear. "Will you marry me?"

"I'm not free to marry, Henry."

"Just a nit," he said.

"Let me guess, you have a relative who is a judge or lawyer or a high-up person?"

"Not a relative. Five years ago, I rescued a kid who was drowning at Presco Lake. His father was a state representative who said he owed me forever. I never asked a favor before, but I would."

Sandy fell back on the pillows, still short of breath.

Henry stood up. "Can't stay. Eddie's alone at the house." He stuffed flesh into taut jockey shorts. "I'm gonna leave you alone to think for a week or so."

"Okay, Henry. That's enough time."

CHAPTER 58

Several weeks had passed since the wedding. Enough time for Sandy to reflect on her voyage into the land of sensory encounters and contemplate her life and her future. She wondered about Oggie and his mission, anxious for his safety. Oggie the Eel had always been able to take care of himself. He'd be okay.

Thinking about Vance's quest to find Helen, apologize, and ask for a divorce, she questioned if he had mellowed enough to handle the situation delicately.

Henry, true to his word, had given her time and space. Even Eddie hadn't come for his lessons. Wes and Miles missed him.

Cam, her nearest neighbor, had kept himself scarce.

One morning, Cam showed up at the door, an envelope in hand. "I need to talk to you."

"What is it?"

"I'm thinking about taking an offer. Look." He spread papers around the dining room table. "A private agency contacted me to head a study on using soil to its best advantage. I'd be on the road for most of the year gathering samples and talking to farmers, and then I would be working with the researchers. It sounds exciting, but I am leaving the decision up to you, Sandy. If you and I can reestablish our marriage, I'll stay here and work on our collective farms."

When did Cam go green? "It sounds marvelous, Cam. Who knew you would embrace farming?" *This has Oggie's name all over it.* "It's up to me?"

She studied Cam, handsome, a good lover, and the father

of her children. "I don't want to hold you back. Wow. You've embraced farming. That's amazing. I'll think about it."

"Fair enough," he said.

Sandy eyed him carefully. *When did he ever back off and give me the choice?*

"I know what you're thinking." He took her hand. "But this time, I'm not trying to manipulate you. I love you and want the family together again. I also understand it has to be your decision, or it won't work."

He stayed for lunch, invited the kids to visit his farm for the day, then gathered his materials and went home.

Later that afternoon, Henry visited, once again dressed up and well-groomed. "Things have been happening. You were right about my faith in God. As soon as I started attending church again, I met people, and things have been revealed to me. Plus," he showed her a large envelope.

"I got this here letter from the University of Tennessee asking me to teach survival skills." He removed a paper from the pack. "It's what they call a grant. I'd go to this big ole farm and show people how to eat off the land. You know, hunt, field-dress the kill, and identify edible plants. I never thought a university would want me. And, they've hired a lady at the church who knows herbal medicines. We'd work together. She's a widow with two boys Eddie's age." Henry showed the pictures of the farm and the details of the grant.

"Henry! The annual pay is $150,000 a year!" Sandy recognized Oggie's work once again. "What do you want to do?"

"I'm leaving it up to you. I asked you to marry me, and that's what I want. But, if you decide against it, I will accept this offer."

"Give me a little more time, Henry."

Henry pulled her close for a moment. "All right." He gathered his papers and left.

Sandy stood in the doorway and watched Henry's truck leave dust in retreat. *Oggie! Even on a mission, you find a way to come up with these too-good-to-resist opportunities, eliminating the competition one at a time.* Sandy pictured a giant spider web with Oggie, the eight-legged creature, pulling on a string, making the outer portion of the web move to his call. When he was through with that string, another leg would shake, and a new portion of the web would move. *What would he do next?*

The following day, she got a call from Vance saying he was on his way to visit her.

When he got there, he kissed her and held her for a long embrace.

"You have news, right? An irresistible offer?" She waited for the punch line.

He relaxed his hold. "When did you become a psychic?"

"Sometimes," she took a breath, "I know things."

He ran his hand up her arm and massaged her shoulder. "Years ago, I treated a calf with an unidentifiable condition. I suspected something in the soil caused the problem."

"Soil?" A surge of heat crept across her cheeks.

"I sent a sample of the pasture's dirt and grasses and a scraping of the animal's skin to Vanderbilt to see if we could learn something. Nothing happened, and I forgot about it."

"And?" The voice inside her squealed. *Damn you, Oggie. Enough with the meddling.*

"Well, the University received a huge private grant to identify soil-borne diseases. Somehow, the work I did came to their attention, and they would like to pursue my theories, calling it the Chambers Study. Two hundred thousand a year as salary. Five fully-equipped veterinary buses are being outfitted to travel in the South, training students and offering free medical exams for farm animals and pets. While they travel, they will take samples of animal tissue and the surrounding soils for research.

The University wants me to head the program. Imagine that."

"Imagine that. And the decision is mine, right?"

"Hell, no. It's mine."

"And what, pray tell, have you decided?"

"I've decided I'm too damn old to be doing shit like that. I gave it to Gene. He's a Chambers. I'm going to run the clinic until I can't practice anymore."

"Oh." *One of the bugs on Oggie's spider web just freed itself.* "Um. I didn't ask how it went with Helen. Did you make things right with her?"

He scratched his chin. "You might say that. I called ahead to see if she'd even talk to me. When she let me in, I came straight to the point. I said I had been a shithead and sincerely apologized for the grief I gave her. I accepted all of the blame for our trouble." He scratched his chin again. "She threw her arms around me and said how badly she'd missed me, plus I looked so damned good now. She kissed me and pulled me toward the bedroom."

"Oh, Vance," Sandy said, putting her hand to her mouth. "And you—"

"I stopped her. I told her I wasn't there for that. I came to ask for a divorce."

"Was she upset?"

"Oh, yeah. After a while, though, she knew it was over and agreed. I gave her the land I had along the river. She didn't want the house. I filed the papers yesterday."

"So, what now?"

Vance took her hands in his. "*That's* the part that's up to you." He kissed her. "I'm going to the clinic to make arrangements. Gene and I have a lot of stuff to do." He pointed to her purse. "Let me see your cell phone."

Sandy gave him the phone. He pushed the buttons for a few minutes.

"Okay. I'm on speed dial, number one. Get in touch with

me later, okay?" He kissed her forehead, hugged her, and then kissed her lips.

She placed her fingers against her lips as Vance got into the Jeep.

That afternoon, Sandy sat on the front porch with a fragrant cup of coffee. The hummingbirds had returned. Cam had all of the kids at his place for the day, allowing her hours of thoughtful quiet.

She considered her lovers, their attributes, and how she felt about spending the rest of her life with one of them. Cam had taken her away from a boring life and given her a higher standard. Yes, he'd been manipulative and controlling, but she believed he had changed. Oggie, brilliant and unpredictable. Life would be exceedingly interesting with him. Wow, all of that wealth. Henry. Down to earth, strong, and resourceful, he'd move mountains to please her. In a crisis, Henry would protect the ones close to him. And Vance. Under his grouchy, acid wit existed a cultured man, a man of his own mind, a man who made her laugh.

All four had attractive qualities that would make marriage unique. She was sure she could be happy with any of her suitors, each with a special advantage. Taking Derrick's advice, she had sampled all of life's senses. Cam, Oggie, Vance, and Henry. They loved her. And she loved each one. All of them had changed for the better and improved her, too. Was there one man who made her senses more intense? Did she love one above the others?

Yes! That day, sitting on her front porch sipping coffee and admiring the tiny creatures that lived with vigor and liveliness, she made her choice.

CHAPTER 59

Sandy sat upright, knees to chest. The man next to her fidgeted as the sheet pulled away.

"Sorry," she whispered and ran her hand along the groove of his back before she restored the cover. She kissed his shoulder and breathed in the smell of his skin.

Sandy couldn't sleep, but not from stress or worry. She was happy. This wakeful night would be one of reflection. So much had happened. After Oggie returned from his mission, he called and said he had to talk to her about things she needed to know about him so she could make an informed decision about marrying him. Mind-blowing information— She remembered bits about the talk. But only a few things because she agreed to *forget* the secret parts—a whole bunch of secrets. After the discussion, he used what looked like an ophthalmoscope, and the memory of the talk faded. She remembered that Oggie wanted more than anything to be with her forever. And forever could mean more than a typical lifespan. She cared for him, the most unusual person she had ever met. Did she want to worry about him each time he left to save the world? After their talk, she said she needed more time.

He had returned the next day, somewhat sad. In his bid to win her for himself, he admitted he used his most complex invention —the one the government insisted he not sell or use— and peeked into the future. What he saw both pleased and disappointed him because he saw her happy and living a happy life, but with someone else. And he loved her enough to allow her to enjoy that particular future. But he would keep his residence next door and would be there for her at any time in any way, his devotion to her being boundless. He added that sometimes futures changed. If that happened, he would be ready. She loved and appreciated Oggie, the weirdest person she had ever met. Weird and wonderful.

Henry — Sandy had a new appreciation for the man. Strong and sexy, able to provide for her and her family under any circumstances. He knew how to run the farm and would take care of her and the children. He would gladly give up the offer to teach others how to survive if she said yes to him. She could love him and spend her days on the farm with Henry at her side. But Henry needed to share his skills with others. She declined his marital offer.

Cam — her legal husband and father of her children — lived on the farm adjacent to hers. Together, they could have one of the largest properties in the area. She believed he had stopped steamrolling or enough that she could manage him. And after all the years together, he knew how to please her in bed. He had enough money from the sale of the Manhattan house to last their lifetime. He had asked if they could reunite, then stepped back to let her choose. She could easily let him move into the farmhouse and be her husband again. With his newfound attraction to soil and growing things, they could enjoy life together on the farm.

Vance — an older man, grumpy at times, witty always. Outspoken. Intelligent. Thoughtful. A lover of classical music who quoted poetry but could use a rifle if needed. Nothing spectacular — not a spy, a survivalist, or a brilliant attorney. Good enough in bed.

They all loved her. And she loved them. Listening to her heart, the choice came easily. On the afternoon that she watched the hummingbirds flit and dart, she grabbed her cell phone and called.

He had moved in over a month ago. Each day, she was

more certain of her selection.

Jeanette was two now. Maybe they should have a baby. He would be thrilled if she became pregnant.

Visions of the past twelve years flashed through her mind like a fast-forward movie.

She had traveled light years from that timid, plain, unassuming girl. She stretched and brushed against her husband's leg.

He stirred and sat up. "If you can't sleep, let me distract you."

"You need your rest."

"I can spare some time for you." He pulled her close. "But let's not do it for hours. I have two neuters and three spays tomorrow. I can't afford to get worn out."

"Just this side of exhaustion? You're on, old man."

"Oh, hell. Exhaust me."

<End>

Patricia is a former art teacher and high school librarian. She lives in South Florida with her husband and three dogs. She writes short stories, novellas, and novels, mostly fantasy and Sci-Fi. She has also written three Romances, a Sci-Fi, a Victorian, and a Contemporary. Her stories revolve around action and deep relationships, allowing the reader to watch the scene unfold as if present. Patricia is active in three critique groups and often helps new writers learn the ropes. She is an active member of the Florida Writers Association, Mystery Writers of America, and Romance Writers of America.

When not writing, Patricia enjoys painting watercolors and drawing in several media. Currently, she is learning illustration techniques for future books. Her frequent travel provides opportunities to check off bucket list items and sometimes inspires new stories. She is a voracious reader and loves a good book talk.

Check out her Facebook page at Carpewordum@gate. net.

www.ingramcontent.com/pod-product-compliance
Lightning Source LLC
Chambersburg PA
CBHW050559260626
47157CB00002B/636